Tears of the Forsaken

A SPENCER & REID MYSTERY
BOOK FIVE

CARA DEVLIN

First Cup Press

Edited by Jennifer Wargula

ISBN paperback: 979-8-992305746

Chapter One

October 1884

Leonora Spencer stepped down onto Harrow's busy train station platform and drew in a steadying breath. The oily scent of machine smoke, the whistles and shouts of porters, and the chatter of dispersing passengers filled the air, and yet, even with all the commotion, Leo immediately felt his eyes upon her. It was a brush of intuition, and one she trusted.

She took a step forward, through a drifting cloud of smoke, her fingers clutched around the handle of her handbag. She was eager to see him, and yet also uncomfortably tense. Nearly four months had passed since she'd last set eyes on Detective Inspector Jasper Reid, and during that time, a small part of her had questioned if she would ever see him again.

In early July, he had taken Leo to dinner—only their

second such outing as a couple. Before she'd even sipped her wine, Jasper made an announcement: He'd been seconded to Liverpool. The police there had been struggling to bring down a counterfeiting operation, and they needed greater manpower to get it done. All this Jasper explained as she sat across from him at the small table, the rest of the chophouse becoming a haze in the periphery of her vision. It wasn't a permanent transfer from the Met. He'd be away two months. Three at the most, he'd said. When he'd stopped speaking, the only thing her stunned and overwhelmed mind could think to ask was: "Did you request this secondment, or was it assigned?"

She now wished she had said anything other than that, for Jasper's injured expression had permanently seared itself into her memory. A spear of guilt had lanced through her at his reply: "I would never ask to be sent away from you, Leo."

He'd known why she'd suspected it.

In July, Andrew Carter, the youngest of the five brothers who ran the vicious East Rips gang out of London's East End had approached Jasper with a warning. Unless the detective inspector bent to his will, in whatever capacity Andrew desired, he would expose what he'd discovered to the public: that Jasper Reid was, in fact, James Carter, Andrew's cousin who'd supposedly drowned in the Thames sixteen years earlier. Jasper's blood ties to the East Rips would not only damn his career at Scotland Yard, but when the remainder of the Carter family learned what James had done, his life would be forfeit. The Carters would surely seek revenge for his abandonment and deceit, and Jasper had worried Leo would be caught up in the violence or used as a pawn.

When he'd come to her, explaining the new predicament Andrew Carter had presented, Jasper had tried to end their fledgling relationship, claiming it would be safer for her if he were to keep his distance. She had refused, of course, unwilling to run scared or walk away from him. Jasper had relented, but with the announcement that he'd be leaving for Liverpool, far from Andrew's reach, Leo couldn't help but wonder if he'd designed the secondment himself.

Now, after months apart and dozens of letters exchanged between them, Leo still wasn't sure if he planned to return to London. Jasper was stubborn enough, and fierce enough about protecting her, to think staying away was the right thing to do.

The uncertainty kept her stomach in a rigid knot as she searched for him on the station platform. It was cool and damp, and the autumn sky dark purple with the threat of a storm. She shivered, and then, the prickling of gooseflesh accompanied a deep voice behind her.

"Your train was three minutes late."

Despite the complaint, Leo's mouth bowed into a grin. She turned, and the knot in her stomach released. Jasper's sooty green eyes, the color of the Thames on a rainy day, locked onto her. For the barest moment, she was struck mute. He'd removed his bowler, allowing the strands of his honey-blond hair, longer than usual, to slip forward over his brow. To her astonishment, he'd allowed a beard to come in.

"You cannot blame me for that," she replied, growing warm under his steady stare. He took in the sight of her, his eyes conveying the same longing she had been plagued with since his departure to Liverpool.

Jasper formed a slow, crooked grin. "You dislike my beard."

"Not at all." It was trimmed neatly, and to her surprise, it gave him a distinguished appearance. She suppressed the urge to reach for his cheek and scrub her fingers through the golden bristle, dusted through with darker shades of burnt umber. "You've grown a beard in the past."

"Which I needed to shave when you would handle it and call me a grumpy walrus."

"I did not handle it!" she exclaimed, even though that was exactly what she'd just been wanting to do.

Leo laughed, her relief at seeing him clear away the hesitance she'd felt while taking the train from London's Paddington Station to Harrow. It didn't, however, settle the confusion over why the two of them were here to begin with.

Three days ago, a letter from the solicitor of a Mrs. Francine Stroud had arrived for Leo at her home on Duke Street. Standing in the front hall, wondering who Mrs. Stroud could be, Leo's pulse had slowed. It turned out to be a summons to Cowper Fields, the sprawling estate that was home to Lord Richard Cowper, the Viscount Cowper.

Cowper was a name Leo did not often think of. The late Honorable Emmaline Cowper's father had bitterly disapproved of his daughter's inequitable marriage to Gregory Reid, a working-class Metropolitan Police officer. His disapproval had turned into loathing when Emmaline and their two young children perished in a disaster on the half-frozen lake at Regent's Park in 1867.

According to the solicitor's letter, the viscount's eldest daughter, Francine, had recently passed away, and Leo was invited to the estate for the reading of her last will and testament.

Other than a date, time, and place—and a postscript note that Jasper Reid had also been summoned—there had been no other information. She couldn't understand why she was being summoned. She had not even known Emmaline Reid had had a sister. The Inspector, as Leo had always referred to Gregory Reid, had spoken of the animosity between himself and the viscount but hadn't uttered a single word about anyone else in his late wife's family.

Later that same evening, Leo received a telegram from Jasper about the strange summons to Cowper Fields, and they had arranged to meet at the Harrow station on the allotted day.

Now, they stood an arm's length apart, a curious and awkward friction filling the space between them. Leo cleared her throat. "Should we be on our way? Thanks to my train, we're running late."

He held out his arm, bent at the elbow, in invitation for her to join him. She hooked her arm through his, and without saying another word, they walked from the platform to the station yard. There, a disorganized queue of carriages, coaches, and wagons awaited passengers. Jasper hailed one such carriage for hire and helped Leo inside just as the first drops of rain fell from the bloated clouds. After directing their driver to Lord Cowper's home, Jasper slipped onto the bench next to her. With no foot brazier lit on the carriage floor, she was grateful for the small lap blanket she could pull over her legs and feet. Still, she shivered—though she acknowledged that seeing Jasper for the first time in months might have been partly the reason why. That, and the uncertainty of what awaited them at Viscount Cowper's estate.

They'd been driving for a minute or so when Leo broke the silence. "Do you know anything about Mrs. Francine Stroud?"

That curious topic would be much easier to discuss than how much she'd missed him, or if he was ever planning to return from Liverpool. They had not broached the subject in any of their letters, and Leo counted herself a coward for continuing to avoid the question.

Jasper kept his bowler in his hands, on his lap. "Nothing. My father never mentioned her."

Though they were not related by blood, the Inspector had been exactly that to Jasper—a father. Since Gregory's death late last January, it seemed to have become somewhat easier for Jasper to acknowledge this truth. Before that, he'd always appeared a bit uncomfortable being called the Inspector's son. Perhaps that was because the Inspector did once have a son by birth, Gregory Junior, and Jasper had felt somewhat of an imposter. But Leo was convinced that blood did not matter to the Inspector; he'd loved Jasper as he would his own kin.

"I'm not looking forward to seeing the viscount," Leo admitted, the curl of nervousness in her stomach returning. "I wish I could forget the way he looked at me and the Inspector that one time we saw him at the cemetery. It was a look of sheer disgust."

Jasper had not been with them on that anniversary of Emmaline, Beatrice, and Gregory Junior's deaths. Every year, the Inspector would visit the stone mausoleum within Kensal Green Cemetery that the viscount had erected for his beloved daughter and grandchildren. One time, a young Leo and the Inspector had crossed paths with the viscount there. No words had been exchanged, only the older man's hateful glare with the Inspector's patient, sorrowful one. He'd never blamed Viscount Cowper for his reproach, though Leo had not been so generous.

"I've never met the man," Jasper said. "I honestly don't know what to expect when we arrive. And that is something I don't like."

Neither did she, but she was too curious to ignore the summons—even if it meant encountering Viscount Cowper again. He likely would not recognize Leo from that one wordless meeting at Kensal Green. It was only her strange memory that held onto those images in perfect detail. Even now, over a decade later, she could still draw up the raven-black stovepipe hat he'd been wearing, the dark, midnight-blue greatcoat, his black ascot, threaded with blue stitching, and the walking stick, topped with a polished jet ball. She could still see the red rims of his eyes and the evidence of crystalline tears on his lashes.

"Perhaps it has something to do with the Inspector," she suggested. "And since he is now gone…something falls to you?"

"That might explain my invitation. But what of yours?" He shook his head. "I suppose we'll find out in short order."

There was no use in speculating further. And after the next few moments of uneasy silence, she knew there was no use avoiding any discussion about his secondment, either.

"Will you tell me about Liverpool?" she asked.

He tapped the brim of his hat in his lap. "It is wholly unremarkable."

"I meant the investigation," she said, knowing he was only teasing.

He grinned with good humor, his gaze lingering on her. "I'd rather tell you how beautiful you look."

Leo wasn't accustomed to such compliments, and as she grinned, heat licked her cheeks. He'd called her beautiful once before, even though she'd been a complete mess after a long day at the Spring Street Morgue. Today, however, Leo had done up her sable hair differently, and she'd worn her best dress. The dark purple ensemble had a swagged pannier overskirt that revealed a lighter purple underskirt. According to her good friend Nivedita Brooks, who had thankfully returned from a long stay with her aunt in Birmingham, the rich color complimented her dark hair and fair complexion.

But she knew it wasn't her hair or dress that Jasper was complimenting.

"I've missed you," she replied and, though speaking her feelings had never been very easy for her, added, "I want you to come home, Jasper."

He was only here with her now because he'd taken a day's leave to see to this strange matter.

The last of his smile disappeared, and he turned serious. "I am, Leo."

"Are you?" She let out a gust of bated breath. Her relief was evident enough to earn a questioning frown from him. She tried to explain. "It's just that I know Andrew Carter can't reach you in Liverpool, or at least, not as easily. I thought you might prefer it that way."

The muscle along his jaw tensed. "No Carter is going

to keep me from my life in London. Or from you, for that matter." Jasper shifted his position on the bench to face her more fully. "The counterfeiting investigation is over. We cracked it the day before I received the solicitor's letter. There is paperwork to do, and I'll need to testify in court, but I'm essentially done there."

Her tentative relief now jolted to full pleasure, and she was still smiling when he took her hand and laced his gloved fingers with hers. Leo thought he might kiss her then, as he'd done a few times before leaving for his new post, but the unwieldy friction between them remained; a result, most likely, of them having spent so much time apart.

"I considered taking a train to London to see you, if only for a short visit," he said, looking intently at their joined hands. Leo, too, had secretly wished he would have, but her doubt about his planning to come back at all had kept her from asking. She'd been wrong to assume what his plans were and could have spared herself so much turmoil if only she had taken the chance.

"Why didn't you?" she asked.

"Because I knew I would not want to return to Liverpool."

He brought her hand, encased in soft leather, to his lips. The strange tension between them began to diffuse, but Jasper didn't lean closer to kiss her. He lowered their hands to the bench, keeping their fingers threaded.

The rain had started in earnest as they'd been driving along a country road toward Cowper Fields. It pelted the roof of the carriage and the glass windows, darkening the afternoon light.

"I suppose you still want to hear about the case?"

Jasper teased, a small smile curving his lips as he gazed at her.

She did, and over the next several minutes, he laid out a complex counterfeiting operation, in which a criminal family, previously unknown to the police, were producing false notes and using one of their businesses, a manufacturer of coffins and caskets, to transport them. The counterfeit notes were sent to select funeral directors throughout Liverpool, Birmingham, Leeds, and London, sewn within the coffins' silk linings. The operation had planted their men within these funeral services to strip the bank notes from the caskets and distribute them in different cities.

"Clever," Leo said. "How did you solve it?"

Jasper cocked his head. "At times, it seemed we never would. They were incredibly careful and methodical. Eventually though, they made a mistake. An unsuspecting funeral director witnessed the extraction of the notes. He was stabbed and left for dead, but he lived long enough to tell the police what he saw. From there, we followed the lead back to the source."

Leo was glad for him. He'd been sent to Liverpool not as punishment, but because he'd done well in solving a few high-profile cases in London as of late. This success would be yet another feather in his cap.

They sat next to each other in companionable silence, their hands still clasped on the seat between them. The carriage soon slowed and turned down a long, gravel drive, toward a large, stone Tudor manor with numerous turrets and leaded-glass windows. Vines with withered brown leaves clung to the exterior, adding to its foreboding air. Leo was grateful for her gloves, as her palms began to sweat as they reached the terminus of the drive, where a small fountain centered a graveled yard.

Jasper opened the door, and a gust of wet wind nearly ripped it from his hand. He helped Leo to the ground and shouted to the driver above a clap of thunder to wait. They expected to return to the train station immediately after the reading of the will, which was to commence on the hour.

Fighting the pummeling wind, they dashed toward the open front door, where a younger man in footman's clothing, and an older man in more formal butler's attire, stood waiting for them. Both had grim countenances, which were in line with the rest of the intimidating manor.

"Welcome to Cowper Hall, Miss Spencer, Inspector Reid," the older man said in a placid, solemn tone as they entered.

The sound of their arrival echoed off the ceiling of a large entrance hall. It was cold and dark, except for the glow of a few electric lamps. A luxury, Leo imagined, for a home so far out of town. Tapestries and paintings of hunting scenes hung on the walls, but her eyes were drawn to movement at the first-story balustrade above. There stood an older man, tall and lean, draped in dim light. He turned swiftly and strode away before she could see his face.

"I am Decamp, Viscount Cowper's butler. The family is waiting for you in the library."

Leo returned her attention to the two men who'd admitted them to the manor. The footman came forward to take her coat, hat, and handbag. As Jasper removed his damp hat and overcoat, the panels of his suit jacket shifted, revealing the leather sheath strapped to his side. His police-issued revolver was secured in it. Police constables and sergeants weren't offered weapons; however, detectives were, and Jasper didn't go many places without his, especially after it had come in useful a few times. Leo didn't expect any trouble at Cowper Hall, but the sight of his Webley put her a little more at ease.

They followed Decamp through the entrance hall in silence, their footfalls muffled by the length of an enormous runner laid over the entirety of the entrance hall floor. It was not an exaggeration to say her whole house on Duke Street could have fit inside this one room.

While walking at a brisk pace, Leo stayed close enough to Jasper to feel the brush of his sleeve. Decamp turned through a pair of tall doors that led into a library that was just as overwhelming in size and formality as the entrance hall. Somber and masculine, with mahogany-paneled walls, green baize carpet, and bookshelves packed with leather-bound tomes, the room also had a long reading table set near the hearth. Four people were seated there, waiting, all attired in mourning black. Their eyes, filled with suspicion, settled on the newcomers.

"Detective Inspector Jasper Reid and Miss Leonora Spencer," Decamp intoned, before sweeping out an arm and indicating that they should approach and take their seats.

At the head of the table, a man in a gray tweed suit and a pair of gold, round-rimmed spectacles stood quickly, as gentlemen often did when a woman entered a room. The only other man at the table uncurled from his chair with reluctance, barely straightened his back, then dropped into his seat again.

"Thank you for attending, Inspector Reid, Miss Spencer," the bespectacled man said. "I'm Mr. Corman. I wrote to you both on behalf of my former client, Mrs. Francine Stroud. Please do take a seat, and we can begin."

Jasper pulled out a chair for Leo, who sat stiffly while the two other women seated at the table, somewhere in their late twenties to early thirties by Leo's estimation, looked on with barely concealed hostility.

"Thank you for waiting," Leo said, her voice slightly tremulous. Jasper took his seat next to her.

Only the solicitor replied, with a polite "Of course."

Clearly, Francine Stroud's decision to include two strangers in her will had upset the rest of her family.

Glimpsing toward the doors to the library, which Decamp had closed firmly behind him when he'd left, Leo wondered why the viscount was not present. It had been he, she gathered, standing at the balustrade. Had he not been invited to the reading of his own daughter's will?

"It would be prudent for introductions first, perhaps," Mr. Corman said. "Inspector, Miss Spencer, may I present—"

"Can we just get on with it, Corman?" the man sulking in his chair spat.

The woman seated next to him, her blonde hair pulled back into an austere bun and bound in black netting, tried to lay her hand on his. He jerked away and muttered something under his breath.

"Forgive my husband," the woman said after being rebuffed. "This is a difficult time, and my mother's request for the two of you to attend, that she has perhaps bequeathed you something…well, it is terribly strange."

"We are in agreement," Jasper replied. "I take it you are

Mrs. Stroud's daughter?" He looked to the woman seated one chair down from the solicitor. The two women were similar in looks, though Leo thought the one who'd spoken was slightly older and possessed more refined features.

Mr. Corman cleared his throat. "Yes, as I was saying, may I introduce Mrs. Stroud's daughters, Mrs. Helen Dalton and Miss Nadia Stroud."

"And this is my husband, Anthony," Helen Dalton offered.

Leo suppressed the automatic urge to give the standard reply: *Pleased to meet you.* It wasn't pleasing to her at all. Nadia Stroud, less attractive than her older sister, appeared bored and slouched back in her chair in a masculine manner. She had a cut crystal glass of spirits in front of her, as did Anthony Dalton.

"We are as confounded as you appear to be as to why we were summoned," Leo said. "Mr. Corman?"

The solicitor was the only one here who could put everyone's confusion to rest. He took his seat and opened a leather briefcase on the table in front of him.

"There is the usual business to discuss, of course, however, recognizing that Inspector Reid and Miss Spencer would be strangers to the family, Mrs. Stroud had asked that I first address the bestowment of their portion and then allow them to depart."

Leo exhaled in relief, even as Anthony Dalton again huffed and muttered to his wife, "Why do they even *have* a portion? What was your mother about?"

Next to her, Jasper tensed as he directed a probing glare across the table toward Mr. Dalton. Although, as rude as he was being, Leo understood the man's question.

She'd tried—and failed—to speculate what Francine Stroud could have possibly wanted to bequeath to the two of them. The woman had been Emmaline's sister, and she would have known Gregory Reid. But how had she known of the two children her former brother-in-law had taken under his wing after the deaths of her sister, niece, and nephew?

The solicitor overlooked Mr. Dalton's complaint. Opening a folio, he withdrew a sheet of paper. Peering through the thick lenses of his spectacles, he read, "To Mr. Jasper Reid and Miss Leonora Spencer, I bequeath all property title to, and ownership of, the residence at Number 19 Craven Hill, London."

A hot bolt of shock traveled down Leo's spine and threatened to send her up from her chair. She stayed seated; however, Anthony pushed his own chair back in a clatter as he leapt to his feet. Helen's face went slack, and she let out a strangled cry. Leo, whose confusion had turned back in on itself, warping through her into yet another knot, turned to Jasper. He'd gone stone still. His dark green eyes met hers briefly before hinging on the solicitor.

"Mr. Corman, there must be some mistake," he said slowly.

"She…she gave them the London house?" Nadia Stroud sat forward in her chair, finally looking as if she cared about what was happening. "She can't have done."

Located in the distinguished Lancaster Gate neighborhood, just north of Hyde Park, Craven Hill was one of the finest streets in London. Finer even than Charles Street, where Jasper lived in the Inspector's old home. That property, too, had been gifted by a relative of

Emmaline's—in that instance, by her grandmother to Gregory Reid.

"Inspector Reid is correct," Leo said, raising her voice to be heard above Anthony and Helen arguing between themselves about what Francine had been thinking. "It doesn't make any sense for Mrs. Stroud to have left us property."

The solicitor appeared as if he had been prepared for a storm wind of arguments. Fitting, as the gales of rain outside had intensified. The electric chandelier overhead seemed to brighten as the storm further darkened the evening skies.

"Be that as it may, the two of you have been granted equal ownership of the Craven Hill address." Mr. Corman came away from his seat to bring them a thinner folio than what he'd opened previously. "This is the deed to the home and some other documents you will need for the property, and the keys, of course." He gave this to Jasper, who stared at the folio in his hand with plain skepticism.

He pushed back his chair and stood. "I'd like some explanation, Mr. Corman. Miss Spencer and I did not even know Emmaline Reid had a sister. We'd never met Francine Stroud in our lives."

"Do you see?" Anthony hissed to his wife, gesticulating toward Leo and Jasper. "Your mother had gone mad! Corman, there must be a way to obstruct this bestowment."

The solicitor did not respond to Anthony but extended something more, this time to Leo. It was an envelope.

"Mrs. Stroud assured me that all will be explained

within the contents of this letter," he said, as Leo took the envelope.

"You are to read it together," he instructed. "Apart from the rest of the family."

Their names, Leonora and Jasper, had been scrawled on the front, in looping, unfamiliar handwriting. Leo rose from her chair on numb legs. The other three people at the table had all gone utterly silent when the letter had been presented.

"We'll take our leave then," Jasper said and, with his hand coming to rest on Leo's lower back, led her from the library.

Chapter Two

Decamp was waiting for them in the hallway. Jasper kept his hand on Leo's back. Her gait was unusually stiff and halting. Understandable. The muscles in his own legs were strung tight, his head swimming after the last several staggering minutes.

"If you will follow me," the butler intoned.

He led them toward another corner of the entrance hall, past the bottom of a wide staircase. The solicitor had likely explained to Decamp in advance that they would require a private room to read the proffered letter. It was all smoothly done and meticulously planned. Jasper didn't like it at all.

"What just happened?" Leo whispered to him as they trailed the butler.

"I'm not entirely sure," he answered. But he was damn well going to find out.

They were brought into a small sitting room. Two electric lamps had been switched on, and a small fire had been stoked in a white marble hearth in preparation for them.

"Tea will be delivered shortly," Decamp said before disappearing from the threshold.

Alone at last, Jasper rolled his shoulders, releasing the tension that had built up. It had all but wiped away any pleasure and relief he'd felt at seeing Leo again. He dropped the folio of papers onto the low tea table in front of the settee and raked his fingers through his hair.

"She's given us a bloody house?" he remarked as he walked toward the window. Rain lashed the glass, and a shudder of lightning brightened the room momentarily.

He'd had misgivings about this visit to Cowper Fields. Now, he was confounded enough by it to become irritated.

He didn't understand how Mrs. Stroud had known about him and Leo, or why she had thought about them enough to include them in her will. Not to mention that she, or perhaps her solicitor, had known to send his summons to the police department in Liverpool, rather than to Scotland Yard.

"It makes no sense, Jasper. Mrs. Stroud's daughters should have inherited the property," Leo said as she opened the sealed letter without first looking for a penknife. The envelope tore, and she cast it aside as she came to stand with him by the window.

"The husband seems to agree with you," Jasper replied.

Anthony Dalton had every right to be upset, but the man had still grated on Jasper's nerves in the library. His petulant arrogance had made him sound more like a spoiled child than a grown man.

"I would wager Mr. Dalton would be unpleasant even

if his late mother-in-law hadn't cheated him out of an expensive property," Leo replied, unfolding a single sheet of thick, cream-colored paper. Handwriting filled the page, front and back.

She began to read aloud, and Jasper quickly crossed the room to close the door. If Francine Stroud had wanted them to read her letter privately, she hadn't intended for any servants to eavesdrop.

"To Detective Inspector Jasper Reid and Miss Leonora Spencer," Leo began.

"As we have never met in life, I understand if you are bewildered to find yourselves at my father's estate for the reading of my will. I cannot explain everything to you, as many details are private and have been kept as such over the years, at Gregory's request. However, I wish you both to know that I esteemed him greatly, and that I supported my sister's decision to marry for love. He spoke and wrote of you both quite often and with great affection. I know that you, Jasper, are a skilled detective, and that you, Leonora, have a stalwart constitution as well as a steel trap of a memory. For these reasons, and because Gregory believed so highly in you, I know I can trust the two of you now with a most significant task. I would like you to discover the truth surrounding my son's death twelve years ago."

Leo paused and looked up from the page. He'd begun pacing in front of the fireplace, a worrisome suspicion settling in his stomach, but now, at this last sentence, he paused, his attention sharpened.

"Go on," he urged Leo. She continued with a nod.

"Theodore was just ten years old when, one night, he fell from the roof of the house on Craven Hill. It was judged to be death by misadventure, but there is something I kept hidden away from everyone, even Gregory. It is known that I was the

unfortunate one to find my son's lifeless body behind the house, where he came to rest. However, I never spoke of a small glass trinket I found clutched in his hand. The trinket, still strung to a length of ribbon, belonged to my older daughter, Helen. In that wretched moment, I suspected something wicked, something that went against the very nature of my being a mother. I was terrified and ashamed to question if Helen had anything to do with Teddy's fall. So, I hid the trinket, a small vial, before anyone could discover it.

I kept it hidden away, unwilling to face my suspicion. However, recently, I learned that I may have been mistaken. The glass vial might not have been in Helen's possession at the time of Teddy's death. Who did possess it, and whether that person was on the roof with Teddy that night, is unknown. I am too ill and much too ashamed of what I believed about my daughter to begin my own inquiry now. However, I am aware that I failed Teddy by forsaking any opportunity to discover the truth about what happened that night. My dear boy deserves justice. I would like you to find it for him."

Leo flipped the page and continued to read.

"You should begin your inquiry at Craven Hill. The home has been vacant for over a decade as I could not stay there after Teddy's death. Go into the first-floor bedroom that overlooks the street. Count six floorboards from the heat register and look for a small graze in the wood. Underneath the plank, you will find the vial. It may help you in your investigation. At the very least, I would like it to be returned to my daughter.

It is by design that I will not be alive to hear the outcome of your inquiry. I cannot confess to Helen what I suspected all these years, and what has kept me from loving her fully, as I should have done. I hope she will know how ashamed I am of my betrayal."

Leo lowered the paper. "Signed Mrs. Francine Stroud. It's dated just two weeks ago."

There came a light rap upon the door. A maid entered carrying a tray laden with biscuits and tea. At the sight of it, Jasper's stomach rumbled; he'd left his lodgings in Liverpool early that morning to see to a few things at the police station before rushing to catch his train. The journey had taken hours, and he hadn't eaten anything since breakfast at Mrs. Hart's. She was no Mrs. Zhao when it came to talent in the kitchen, but at least he hadn't starved during the last four months.

The maid settled the tray onto an occasional table, and after she left, Leo let the silence stew a bit longer as she poured for them. Jasper was grateful for the delay. He hadn't any idea what to say in response to the extraordinary letter. Mrs. Stroud had given them an assignment, for all intents and purposes, but as a detective inspector with Scotland Yard, Jasper did not take on private inquiries. His caseload was already too heavy as it was.

"I'm not sure what to make of it," Leo said as she handed a cup of tea to him and then lowered herself onto the edge of a chair. "She could have asked us to investigate her son's death without bequeathing us the property where he died."

"Which makes me wonder if there were additional reasons she did not want any of her family members to have that home," Jasper replied, taking the seat adjacent to her, on the settee.

"Because she suspected them?"

He reached for one of the biscuits and shrugged. "She'd started to doubt Helen was behind the deadly fall, so that opened the possibility that another person was. Someone who would have had reason to be on the roof of that house."

On its surface, the inquiry did not seem too complicated. A conversation with Helen, then with the rest of the family, followed by the staff employed at the house on Craven Hill at the time, should unlock the truth, something Francine had been too afraid to undertake herself. How had she been able to turn her back on the truth surrounding the death of her only son all these years? Jasper didn't think he could have withstood it. He'd have much rather faced the truth, ugly as it might be, and dealt with the consequences than go to his grave still wondering.

"What are we to do?" Leo asked, her cup of tea forgotten as she held it in her lap. "I could go to the address when I get back to London—"

"Not alone," he said, the reaction automatic.

"But the house is empty," Leo argued.

"That doesn't matter. You shouldn't be entering abandoned homes by yourself."

Even ones located within wealthy neighborhoods. She set her jaw and kept her lips sealed. *Bloody woman.* She was going to go anyway.

Agitated, Jasper set his cup and saucer on the table. "We'll speak to Helen before we leave. With any hope, she'll be able to clear up the question surrounding her brother's death quickly." Or, she could blanch at having been found out, stammer a confession, and then Jasper would place her under arrest. He exhaled and scrubbed his bristled jaw.

He did not want this assignment, especially since it

was being handed down from a woman his father had apparently known quite well. Yet, Gregory Reid had kept his acquaintance with Emmaline's sister a secret. The wording of Francine's letter made it sound as if *Gregory* had been the one to request the secrecy. It bothered Jasper. Perhaps as much as the decade-old mystery surrounding Theodore Stroud's death bothered him.

"Mrs. Stroud didn't provide many details about Teddy's fall," Leo said. "We should find out more about it before we speak to Helen. Do you think Mr. Corman might know?"

"I'll ask, but I think Mrs. Dalton, and maybe Miss Stroud, would be the more knowledgeable about it."

"What about the viscount?"

The mention of him soured Jasper's stomach. Gregory Reid had explained enough about Emmaline's father for Jasper to have already formed an opinion of the man. He did not believe meeting Viscount Cowper would alter that opinion.

"He didn't attend the will reading," Leo commented, after taking a disinterested sip of tea.

Jasper was curious to know why. "Perhaps she left nothing to her father," he suggested. It was the most reasonable answer.

"Or he was upset that two people connected to Gregory Reid were summoned here and chose not to attend," Leo added.

"I'd considered that too."

Richard Cowper had squarely laid the blame for the untimely deaths of his daughter and grandchildren at Gregory Reid's feet, saying that had he not been working as a policeman, he would have been at the boating pond in

Regent's Park that day when the ice broke. He would have been able to stop his wife and children from slipping under the broken sheets of ice and drowning in the deep, frigid water. And though his father had acknowledged that even had he been there, the outcome might have been the same, Jasper despised the viscount for piling onto a heartbroken man and twisting his grief.

He ate another biscuit, though it was bland and dry, and finished his tea. Meanwhile, Leo stared into the fire with a faraway look. She was likely rereading the letter from Mrs. Stroud, which had been emblazoned in her memory the moment she read it.

What he'd said in the carriage on the ride to Cowper Fields was the bald truth: He'd missed her. Not a day had passed during his secondment to Liverpool when he had not thought of her. From sunrise to the moment he dropped into bed each night, thoughts of Leo flowed through his mind like an ever-unraveling length of thread. Sometimes the thread would catch and tug, as it had a time when he'd been walking behind a young woman who looked so much like Leo—her figure, her clothing, her hair, even the set of her shoulders—that he'd needed to cross the street and increase his pace in order to look back at her to be sure Leo had not arrived in Liverpool unannounced. But for the most part, the thread unraveled with a persistent ache. Especially at night, after writing yet another letter to her in his small room at Mrs. Hart's boardinghouse. Christ, he'd never written so damn much in his life. And when her replies arrived in the post, he'd read them with her voice clear in his head.

He'd wanted a different reunion with her than this odd and uncomfortable will reading, and the even stranger news that they were to jointly own a home in exchange for solving an old case. The bizarreness of it all hadn't helped their awkward meeting at the train station. Jasper had wanted to take Leo into his arms and kiss her, and yet, there had been an unexpected wall between them.

A strong gust of wind howled outside, and a clap of thunder shook the glass panes in the sitting room window. The electric lamps flickered briefly and seemed to distract Leo from her musings. She looked at him, and a small frown tugged her lips.

"Have you heard from Andrew Carter at all?" she asked softly.

A bit of tension fed back into his shoulders. "No. Have you?"

She shook her head, and Jasper sat back on the settee, relieved. Part of him had been grateful when Detective Chief Inspector Dermot Coughlan had come to him in July with a request from Liverpool for one of the Yard's inspectors to join them for a complicated case. Superintendent Monroe had recommended Jasper for the secondment, and Coughlan had approved the choice. Whether or not Jasper approved didn't matter; he would go and do the Yard proud. Leaving London and Leo for an unspecified length of time came with one benefit: physical distance from Andrew Carter and his family.

Jasper's inquiry into Andrew's new wife's murder at Striker's Wharf months before had stirred the youngest Carter brother's suspicion over the lead inspector's resemblance to James, Andrew's third cousin who'd drowned nearly two decades before. Eventually, he'd put the truth together and approached Jasper with the threat of exposing his true identity—unless he did favors for his cousin, whenever he might need them. Andrew had mentioned Leo in that same conversation, alluding to his willingness to use her as a means of coercing Jasper, if need be.

His blood ties were complicated and permanent, and Leo would surely be better off with a man who did not have an axe hanging over his neck. But he refused to give her up because of the bloody Carters. Not to mention that he seethed with jealousy at the mere thought of Leo being with another man.

"Then again," Leo went on, her voice turning lighter. "Perhaps I haven't heard from Mr. Carter due to my outings with Lord Hayes." She formed a crafty arch of her brow. "Did you really think I wouldn't know what you were up to?"

Jasper smothered a grin. He'd asked his good friend Oliver Hayes to check in on Leo every now and again and invite her out for dinner or for a stroll. Though Jasper kept his reasons to himself, he'd wanted Oliver and Leo out in public, in case Andrew had his men watching. His cousin had had Jasper tailed for weeks back in July before approaching him to make his demands, and he wouldn't put it past Andrew to have eyes on Leo too. If word got back to Andrew that Leo was stepping out with another man, well then, that wouldn't be so bad. Apparently, Leo had deciphered Jasper's intentions, though.

"I hope Hayes behaved himself," he said, already trusting his friend had been a gentleman, and yet also unable to stifle a jealous twinge.

"He told me to tell you how angelic he was," she replied, her smile growing. "But you should know he is a hopeless flirt."

Jasper groaned. "I am aware."

"We had some lively discussions."

He shifted on the cushion. "Did you?"

"I believe I might have swayed him on the topic of women's suffrage."

As Oliver had once called all suffragists "miserable harpies," Jasper would be astonished if indeed his friend had come around.

"We attended the theatre too," she went on, still grinning, as if knowing the thorns of envy were pushing deeper into him. "He leases his own box. It was very nice."

"How lovely," he forced out through gritted teeth. "I think we should see if Mr. Corman is finished with the rest of the will reading."

He stood up—and the lamps in the room flickered out. The fire provided enough light to see by, but at the next raging howl of wind, something struck the window. Leo jumped to her feet and whirled, but Jasper raised a hand to calm her as the shadow of the object fell.

"It was just a tree branch," he said.

"The wind must have taken down some electrical wires," she supposed.

Jasper started for the closed door to the sitting room, still aiming to see if the solicitor had finished the reading of the will and if Helen Dalton was available for an interview. In the entrance hall, servants had already lit candles and paraffin lamps. The butler, Decamp, strode toward him, hands clasped behind his back.

"Inspector, I've just received word from one of our footmen returning from town. Floodwaters have submerged multiple portions of track north and south of

Harrow, and there are several trees that have come down along the route to town. Travel is not advised at this time."

The cramp present in Jasper's stomach since receiving the solicitor's letter started to feel permanent. *Of course,* they would be prevented from leaving Cowper Hall. He kept his displeasure from showing as Decamp continued, "His lordship will have rooms prepared for you and Miss Spencer."

Leo had come into the threshold behind Jasper. "That isn't necessary," she replied. "Harrow is large enough. I'm sure that if we can travel around the downed trees, we can find lodging in town."

"The viscount will not hear of it," Decamp insisted. "And the driver waiting for you has gone. As soon as your rooms are ready, you'll be shown to them to freshen yourselves before dinner, which will be served in the dining room at eight o'clock."

So, not only would they be stuck here for the night, but they were to dine with the family. *Hell.* At least they would have plenty of time to question Helen. Although as soon as the topic of Theodore's death came up, Jasper wasn't certain the viscount and the Daltons wouldn't boot them both straight out into the storm.

Chapter Three

The dining room glittered with candlelight. To combat the cut to the electric supply, an excess of tapers and paraffin lamps had been arranged down the long table, along with two floral centerpieces that reminded Leo of funereal sprays. The storm had lessened, but it hadn't abated, and even now, a few hours after being shown to her guest room, intermittent winds hammered at the manor's time-weathered exterior.

As Leo entered the dining room, she noted all but two place settings at the table had been claimed. Her own spot, of course, and the one at the head of the table. The viscount's, she presumed. To Leo's relief, Jasper was already present. He, along with Anthony Dalton, the solicitor Mr. Corman, and another man in a handsome wine-red velvet dinner jacket who had not been present at the will reading, stood politely as she entered the dreary room. The three women, Helen, Nadia, and a third around their same age, remained seated and quiet.

Leo met Jasper's eyes, which narrowed and seemed to

inspect her for anything that might be wrong. She'd missed the vigilance of his gaze these last months; the way it lent her a sense of security. A footman pulled out a chair for her, and with some unease, she took her seat. Thankfully, she sat directly across from Jasper. The unpalatable Anthony Dalton was to her right, and Mr. Corman, to her left.

"We were beginning to fear you'd lost your way in the dark," Nadia Stroud said as she was just about to sip from her glass of wine. "But how could you, I suppose, when you possess—what was it you said, Mr. Corman? A photographic memory?"

Leo pinned the young woman, and then the solicitor, with a startled stare.

Mr. Corman's cheeks reddened with remorse. "Ahem, yes," he said, clearing his throat as if nervous. "Mrs. Stroud did mention as much to me when arranging for her will."

It was information that only the Inspector could have provided Francine with. Strangely, a sour sense of betrayal made its way through Leo. Why would he have been speaking to Francine Stroud about her unusual memory?

"How very special, Miss Spencer," Nadia said, though the teasing curve of her lips was not meant to be friendly.

While in school, when she'd been younger, Leo had not had many friends among the other girls. She'd known, even then, that she came across as too serious and standoffish, and she had not been interested in changing those qualities about herself just to fit in. However, not being part of any particular circle of friends had allowed her the opportunity to observe them. Francine Stroud's younger daughter had the pinched expression of someone who was secretly eager to see how her veiled barb would land.

Leo paid her little mind as she unfolded her napkin and placed it onto her lap and decided not to respond to the comment about her memory. Nor would she point out that since she had not yet visited the dining room, she could not have remembered the way. It would only sound peevish, and it was clear Nadia's intent had been to provoke her.

"A footman was kind enough to show me the way," she said.

In fact, the uniformed young man had been waiting at the landing of the stairs as if he'd been assigned to do just that. She'd been impatient to escape her room almost as soon as she had been shown into it earlier. A maid named Ursula had immediately come to draw a bath, which Leo had initially refused. She only wanted to rejoin Jasper and seek out Helen Dalton for their interview regarding Teddy Stroud. However, the young maid had informed her that Mrs. Dalton had gone to her room with a megrim and that she'd taken a draught to help her rest.

Then, as Ursula turned on the taps in the small bath chamber attached to Leo's room, the hot water steaming the air as it pooled into the white enamel tub, she'd given in to the luxurious temptation of a bath. At her own home, she had but a small metal tub in a backroom off the kitchen that she would fill with water heated on the hob. When cool water was added to the hot, the tepid result left her riddled with gooseflesh, so she bathed as quickly as possible.

The cost for installing pipes for indoor plumbing would be far too costly for Leo and her aunt and uncle,

Flora and Claude Feldman. Jasper, she knew, had plumbing at his much finer home on Charles Street. And as she disrobed and settled into the hot water, scented with rose oil, she considered that the house on Craven Hill would likely have it as well. She'd spent far more time bathing than she usually would, her hair pinned up high so that it wouldn't become wet. Her mind had wandered through the details of Francine Stroud's letter, the reactions of her family when the solicitor had read the bequest to Leo and Jasper, and the curious absence of the viscount.

She looked again toward his empty chair at the head of the dinner table, and her eyes met with the man in the velvet dinner jacket. He was in his mid- to late thirties, with dark hair and eyes, though the poor lighting could have been the cause for his irises to appear fathomless. He dipped his chin in a polite nod and, as gentlemen were trained to do with ladies, withheld from speaking or introducing himself until someone else did so. Helen Dalton took up the task, her hand clutched around the stem of her wine glass.

"Miss Spencer, I should introduce my uncle, Frederick Cowper, and his wife, Millicent. Frederick, Millicent, this is Miss Leonora Spencer."

Leo felt her brow twitch before she could school her immediate reaction. *Uncle?* Gracious, Mr. Cowper appeared no more than a handful of years older than Helen and Nadia. She would have guessed him to be a cousin or brother.

"Pleased to make your acquaintance," she said to him and to his wife, the latter of whom had no qualms about appearing utterly bored.

Beside Leo, Mr. Dalton snorted a laugh.

"You are wondering how they can possibly be uncle and niece," he remarked, having noted Leo's surprise after all. "Frederick is the issue of the viscount's second wife," he explained, his voice too loud, his tone unmistakably mocking. His glass of wine was empty, and with an impatient gesture, he indicated the footman should refill it.

Mr. Cowper glowered at Mr. Dalton before cutting his attention to Leo. It brightened visibly as he tried to be courteous. "Miss Spencer, a pleasure to meet you. I am sorry you've been detained from returning home this evening, though I hope your stay here will be comfortable."

The greeting was more welcoming than anything had been so far at Cowper Hall. She offered her thanks, though it was drowned out by Mr. Dalton's guttering laugh. "Ah, yes, ever the gentleman, Frederick is." He leaned to the side, closer to Leo's shoulder. She resisted leaning away from him, though she was tempted, especially as he brought with him the sour odor of whisky. "And the irrefutable apple of the viscount's eye."

This made him laugh again, though Leo could see nothing humorous about the statement. Neither could anyone else, apparently. Helen tried to disappear into her glass of wine, while Nadia rolled her eyes and sighed.

"Will the viscount be joining us?" Jasper asked, his voice firm enough to steal Mr. Dalton's attention, which had drifted toward Leo's lap. The man was utterly soused.

"Not if we are lucky," Mr. Dalton said as he straightened again and leaned away from her.

A footman came forward to pour wine into Leo's glass, and she readily sipped the claret. The sooner this dinner was over, the better. Jasper's livid stare as he leveled it at her drunken neighbor hinted that he felt much the same.

Then, in a flurry of motion, another person joined them. He entered the room with swift strides, making his way to the head of the table without so much as a greeting for any of the seated guests. It was the same tall, silver-haired man she'd seen turning away from the balustrade upon their arrival—and the same bitter-faced man she recalled from the Kensal Green Cemetery all those years ago.

Viscount Cowper did not introduce himself to his guests as he sat down and snapped his fingers for the dinner to commence, nor did he make any excuses for his tardiness.

"I've been informed that the electric should be fixed by tomorrow, mid-morning," he said. His deep voice cut a path down the table, and oddly enough, the lit wicks on the tapered candles all flickered.

Mr. Corman cleared his throat. "That is excellent news, my lord."

The solicitor's reply drew the viscount's steely blue eyes in Leo's direction. He assessed her for one or two seconds, then averted his gaze as if bored. Judging by the age lines and mottled spots on his face, and the hollows of his cheeks and eyes, she guessed he was probably seventy-five or eighty years old. However, he'd moved with a younger man's agility, and he did not wear spectacles. His son, Frederick, greatly resembled him, though he did not possess the viscount's same grim slash of a mouth.

The footmen arrived with tureens of soup, and the next several minutes were busied with settling into the first course. At the arrival of the food, two shaggy-looking dogs popped up from where they must have been lying next to Nadia's chair. They were Irish Wolfhounds, Leo suspected, and they stared at Nadia as if hoping she would feed them. Helen shook her head at the dogs' begging, but other than an exchange of pointed looks between the sisters, nothing was said.

The silence around the table was so fraught that Leo hardly tasted the soup. She crossed glances with Jasper multiple times, wishing they could have taken supper alone somewhere else rather than with the family.

When their bowls were being cleared away, Helen broke the uneasy quiet.

"Miss Spencer, Inspector," she began, her nervousness betrayed by a quaver in her voice, "I think we are all quite curious as to the letter my mother left for you to read privately. Did she explain what your presence here has all been about?"

The solicitor dabbed the corner of his mouth with his napkin and stammered the beginning of a response. "Mrs. Dalton, I must reiterate that your mother's request was that—"

"Yes, thank you, Corman, we are aware of her request," Mr. Dalton interrupted, the snide remark enough to silence the solicitor. "However, as all of us wish to know exactly why Francine gave two people she has never met —not only that, but the two *proteges* of her late sister's husband—an obscenely expensive property, I think it only fair they explain why."

The intensity of his stare bored into Leo's cheek. "Whether you think it fair or not, Mr. Dalton," she replied, turning to face him, "the contents of that letter are private. As Mrs. Stroud wished them to be. I imagine, as her family, you would want to respect her final wishes."

He sneered. "Do you have even the slightest idea how much a property at that address in London is worth? It certainly is not meant to house those of the working class."

At the barefaced insult, Jasper looked as if he'd have liked to clock the man in the jaw. Leo would have enjoyed seeing it done, too.

"Tony, that is quite enough," Frederick said, slapping his hand once upon the table. It wasn't violent, though it did startle the two wolfhounds flanking Nadia's chair. "I'll ask you to respect my late sister's wishes and to treat our guests with the same respect."

Mr. Dalton gurgled some more laughter, the hysterical sound of it a bit alarming. "Of course, my lord. Whatever you say, my lord."

"Do shut up, Anthony," Viscount Cowper said smoothly, paying more attention to the claret in his glass than to anyone else at the table. "Mr. Reid and Miss Spencer, what my grandson-in-law says has merit, even if he is acting like a drunken buffoon."

At the rebuke, Mr. Dalton shrank back into his seat with a pout.

"Inspector," Jasper said.

The viscount frowned. "Pardon?"

"It is Inspector Reid, not 'Mister,'" he replied evenly, even as Viscount Cowper's mien darkened. "And while Miss Spencer and I understand the frustration over the ambiguity of this bequest, we intend to honor your daughter's wishes by withholding the contents of the letter." He paused. "For now."

Leo stifled a pleased grin at Jasper's pointed rebuke and admired him for not silencing himself in the face of opposition.

She took a furtive glance toward Helen. The woman seemed just as nervous as before. Did she have an idea as to what all this was about? Perhaps her mother had not hidden her suspicions well enough. Nothing could be said on the matter of Teddy here, of course. Jasper would want to question her alone.

"*Inspector*," the viscount echoed, drawling the title with obvious derision. "I must say, I was baffled when I heard Gregory Reid had replaced my grandson with some runty street urchin he'd scraped up while going about his work."

Leo's pulse jumped at the purposefully cruel words. She could barely believe he'd dared say them aloud.

Jasper, however, didn't flinch at the viscount's direct loathing. Instead, he allowed a small twitch of his lips. "That you believe he would attempt to replace Gregory Junior with me reveals how little you truly knew him."

"Grandfather," Nadia began, speaking gently. "Now isn't the time to dredge up the past. Let us eat."

At that word—eat—the wolfhounds yipped and let their tongues loll out of their mouths. Helen scoffed in disgust.

"Must you allow them in the dining room? It is unsanitary."

Nadia stroked the head of one dog. "It isn't unsanitary, Helen; you just hate my dogs."

"One of them bit my maid!" Helen cried. "She is terrified of dogs as it is."

Nadia laughed. "It was a nip. Porthos didn't even break Dora's skin."

As the sisters bickered, the footmen returned with large platters of roasted duck, glazed in an orange sauce. One held the tray to the viscount's side, offering him the chance to help himself. The other footman went to Helen's side. While she took a portion for her plate with shaking hands, the viscount did not. He remained locked in a staring spar with Jasper.

"Perhaps you are right," Lord Cowper finally said, "and I did not know Gregory well. However, it seems both my daughters certainly did."

The words themselves might not have implied anything untoward, but the suggestive sound of them curling off his tongue made his meaning obvious. Paired with the mention of Gregory in Francine's letter and his request for secrecy, Leo's mind reeled to a stop. She could not reconcile what the viscount was insinuating: that the Inspector and Francine had once been romantically involved.

A swift glance across the table showed Jasper grinding his jaw with stifled fury. He would not react, Leo knew. He was too measured, too cautious to be goaded into making a spectacle of himself. He kept his eyes trained on the viscount until the footman intercepted their staring match by leaning forward next to Jasper's shoulder, presenting the platter of duck.

The rest of dinner unfolded at a quick pace; the footmen likely related the strain in the dining room to the kitchen staff, and they knew to hurry things along. When it was time for dessert, only Mr. Corman appeared eager to eat his trifle. Lord Cowper tossed down his napkin and shoved back his chair, rising to his feet like a geyser.

"Gentlemen, you are, of course, welcome to join me in

the billiards room for a brandy and cigar," he said, though the invitation sounded hollow and rote. He immediately left, his pace loping but fast for a man of his age.

Helen also stood. "Ladies, shall we?"

Leo wasn't quite sure what to do. The men and women were now separating to different rooms, as she supposed was their custom. The practices of the titled and wealthy were often a mystery to her. She and Jasper locked gazes, and with his solemn nod, she supposed she would follow the viscount's granddaughter.

The solicitor looked longingly at his barely touched trifle as he and the other men rose from their seats to join the viscount. She didn't envy Jasper; it would not be a relaxing game of billiards, to be sure. As she approached the door, she and Jasper were able to steal a moment together, his sleeve brushing against hers as they walked side by side. He lowered his voice to a whisper, "See if you can arrange for an interview tomorrow morning with Mrs. Dalton."

Leo nodded. "I'll invite her to take breakfast in my sitting room," she replied under her breath. It was all they had time for; outside the dining room, Jasper peeled off with the other men in a different direction.

She pushed aside the odd sensation of disappointment and the desire to rejoin him. After her decadent bath and then the next few hours spent pacing her bedroom and adjoining sitting room, exasperated to have no immediate purpose, she had longed to know where Jasper was and what he was doing. It was just the same as she'd felt over the last four months spent apart. His letters were surprisingly detailed about Liverpool, his lodgings at Mrs. Hart's boardinghouse, and his fellow sergeants and constables. But it wasn't enough. Leo had wanted to be able to see him. Touch him. Feel his sooty green eyes on her. It was a greedy sensation that she wasn't at all sure she liked, and yet, it was also unstoppable.

Helen led them to the same sitting room in which Leo and Jasper had been sequestered earlier in the afternoon. The fire burned brightly, illuminating the room with a cozy golden glow. Nadia and Millicent went to the settee, and each took an end cushion, smoothing out their black skirts after sitting. Somewhere along the way, the dogs had departed from their mistress, but as Helen selected a chair and sat, she was just as rigid and unsmiling as she had been at the dinner table. A maid had come into the room and was pouring what appeared to be sherry into cordial glasses.

Leo lowered herself into another chair, and the silence persisted. Millicent propped her elbow upon the arm of the settee and absentmindedly brushed her fingers against the blue silk damask. Only after the maid brought the tray of cordial glasses around and then left them did someone speak.

"Can't you convince your husband to stop being such a boor all the time?" Nadia asked, directing her question to her sister.

Helen pinched her lips together. "I don't think this is an appropriate topic to discuss in front of our guest."

Nadia waved her hand. "It's not as if Anthony has successfully hidden how ill-tempered he is, especially when he is drunk. Miss Spencer noticed, trust me." She turned toward Leo and pinned her with a pair of hard brown eyes. "Didn't you?"

As platitudes were not her forte, Leo replied, "I noticed some discord, yes."

Nadia crossed her arms and smiled smugly at her sister. "See?"

Helen lifted her chin and turned her head, as if to dismiss them all. Lounging against the other arm of the settee, Millicent sighed heavily. "Nadia, dear, if you had ever married, you might understand that it isn't so easy to change the nature of a man."

The affront struck precisely as intended; color bloomed on Nadia's cheeks.

"Millie, dear," she replied, parroting the tone Millicent had just used, "If I marry, it won't be to a man whose nature I regret not being able to change."

Leo sipped her sherry, observing the three women, happy to be mostly overlooked.

"Lord, but your superiority is exhausting," Millicent said, setting down her untouched sherry. She got to her feet and, for the first time, addressed Leo. "My apologies that you've been subjected to this family. Luckily for you, it is only for one evening. Good night."

She swept out of the room.

"Oh, poor *Aunt* Millie," Nadia opined while shaking her head. "See what marrying for a title does, Miss Spencer? I suggest you never consider it."

"I don't believe I will ever have reason to, Miss Stroud," she said, slightly amused by the impractical advice. The only titled person Leo knew was Oliver Hayes, and there was no chance he would offer marriage to her. Nor would she dream of accepting should he do so.

"I imagine it is strange having a woman so close to

your own age as an aunt," Leo said. She was curious about the stark disparity in age between the viscount's first two children—Emmaline and Francine—and his third, Frederick.

"No stranger than having an uncle who is just a handful of years older than we are," Nadia replied lightly. She had finished her sherry. Now, with any hope, she would leave, and Helen would remain long enough for Leo to invite her to breakfast the following morning.

"Were your mother and Emmaline Reid close in age to the viscount's second wife, then?" Leo asked. It might have been an ill-mannered question but considering how the Cowper and Stroud families had behaved thus far, Leo wasn't going to lose sleep over it.

Nadia chuckled. "The very same age. Lucy was their friend, if you can believe it. Imagine! Having to call your once bosom friend 'Mama!'"

Helen chastened her giggling sister with a piercing glare. She then attempted to maintain her poise as she explained further to Leo, "Lucy gave our grandfather his heir, Frederick. Sadly, she passed shortly afterward. Freddie has been more like a cousin or older brother to my sister and me than an uncle."

Leo had known that the viscount was a widower, though she had not known it was twice over.

"And your father?" Leo inquired, curious about Mr. Stroud. "He has passed as well?"

Helen's prim mouth turned downward. "Many years ago."

On the settee, Nadia began to appear weary again, her index finger twirling a curl of her dark hair languidly as she stared into the fire. Just as Leo began to hope she would grow bored enough to leave the room, they were joined by a middle-aged woman, dressed in the utilitarian garb of a maid.

"Madam, I've been sent to tell you that Mr. Dalton is leaving for Field's End Hall."

Helen started in her chair. "He is going home in this weather?" Outside, the rain was still falling heavily, but the winds had died down somewhat.

"Is it very far?" Leo asked.

"No, I suppose not," Helen replied, rubbing her temple.

A commotion burst into the sitting room in the shape of the two startlingly tall and lanky wolfhounds. They ran past the maid, who yelped and jumped with more alarm than was necessary, and converged on Nadia. One leapt onto the settee and tried to lick her cheek, while the other sat directly on her feet.

"Oh, those beasts!" the maid cried.

"Dora, I don't know why you mind them so. Porthos and Aramis have utterly ignored you since the little nip on your hand," Nadia said as she lovingly scrubbed their wiry gray fur.

Helen stood up. "It was more than a nip. And you know my maid was attacked by a dog as a child," she hissed, her firm hold on her temper cracking. "You should be more thoughtful, Nadia."

"She has had ample time to get over her fear of dogs," her sister muttered.

Helen started forward, intending to quit the room and perhaps even the house, if she chose to follow her husband. Given no choice, Leo stood up.

"Mrs. Dalton, Inspector Reid and I would like a private

audience with you before we leave tomorrow. Perhaps you will join us for breakfast? In my sitting room?"

It was inelegantly done, she knew, but it had the effect she'd wanted. Helen stood immobile near her maid, staring at Leo with curiosity. Slowly, she gave a nod.

"Of course. I will see you at, say… eight o'clock?"

"Thank you," Leo replied. Then, blinking as if a bit stunned, Helen continued toward the door. Her maid, Dora, gave Leo a quick, head-to-toe glance before trailing her mistress out of the sitting room.

"Does this *private interview* have to do with the letter my mother gave you?" Nadia asked with frank interest.

"I am certain you will find out in time, Miss Stroud."

Leo decided it was time for bed, and she'd never been more ready to retire for the evening. She bid Nadia a good night and left the room. In the entrance hall, candles and lamps showed the way to and up the main staircase, but as she turned to the right on the landing above, the corridor leading toward her guest room was much darker, with only a few pockets of candlelight along the way.

She felt a shift in the air and then heard a rustle of clothing behind her. Leo whipped around, aware she wasn't alone. Jasper emerged from a shadowed corner, hands in his pockets, his chin tucked. The dark gleam of his eyes cut through the dusky lighting as he said quietly, "Your room, or mine?"

Chapter Four

The sitting room had been prepared for Leo's return, with lamps lit and a wood-burning fire crackling within the small, tiled hearth. As Leo closed the door behind them with a soft *snick,* Jasper had a moment's doubt that this had been the right choice. The doubt wasn't strong enough for him to retreat, however. He'd needed to speak to her alone, especially after their disastrous dinner, and it would have been just as unsuitable for her to have joined him in his guest room.

It was possible a maid might return to see if Leo needed anything else before taking her leave for the evening, but with the collapse of all civility within the manor so far, the impropriety of his being in an unmarried woman's guest room would not be the straw that broke the camel's back.

"Helen has agreed to meet us for breakfast tomorrow at eight o'clock," Leo informed him as she reached one of the chairs set before the fireplace. She didn't sit but stood behind the chair, resting her hands on the back of it.

"She's quite nervous, I think, and I'm not sure if it's all due to her husband's ill-mannered behavior."

Jasper's first impression of Anthony Dalton earlier that day had only been cemented during dinner. It seemed everyone at the table, including his own wife, disliked him, but there had been a distinctly different strain of hostility between him and Cowper's heir, Frederick.

Dalton had left almost immediately after the men arrived in the billiards room. He'd downed a dram of whisky and then barked at the butler, Decamp, for his curricle to be brought around. No one had tried to dissuade him from returning to his home, located less than a mile away from the viscount's manor.

"Do the women hate each other as much as the men seem to?" Jasper asked as he began to walk around the small sitting room. There wasn't much to see, but it at least kept him from drifting toward Leo.

"They're an awful family, aren't they?" she said with a disbelieving shake of her head. "I'm of a mind to believe it all stems from the viscount himself. I learned he married Emmaline and Francine's good friend after the death of the first viscountess. The second wife passed away shortly after giving birth to Frederick."

An older man marrying someone half his age wasn't unheard of, but that he would select one of his daughters' friends was, at least to Jasper's mind, a touch perverse.

Hands in his pockets, Jasper rounded the room again. "Frederick and his father seem to be on good terms, at least. I asked why they were not present at the will reading, but they gave no answer."

It was a nice way of saying they'd ignored him entirely as they'd chalked the tips of their billiard cues, though they had exchanged a look between themselves. Mr. Corman had cleared his throat nervously and announced that he would retire for the evening, if no one minded. No one had, and he'd slipped out as if in great relief. Jasper had followed him into the corridor, but the man was a professional. He would not budge when pressed for information on why the viscount and Frederick had been absent earlier that afternoon.

"I don't think I've ever so desperately wished to leave a place before," Leo said as she wrapped her arms around herself.

"You aren't alone in that." The knot in his stomach hadn't relented all day, and he knew it wouldn't until they'd left not just Cowper Hall, but the estate in its entirety.

Then again, he wasn't eager to leave Leo at the train station and return to Liverpool. The counterfeiting investigation had been concluded, but there were mundane tasks to see to, and it would still be a few weeks before he was released from his secondment.

She cocked her head, as if thinking of something. "I must admit, though, I haven't ever had such a pleasurable bath before." A nostalgic smile touched her lips. "Hot water, straight from a tap. It felt nearly sinful."

Every muscle in Jasper's body tensed as a delectable image instantaneously formed in his mind. She hadn't meant for her comment to be provocative, and if Jasper had been anyone else, it wouldn't have been. The vision of her lounging in bathwater, her skin wet, her shoulders bared—*everything* bared—wasn't just a result of being too long without the company of a woman. It was due to being too long without *her*. Opportunities had arisen in

Liverpool; taking advantage of them would have been easy. But the temptation had never been strong enough for him to set aside his thoughts of Leo. Or the promise he'd made to her, even if he had only ever voiced it to himself.

Jasper had every intention of forging ahead and pretending the comment about her luxurious bath had not affected him. But when she emitted a small sigh of contentment at the memory, he broke. A soft groan squeezed from his throat.

Leo peered at him with a questioning look.

"There is no chance your bath was sinful," he said, sensing the line of impropriety nearing, and yet not caring enough to shut his mouth. "But the picture you've just put into my mind certainly is."

His meaning instantly clear, Leo's cheeks pinked. She looked away, lips bowing into a grin. "That was most definitely not my intent."

He quit his pacing and came to stand in front of the chair where she stood. "The fault is all mine. And I'm sure I've said too much. I should go."

Should.

Leo stepped out from behind the chair. "Must you?"

Jasper had not yet moved to leave and now knew he would not. Not yet, at least.

He gravitated toward her, his gaze locking on her mouth. "I probably should."

There was that word again: *should*. He'd never realized how ineffective a single word could be.

Jasper reached for her, and then Leo was in his arms, her lips against his. In an instant, all the awkward friction that had held them apart on the carriage ride to the manor vanished. They stood still, Jasper indulging in the feel of her lips against his. Of her hands coming up to rest on his chest. And then, of the gentle nudge of her mouth, as if to tell him, *yes.*

They dropped into the kiss as easily and naturally as they had the few times before he'd left London. There was no awkwardness as her lips moved against his, then parted so he could taste her. He tucked her closer to his body with the urge to consume her. Every inch of her. The scent of rose oil warming between them brought the wicked vision of her in her bath flaring to life in his mind again. A deep ache fissured through his stomach, and lower still. It was on a mindless, dangerous course, and with Leo quicky becoming soft and pliant under his hands and against his body, the part of his brain dedicated to reason and caution began to mute. The world narrowed to two spaces as Jasper led her toward a small writing desk: the desk itself—he took her hips in his palms and lifted her to sit upon the edge—and the bedroom behind them. His heart pounded at the thought of bringing her into that room.

He pulled back, though only so that he could set his mouth to the curve of her throat. Her skin was hot and sweet, and he nuzzled her with his tongue and teeth with that same need to consume her.

"Jasper."

He went still, her ragged whisper having reached past his depraved thoughts. Only then did he realize that his hands had gathered fistfuls of her skirt—and that one palm gripped the back of her thigh.

Hell.

He started to release her leg, but her hand came down

over his to stop him. He groaned against her throat. "I need to go."

"I know," she said, even as her fingers raked up the nape of his neck into his hair. She kept her hand on his, pressing it back against her thigh.

"Leo," he said, his voice strained. "I've taken this too far. I shouldn't be here."

And he definitely should *not* be attempting to reach under her skirts. Christ, what was wrong with him? It didn't matter if she was welcoming him, or that his blood was singing and his pulse thrashing—Leo was far too important to him to treat with such frenzied lust.

"You're right," she said after a protracted moment, during which Jasper nearly wondered if she would say something different, if she might ask him to stay. Had she, he wasn't sure he would've had the strength to tell her no.

Leo's fingers lowered from his scalp, and her hand lightened, then lifted, from his. He eased her from the edge of the desk down to the floor. Her flushed cheeks and lips, and the abraded skin of her neck threatened to undo him. Gingerly, she touched her chin. The friction of his beard had chafed it as well.

He laughed shyly. "Sorry about that. I will shave, if you prefer."

Leo reached for his cheek and scrubbed her fingers through his bristle. "Don't you dare. I like it."

It took everything honorable in him not to pull her back into another kiss. She slowly retracted her hand, then checked the placement of her hairpins as she walked toward the door. After peering into the corridor, she pulled her head back in.

"It is clear," she announced, her blush still high.

His muscles were tight, and evidence of his desire alarmingly close to being noticeable, as he met her at the door. "Goodnight, then."

He lingered only a moment before leaving. As he took long strides down the shadowy corridor, back toward the grand staircase, he rubbed his lower lip and the lingering sensation of Leo's tongue drawing along it. Sleep would not come easily tonight.

At the top of the central staircase, one could turn left or right down wide corridors leading to different wings of the manor. There were also two slim corridors edging the balustrade that overlooked the grand entrance hall. Down one of these corridors was the billiards room. The door was open, spilling out lamplight. Two voices sounded from within. The first, belonging to a man, was angry and loud. The second belonged to a woman, who sounded frightened. Her small figure emerged onto the landing, her hands clasped together in a sort of pleading gesture.

"Please, I didn't mean no harm." It appeared to be a young maid. Jasper retreated a step, pulling himself behind a corner, then peeked around the edge. Frederick Cowper came out after her, still in his dark red dinner jacket, and billiard cue in his hand.

"You would do well to mind your own business," he said through what sounded like clenched teeth. "That is, if you would like to keep your position here."

"Of course, I do, sir. I'm sorry, sir. It won't happen again." The maid bobbed her head and curtseyed skittishly before hurrying toward where Jasper stood. He pulled back out of sight, and to his relief, the maid continued swiftly down the stairs, stifling her sobs.

He gave Frederick several more seconds to return to the billiards room. When Jasper heard the door click shut, he exhaled. Whatever that had been about, the heir to the viscountcy had not been nearly as pleasant toward the maid as he'd been toward his guests at dinner. Jasper wasn't curious enough to find out what the maid had done wrong. All he wanted was to question Helen Dalton in the morning, then take Leo and leave this bloody house for good.

Leo drew back the heavy velvet drapes in her room before going to bed. Should the rain and wind pull away during the night, she wanted the morning sun to wake her as quickly as possible so that she and Jasper could speak to Helen, then depart for the train station. As she lay in bed after changing into the nightdress the maid had laid out for her, Leo listened as the storm relinquished its wrath. Her body, however, still felt as though she'd been caught in a whirlwind.

Her skin felt tight and sensitive underneath the linen nightdress, and her chin was lightly scuffed from Jasper's new beard. Her breathing was still off-kilter, and when her fingers drifted over the column of her neck where Jasper's teeth had gently nipped, she closed her eyes and allowed herself to indulge in thoughts of him. Of course, she had indulged in these thoughts before but never had the reality of them been as close as when he'd been kissing her on that desk.

She wasn't disappointed he'd pulled away—at least, not entirely. Leo knew well enough that she wasn't ready for what might have unfolded had they not come to their senses. But that didn't mean she disliked imagining it.

Surprisingly, sleep claimed her quickly, and she didn't wake to the rising sun as she'd planned. Instead, a woman's timid voice pulled her to consciousness.

"Miss? Ever forgive me, miss, but I've come to wake you."

Leo lifted her head from the pillow and met the maid, Ursula, with a sleep-fogged frown. "Oh. Hello."

She wasn't accustomed to waking up to people hovering by her bedside. The young maid wore a fraught expression as she scurried from the bedside toward Leo's garments, which were draped over an upholstered bench.

"I was supposed to come last night to help you undress," she said as she picked up the dark purple jacket and held it up for inspection. "I'm so sorry, miss. Mrs. Renwick will have my head on a pike if she finds out that I didn't come."

Leo sat up and reluctantly ceded the sumptuous cushion of the mattress and down blanket. Hot baths and cozy, plush beds were the only things she would miss about Cowper Hall.

"I did not mind, Ursula. As I've never had a maid, I didn't miss the help," she said. Though, she was curious as to why the maid had not come, especially as she seemed so distraught and guilty for it now.

"You won't tell Mrs. Renwick?" she asked, looking back at Leo with a genuine glimmer of tears in her eyes.

"You have my word," she promised and then rose from the bed. Outside, the sunlight was fickle, but at least the rain and wind had ceased.

"Oh, thank you ever so much, miss," the maid replied

with a gusty exhale of relief. She rushed forward with Leo's chemise and bloomers in her arms. "I've been told you're expecting Mrs. Dalton for breakfast."

Leo checked the clock in the corner of the room. It was just past seven now.

"I can dress myself, truly," she said.

But Ursula, likely feeling remiss in her duties, shook her head. "I'll hand your things over the screen, miss, if you prefer."

She found she did prefer that. So, after stepping behind the trifold screen, she removed her nightdress and took her garments one by one from the maid. Afterward, Ursula guided her toward a mirrored dresser, where she insisted Leo sit and let her style her hair. As this task was one that she'd never been very patient with, nor fond of, Leo assented without complaint. The maid happily shook loose the hasty plait Leo had created the night before and began to brush her dark hair with a soft-bristled hairbrush.

"I usually style it in a low bun or sometimes, I pin it up, but..." Leo shrugged, more than aware that fashion was not her forte. It had never seemed to matter much, considering she was usually only going to work at the morgue.

Ursula smiled as she started to expertly loop, twist, and pin strands of Leo's hair. She watched carefully in the mirror's reflection, so that she could remember the steps later. When finished, her hair was pinned up in a lovely loose bun, circled by a thin braid. A few artful strands of hair had been left to frame her face, curled with the help of a hot iron.

"There, miss," the maid said proudly as she stepped

back to admire her work. Leo did as well, turning her head side to side while gazing in the mirror.

"It's beautifully done, Ursula. Much better than I could ever do for myself." She acknowledged that there were now three things she would miss about Cowper Fields.

"It shows off your heart-shaped face," the maid complimented. Then, her smile grew conspiratorial. "I'm sure the detective inspector will notice. Is it true you and he are a couple, miss?"

Leo met the maid's eyes in the mirror, taken aback. "Who has told you that?"

Ursula's eyes widened, again with guilty terror. "It's just what a few other servants were saying, miss. I shouldn't have asked. It's none of my business," she said, then started to tidy up the brush, hairpins, and hot iron. "I keep mucking everything up lately, saying the wrong thing. Do forgive me, miss."

Leo stood up from the cushioned stool. "There is no need to keep apologizing, Ursula. You've said nothing wrong. You are right. We are a…couple." It felt strange to say it, but also remarkably satisfying.

Ursula paused, her contrition transforming to girlish glee. Before she could say anything, Leo held up her hand. "It is new. Very new."

And that was exactly why Jasper had been wise to rein in their kiss last night.

"And the inspector doesn't mind that you work with the dead?" Ursula asked next, though as soon as she finished her question, her eyelids popped wide again. No doubt horrified she'd said something wrong again.

"He doesn't mind," Leo answered, smiling at the idea of the servants whispering about her belowstairs. She understood how strange she must seem to them, considering they served proper ladies and gentlemen.

"I've never met a lady like you before, miss," Ursula said as she continued to the other side of the changing screen to gather the discarded nightdress.

"I'm not a lady," Leo was quick to note. "Not a titled one, at least."

"Well, you're much nicer than any of the ladies in this house," she replied, then froze. "But I shouldn't say that."

Leo was about to assure her, once again, that she would keep the maid's confidence when the door to the attached sitting room opened.

"Miss Spencer?" a voice called.

It was the housekeeper, Mrs. Renwick, whom Leo had met briefly the previous day. Ursula straightened like a soldier as the older woman entered.

"Good morning, Miss Spencer," she said with heavy breaths, her eyes darting around restlessly. "I was hoping to find Mrs. Dalton with you."

"We're not meeting until eight o'clock," Leo explained.

Mrs. Renwick turned to the maid. "Have *you* seen Mrs. Dalton, Ursula?"

The maid shook her head, the lace on her mobcap trembling.

"Is something wrong?" Leo asked, a crimp in her stomach beginning to form.

The housekeeper's lips pursed. "It seems she cannot be found."

"Mrs. Dalton wasn't in her room when her maid entered this morning?" Leo asked, presuming that her maid would have done exactly as Ursula had with her.

"Dora said the bed hadn't been slept in," Mrs. Renwick revealed.

Leo squeezed her eyes shut and dragged in a breath. Helen Dalton had left the manor during the night. Leo had a good guess as to why.

"I need to see Inspector Reid, Mrs. Renwick," she said.

The housekeeper led Leo to the breakfast room, where Jasper was standing in close conference with Mr. Corman and the butler, Decamp. The viscount sat at the head of the table, reading a newspaper and eating. When Jasper turned to greet her, she fought back the errant memory of his palm gripping the back of her thigh and the deep stroke of his tongue and instead forced her mind to the problem at hand.

"Mrs. Dalton has left," she said after she joined him and the other two men. He nodded.

"Decamp says no one in the stables was summoned during the course of the night to bring a carriage for her."

"And Mr. Dalton left earlier with their curricle," Leo mused aloud. Had Helen walked? But, as Leo recalled, the rain had still been pouring near midnight.

"Her maid said she left Mrs. Dalton around eleven last evening. Dora has been to the Dalton residence and back this morning already," Mr. Corman put in. "Mrs. Dalton has not been seen there."

"Anthony was an ass last night," the viscount said, turning a page in his paper as he continued to read. "My granddaughter is likely taking one of her dramatic breaks from him, and by leaving in the middle of the night, she is surely all too happy to be causing a stir."

Leo kept her mouth shut against voicing her own theory: that Helen had fled the manor before having to speak to a detective inspector about Francine's mysterious letter, and that she had a notion as to what his questions would be about. Had Helen indeed played some role in Teddy's death, as Francine had always feared? It made Leo feel ill to consider that possibility.

"Her maid is quite concerned, however," Decamp said cautiously after the viscount had finished speaking, "as in the past, Mrs. Dalton has always taken Dora with her."

Jasper turned to Leo and quietly said, "The interview."

She nodded.

"What?" The viscount's charade of feigning disinterest while reading the morning paper fell apart. "What interview?"

"That is confidential," Jasper replied. "As Decamp has informed us that the roads and tracks are now clear for travel, Miss Spencer and I will be taking our leave."

He knew her well enough to know Leo would not wish to sit down and break her fast with the viscount or anyone else who arrived in the breakfast room. Nadia, Millicent, and Frederick were not yet present.

"Thank you for your hospitality," Leo added, though she directed this toward the butler and Mr. Corman.

The viscount grunted, then returned to his paper. "Enjoy your new home, won't you?"

Jasper and Leo approached the door at the same time as Frederick was arriving. His hair was combed back and still damp, as if he'd just bathed. But Leo noted he was again wearing his burgundy dinner jacket. An odd choice for an informal breakfast, she thought.

"Am I catching you on your way out?" he asked.

"Don't keep them," the viscount interjected. "We wouldn't want them to miss their train."

"Good day, Mr. Cowper," Leo said, with a vexed glance back toward the old man.

A footman was waiting for them at the front door with their coats, hats, and gloves, along with Leo's handbag.

"I've decided to come to London for a few days," Jasper said as they waited in the entrance hall for one of the viscount's carriages to pull up outside.

Leo whipped her head around to peer at him, a warm bolt of happiness rippling through her.

"I thought we might take a look at the house on Craven Hill," he explained.

"And pry up the floorboard to find the glass vial Mrs. Stroud wrote about?"

Jasper laughed as the carriage arrived. "I should have guessed you'd be more interested in the mysterious vial than the fact that we now own a home in a posh neighborhood."

Chapter Five

The cushions on the train were flat from overuse and the braziers poorly stoked. As uncomfortable and chilly as she was, Leo would not have dreamt of complaining. It had been a relief to depart Cowper Fields, and knowing Jasper would be staying in London for a day or two made that relief even greater. Whether he'd changed his plans to be sure she did not visit the uninhabited home on Craven Hill alone, or because of Helen Dalton's disappearance, or because of what had nearly happened between them the night before in her guestroom, Leo did not know. She hoped it was a little of all three, as they were the things she could not stop thinking about as well.

Though the train into London was crowded, they managed to find seats facing one another in the same compartment. Holding any conversation about the events of the last day was out of the question, considering their fellow travelers: two older women, each of whom fawned over Jasper when he asked if he and Leo might join them.

So, to pass the time, they each opened a section of the newspaper they'd purchased at the station from a newsboy and read.

While the train clattered toward the city, Leo peered over the top of her paper to find Jasper doing the same. The fine lines around his eyes creased as he grinned mischievously, before then lowering his attention back to the paper. The meeting of their eyes occurred several more times and soon became obvious to their neighbors. One of the women sniffed disapprovingly, while the other pressed her lips thin in amusement.

As distracting as the glimpsing game with Jasper was, the assignment from Francine Stroud, the gift of the house, and Helen's unexpected, unexplained departure during the night continued to weigh on Leo. Leaving Harrow and Lord Cowper's country seat had loosened the ever-present cramp in her stomach, but a part of her worried that this was only the beginning of a tense association with the Cowpers. She did not want any connection with them at all, tense or otherwise.

As she and Jasper disembarked at Paddington, there was the temptation to travel down the road from the busy station to where Craven Hill was located. But they agreed that neither of them was quite ready to visit the home they'd just been given. They each needed to change their clothing and tidy themselves, not to mention Uncle Claude would be curious, and not a little bit concerned, as to why she had not returned the evening before as planned. Connor Quinn would be wondering why she had not arrived for work that morning. And Jasper would need to wire Liverpool with the news that he would be out for a few more days. Later that evening, he would fetch Leo from her home on Duke Street, and then, they would visit Craven Hill together.

It was still difficult to believe that a deed to such a home had been placed in their names. To jointly own a property was a strange a notion, especially for two people who had just barely started courting. Neither of them would have ever been able to afford such a place, and it felt wrong in principle to be simply handed it. What were they to do with it?

That Francine and the Inspector might have carried on a clandestine relationship, and that it was now benefiting Leo and Jasper, also bothered her.

She tried to shake off her underlying sense of disappointment in the Inspector as she and Jasper shared a cab to Westminster. It wasn't her place to judge Gregory Reid, especially when she did not have all the pertinent information and when both he and Francine were unable to speak for themselves.

Jasper had the cab deliver Leo home first before continuing on to Charles Street. She brought out her key and let herself into the house.

"Uncle Claude?" she called. Even though it was before noon and Aunt Flora would not yet be taking an afternoon nap, Leo kept her voice low. Loud noises perturbed her aunt as of late, and both she and Claude were careful to do all they could to avoid agitating her. For Leo, that meant attempting to stay out of her way as much as possible. What had at first been a slow deterioration of her mind had, for several months now, been gaining in speed and destruction, and with it, more anger, oftentimes directed toward Leo.

In her confused state, Flora blamed Leo for the

murders of Leonard and Andromeda Spencer, and two of their three children, Jacob and Agnes. Leo suspected this was because she resembled her father, whom Flora blamed for the slaughter of her beloved younger sister and her family. Her aunt wasn't entirely wrong to blame him. Recently, Leo had discovered that he'd worked for the East Rips and betrayed the Carter family in some way, and that they had brutally murdered the Spencers as punishment.

Just Leo had been spared, and that was only because Jasper had been sent along with the killers that night. He'd been directed to the attic to look for the little girl who was missing and to take care of her once he found her. It was meant to be his initiation of sorts, as at the age of thirteen, he was considered man enough to silence any enemies of his family. Jasper had found her, but he'd hidden her rather than harm her, even knowing that his refusal to kill her would have dire consequences for him.

"Oh, thank goodness, there you are," Claude called out in reply, his voice emanating from the kitchen. "Was it the weather? There were rather terrible storms here."

Leo made her way to the back of the house, the familiarity of the modest home snug and inviting compared to the yawning spaces of the manor where she'd been trapped overnight. To Leo's surprise, Dita Brooks was seated at the small kitchen table with her uncle. Her circumspect brown eyes locked onto Leo as soon as she came through the door.

"Uncle Claude did not care for my theory, which was that the evil viscount had lured you and Inspector Reid there under false pretenses," she said with a devious arch of her brow.

Leo went to the hob to fix herself tea; she'd had a bitter cup from a vendor at the Harrow station and nothing else all morning. "And what did you imagine he had in store for us?" she asked her friend.

Dita, who had always been more fanciful than Leo, replied, "Oh, I don't know, something having to do with an old grudge and a damp dungeon."

Claude peered over the rims of his thick-lensed spectacles at Dita with the indulgent expression of someone who knew reprimanding her would be ineffective. Leo only shook her head and chuckled at the gothic plot.

"I thought I told you to stop reading dramatic novels," she said. "My uncle is correct; it was the storm that prevented us from returning last night. The tracks were flooded, as were the roads." She poured her tea and joined them at the table. There, Flora sat with some knitting in her lap. Her thin, mottled hands worked a pair of knitting needles expertly, the scarf she was creating well-formed.

"Mrs. Zhao is to be commended," Leo said softly.

Jasper's housekeeper had offered to come sit with Flora a few times a week, and she'd had the notion that a handicraft might calm Flora's otherwise agitated mind. Leo's aunt had often knitted when she was younger, and the skill had returned with astonishing precision.

"I am grateful to her," Claude murmured.

With Jasper planning to be gone for several months, Mrs. Zhao, who was accustomed to being busy, had needed something more to do. Claude had readily accepted her offer to sit with Flora, as he had been given the opportunity to join Tate's Funeral Service. Tate's had often collected the corpses directly from the Spring Street Morgue while Claude had been coroner there, and the owners had appealed to him to join them as their embalmer. The task took a certain steely constitution to oversee, and Claude was perfect for the position. And like Mrs. Zhao, Claude had missed having an occupation. These last few months, he'd visibly been rejuvenated.

Leo's stomach growled, announcing her hunger, and Dita shoved the cutting board with bread and cheese toward her from the center of the table.

"I can't stay long. My new job begins at noon sharp, and it won't do to be late," she explained. "So, do hurry up and tell us what happened at the reading of that woman's will."

Belatedly, Leo recognized that the blue-and-yellow-striped dress Dita was wearing was new. A wide, blue ribbon accentuated the cinched waist, and underneath, an S-shaped bustle looked acutely uncomfortable for sitting. It was clearly a uniform of some sort.

"Where is your new job?" Leo asked. But Dita shook her head.

"I'll tell you after. It's not nearly as exciting as a mysterious will reading."

With her uncle and Dita both staring at her expectantly, Leo took a deep breath and revealed what Francine Stroud had given to her and Jasper. As she spoke, Dita's jaw loosened and dropped, and Claude leaned forward, bracing one elbow on the table and cupping his cheek in awe.

"But that part of town is… well, it's so affluent," Dita gasped, blinking rapidly as if a bright light had shone into her eyes. "Why would this woman have given it to you and Jasper? I thought the Inspector had nothing to do with his late wife's family after she died."

Leo was happy she'd taken a bite of the bread. Chewing and swallowing gave her a few extra moments to sort through her reply. She did not want to tell them about the letter from Francine and the request that they investigate Teddy's death. Not right now, at least, with Flora seated near them. She seemed to be in her own little world as she knit, but any talk of death, or especially of dead children, upset her greatly.

"It seems the Inspector and Mrs. Stroud maintained an acquaintance after all," Leo chose to say. "A friendship even."

"In secret?" Dita asked.

Leo nodded, again feeling the dull cut of something too close to betrayal. The Inspector hadn't exactly lied; but he had concealed this relationship with his wife's sister. Then again, it really hadn't been any of Leo's business. There was no rational reason for her to be upset by it, particularly since both the Inspector and Mrs. Stroud were now dead.

"To give you and Jasper a property that must be worth thousands of pounds and overlook her own children... That is extremely odd, isn't it?" Dita asked. She was right, of course. But Leo had no answer to give.

"Jasper and I are just as perplexed," she admitted before drinking her tea to wash down the dry bread. Her nerves were suddenly jumping again.

"That is quite extraordinary, my dear." Claude's usual calm demeanor was unflappable, even now. "Have the two of you discussed what to do with it?"

"Not really. But he is here for a few days. We came into town together on the train."

Dita's devious grin from a moment ago returned, but

before she could ask about their reunion—something she had been romanticizing about for several weeks, ever since her return from Birmingham—Leo gestured to her dress. "All right, tell me where you are now working, where you must wear that uniform. Those aren't your colors at all."

Dita preferred deep sapphire, bright emerald, and golds, to the tepid, thin, blue and yellow stripes she now wore.

She sighed dramatically as she pushed out her chair and stood. "I know, it's awful, isn't it? But it's what the shopgirls must wear at Gleason's." She struck a pose with one hand on her hip and the other at the back of her head, her glossy black hair styled in upswept ringlets.

"You've landed at Gleason's? Dita, that is wonderful!"

Located on Oxford Street, Gleason's was one of the finer department stores in London. Though Leo had never set foot inside the store, she'd passed it a handful of times. The large building occupied a full block, with three stories devoted to men's wear, ladies' fashions, and home furnishings. The window displays were designed with an artist's eye, staged to lure in those who had the means to satisfy their urge to purchase what they saw, and to draw longing gazes from those who did not. Leo fell into that latter category.

"It's a decent wage, and I won't have to pat down a single customer," Dita said with a wink, referring to her past job as a matron at Scotland Yard. It had been a civilian position, in which she'd had to search ladies and children brought in under arrest and then guard them on the upper floors of the building, for a paltry wage.

"I've got to dash off. They're quite serious about punctuality, and this is only my second day," she said, bustling toward the back door. It put a smile on Leo's face to see Dita's energy and vivacity coming back after she'd lost her fiancé in a bomb blast at Scotland Yard five months earlier. "I'd ask you to come out with me tonight," Dita continued. "But I have the feeling you'll be busy with a certain detective inspector."

She pulled the door shut behind her after sending Leo a suggestive smirk. Claude chuckled and sat back in his chair.

"I believe that young woman will do well convincing wealthy ladies to part with their money," he remarked, then turned a bit more serious. "Is there something more to this house you've inherited? I can't help but feel there must be."

Leo hesitated, peering at her aunt. Claude followed her pointed gaze.

"Ah. I see. Well, you can tell me another time," he said. Leo reached across the table and gripped his forearm, giving it a gentle squeeze.

She finished her tea and went to her room to change out of her purple traveling gown and into one of the serviceable dresses she typically wore to the morgue. They were more comfortable, without thick petticoats or girlish frills like bows or ribbons. The muted shades of gray, green, and blue were also more suitable for the tasks she would undertake while working with Connor Quinn, the new assistant coroner at the Spring Street Morgue. He'd consented to her taking the day yesterday to travel to Harrow and see to the business of the will reading, but he'd expected her back that morning.

When she entered the former church vestry-turned-morgue, it was through the back door, into the office. The autumn and winter months were always much more pleasant inside the morgue, as the chill in the air tamped down the pervasive foul odors associated with decomposing corpses. For that reason, Leo kept a second jacket in the office that she would wear while assisting Connor on postmortems. She slipped it on, along with an apron, and entered the postmortem room.

She expected to find him bent over a corpse on one of the metal slab tables in the large room, where stained glass windows and arched ceiling beams were further remnants of the former vestry. The room, however, was vacant—of any living people, at least.

Leo took a few steps forward, then held still. The hushed sound of sniffling traveled from the direction of the supply closet.

"Connor?" She moved toward the open door to the closet.

"In here," he called, his voice rough. He sniffled a few more times, as if preparing for her, and when she saw him, it was evident he'd been crying. His eyes were glassy, and the tip of his nose was red. He avoided eye contact with her, surely embarrassed to have been found in such a state.

"What has happened?" she asked. He had never been anything but good-natured and smiling.

He grimaced. "It's one of the, ah, bodies that's just been delivered." He coughed to clear his throat, likely tight with emotion.

Leo's stomach plummeted. "Oh no. Is it very bad?" She then had a notion. "Is it someone you know?"

Connor breathed in deeply, then gestured for Leo to

follow him. He led them from the supply closet to a sheeted figure on one of the tables. From the drape of the cloth, she could determine that it was a woman and that she had not yet been disrobed for examination. With slightly shaking hands, Connor reached for the top of the sheet and then pulled it back. The woman who came into view was young, in her mid- to late twenties perhaps. Her white skin had the hard, milky-blue pallor of someone who had been dead for many hours. Telltale bruising visible around the ruffled neck of her bodice pointed toward strangulation as the cause of her death.

"Who is she?" Leo asked as Connor stared at the woman, his eyes full of anguish.

"Her name is Lydia Hailson," he replied, then with a shaky exhale, added, "We were betrothed once."

Startled, Leo looked back down at the dead woman. She hadn't known Connor had ever been engaged to marry. While they were friends, working well and easily together, he had not shared much about his personal life. Now, to have his former fiancée arrive at the morgue… and so clearly dead by violent means. His reaction made perfect sense.

"I'm so sorry, Connor."

Leo's attention drifted to the ruffled collar of the woman's dress again, although this time she didn't look at the bruising. She pulled the sheet a little lower to see more of the bodice. Her pulse slowed as two thoughts battled. The more immediate one won out. "You cannot conduct this postmortem," she said. "Perhaps we could ask my uncle to come in, just this once?"

Connor nodded his agreement.

Leo then voiced her second thought: "Did Miss Hailson work at Gleason's Department Store?"

At this, Connor blinked at her, taken aback. "I don't know. It's been some time since we last saw each other. Why?"

"Her dress," she explained, gesturing toward the bodice and skirt, which were fashioned from fabric with thin blue and yellow stripes, identical to what Leo had just seen Dita wearing. "It is the shopgirl's uniform at Gleason's."

Chapter Six

Jasper leaned the back of his head on the lip of the enamel tub and closed his eyes, happy to be home. The lodging house in Liverpool only had one shared water closet, located off the back of the house, and if a lodger wished to bathe, it was an extra shilling each week for a single bath. Jasper had gone to a nearby bathhouse instead, as the facilities were cleaner and more spacious.

As he soaked in the water now, the sound of Mrs. Zhao humming in the kitchen helped keep the tantalizing image of Leo in the tub at Cowper Hall at bay. He had too many things to see to in the next few hours to indulge in such thoughts anyhow. A stop at Scotland Yard would be necessary, as he needed to send word to his superior officer in Liverpool that he would be out for an additional two days. He also wanted to pull the record the Metropolitan Police had on file for the accidental death of Theodore Stroud.

"Would you like more hot water, Mister Jasper?" Mrs. Zhao called at the closed door to the water closet. Though the house had been plumbed since before Jasper came to live with Gregory Reid, the pipes had since stopped working. They could be repaired, or replaced, but neither he nor his adoptive father had thought the high cost necessary, especially since the water closet was conveniently located just off the kitchen.

"No, thank you, Mrs. Zhao," he said, sitting forward. "I'm getting out."

He'd been soaking for so long the water had turned tepid, and his fingertips had started to wrinkle.

"I have your dinner ready," she replied, the merry tone of her voice enough to make him laugh lightly as he stepped out of the tub.

When he'd come through the front door earlier, Mrs. Zhao had run into the foyer with a rolling pin raised above her head, ready to use it against whoever was breaking into the house. As her eyes took in the sight of him, and not some vile intruder, they had filled with tears. She'd embraced him while scolding him for not giving her advance notice of his plan to return home. Since then, she'd been a whirlwind of energy.

Jasper tied the belt on his dressing robe before emerging from the water closet. He inhaled the enticing scents of Mrs. Zhao's cooking: buttery pastry, roasted lamb, and savory herbs.

"I think I've just gained back a bit of weight," Jasper teased, referring to one of his housekeeper's first observations: that he had lost weight while in Liverpool. He did not think he had, as his trousers fit as they always did, but she'd simpered happily to learn that Mrs. Hart's cooking had been both uninspired and flavorless.

He went upstairs to his room to dress, and by the time

he returned to the kitchen, a plate of piping hot lamb pie was on the table next to a pot of tea. Mrs. Zhao fixed herself a serving as well and took the seat adjacent to his.

"Mr. Feldman said you and Miss Leo were asked to visit the viscount's home," she said as she picked up her fork. Jasper had wondered if Leo's uncle would inform her of the summons, now that Mrs. Zhao saw him more often while caring for Flora a few days per week.

"For a will reading, yes." Since learning of the will's contents, the secret attachment his father seemed to have had to Francine Stroud had troubled him. The questions of when they'd seen one another and how they had kept in touch led him to wonder if there was at least one person who might have known the nature of their relationship.

He split the pastry of his pie with his fork. "I need to ask, Mrs. Zhao…" He hesitated, wanting to know, and yet also not wanting to hear the answers. "It is somewhat delicate."

She dabbed her mouth and said, "This is about Mr. Reid and Mrs. Stroud."

He lowered his fork to his plate and stared at her. So, she had known. "Was it what I think it was?"

Although in her early sixties, Mrs. Zhao's face was not heavily lined. However, two furrows now appeared between her thin black brows. "Yes," she replied simply.

He nodded as a numbness stole through him. "I see."

Mrs. Zhao had been a loyal employee to his father, but she'd also been a loyal friend. It shouldn't have surprised him to learn that she'd known. What did surprise Jasper was the discovery of a facet of his father's life that *he* had known nothing about.

"Was this after Emmaline had died?" he asked carefully.

"Of course!" she gasped, as though offended that he'd considered otherwise. "A few years had passed by then."

Jasper didn't know how he might have handled finding out that Gregory had conducted an affair while still married to his wife. He sank back into his seat with relief.

"Mrs. Stroud was the only person from that family who realized just how devastated Mr. Reid was by the loss of his family," the housekeeper went on. "She would call on him whenever she was in town, and I came to recognize her handwriting on letters that arrived for him in the post. I began to suspect it was more than friendship when, one morning, I came home from my sister's in Limehouse earlier than anticipated." She raised a brow as if to insinuate her meaning. Jasper understood: She'd found Francine had stayed the night.

"It was awkward, and Mr. Reid asked me not to say anything to anyone," she said softly. "She was still married."

Jasper presumed her husband had died, although he had not thought to ask when he'd passed.

"Where was I at the time?" Jasper asked.

"At school in Cheltenham."

He'd attended the private boys' school for four years, only coming home to Charles Street for short breaks. Jasper had never wondered what his father had been doing during those years. Working at Scotland Yard, he'd presumed. He could understand now, however, that Gregory Reid might have been lonely.

"And when did it end?" he asked next.

"When you finished at school."

"Right," he said, experiencing a pang of guilt. Jasper's return to London had meant Gregory could no longer have Francine at the house in secret. Had his father resented that?

"It wasn't just your coming home," Mrs. Zhao said gently, as though reading his thoughts. "Her son passed away, and then, not long after that, her husband did as well."

Twelve years ago, the letter from Francine had stated. Jasper would have been about eighteen years old and in his final year at Cheltenham.

"I heard about her son." He decided not to say anything about Francine's request that he and Leo investigate Teddy's death. He shook his head. "Why did he keep it from me?"

Emmaline had not been Jasper's mother; he'd had no ties to her at all, no allegiance. After Francine's mourning period for her husband had concluded, why had they never rekindled their relationship?

"Shame, I believe," Mrs. Zhao replied to the question Jasper had asked her as well as the one not voiced.

"Because Francine was his late wife's sister?"

The housekeeper pushed her plate away with a sigh. He'd lost his appetite too.

"And because of the money."

Jasper peered at her quizzically. "What money?"

She winced. "Every year, the property taxes for this house were paid in full by an anonymous party; Mr. Reid believed it was Mrs. Stroud."

Jasper slid back his chair and stood as a rush of energy overtook the numbness that had filled him. For the last several months, ever since his father's solicitor had handed Jasper the deed to the Charles Street address, he'd questioned how the property taxes had been paid. Most people of Gregory and Jasper's class leased rooms or houses; they did not own a home—especially not one in a neighborhood as affluent as this one. The land the house sat upon was taxed, at a rate proportionate to the quality of the home and that of the other homes in the surrounding area. The taxes would have drained Jasper's meager savings, and he'd not been able to reconcile how his father had managed all these years.

"Why did no one tell me?" he asked, becoming angry now. Worry had plagued him for months; he'd lain in bed, harangued by the decision to either go broke trying to keep the home his father had clung to, as he had the cherished memories of his wife and children, or sell it.

"I did not know if she would continue with her generosity after Mr. Reid's death," Mrs. Zhao explained, her hands clasped in a nervous, pleading manner. "And the solicitor, Mr. Stockton, he did not know who the anonymous donor was. I believe he was waiting to see if the money arrived as it always had."

Jasper stalked away from the table, raking a hand through his hair, still damp from the bath.

"Mr. Reid could not tell you," she went on, "without also admitting to the affair."

Not to mention, it had likely been a longstanding bruise on his father's masculinity.

Jasper had been shut out, and if his father were still alive, he'd have given him hell for it. But as he wasn't, there was only Mrs. Zhao left, and he would not take his anger out on her.

"I need to get to the Yard," he grumbled.

His housekeeper nodded as if understanding his anger and his need to leave the Charles Street home. Jasper threw on his coat and hat at the door and left on foot for police headquarters. The raw autumn air chilled his temper as he walked, his mind sorting through the mess just revealed to him. Anger, disappointment, hurt—he didn't know which one he felt most keenly.

Once he arrived at Scotland Yard, however, he was able to set it all to the side as he greeted Constable Woodhouse at the front desk, and then the rest of the men in the Criminal Investigation Department. Constable Horace Wiley, who had applied for but been denied the secondment to Liverpool for the very investigation Jasper had just wrapped up, scowled an envious hello, but the others were pleased to see him. Word had come down of the counterfeiters' arrests, and Detective Sergeant Roy Lewis had suggested a round of drinks at the Rising Sun that night to hear all about it.

Regretfully, Jasper had needed to postpone the gathering until the following day, as he was due to pick up Leo. After asking Detective Sergeant Warnock to find the record of Theodore Stroud's death and leave it on his desk, he wired the Liverpool station requesting another two days' leave. Then, he set out for the morgue.

In the dusk, the stained glass windows of the old vestry glowed with lights from the gasoliers inside, and when Jasper entered the building, he heard a sound coming from the postmortem room that he recognized: the jovial whistling of the former assistant city coroner, Claude Feldman.

He pushed open the door to the inner room to find Leo's uncle placing the final closing sutures on the unclothed corpse of a young woman. He averted his eyes out of respect for the woman but was momentarily confused. Claude was no longer coroner here, and yet, when the older man looked up from his work, he brightened visibly, as he had for the last few years whenever Jasper visited the Spring Street Morgue.

"Ah, Inspector, how good it is to see you. My niece has informed me that you're here for a short visit." Claude snipped a length of catgut thread with a pair of small scissors. "How is Liverpool?"

Jasper peered toward the door to the back office, where Leo could usually be found, typing up postmortem reports, death certificates, and any other bit of paperwork that was required.

"Let's just say I am ready to be home," he replied. "I hadn't expected to see you here. What has happened to Mr. Quinn?"

The door to the office opened, and Leo swept into the postmortem room. The morgue cat, Tibia, trotted in her wake, and such was the depth of Jasper's homesickness that he was actually pleased to see the furry, gray-striped monster. Not enough to go in for a scrub of her fur, of course—she would have sunk her claws into his hand had he dared.

"I will tell you all about it on our way to Craven Hill," she said, already wearing her coat, hat, and gloves.

"The bequest is quite remarkable," Claude commented as he covered the young woman with a clean white sheet. "As is the request from the late Mrs. Stroud."

Before the cotton could settle over the woman's head, Jasper saw bruising around her neck and clavicle. This was a murder, then. It distracted him a moment from what Claude had said.

"I'm not sure what we'll find in the matter," Jasper replied. "It has been twelve years, after all."

And he would have a mountain of work on his desk when he returned to Liverpool in a few days. He would not be able to give the death of Francine's son much attention. While Leo might be able to look further into the matter, he did not want her investigating the boy's fatal fall on her own.

They left Claude to close the morgue for the evening, and at a nearby cabstand, Jasper hired a hansom.

"All right," he said after helping Leo into the cab and their driver had started in the direction of Hyde Park; Craven Hill was located on its northern boundary. "Tell me what your uncle was doing at the morgue just now."

The narrow space on the single, forward-facing bench meant that they were seated close together. So, as she told him about the strangled young woman and how she had been Connor Quinn's former betrothed, his attention was repeatedly challenged as Leo's arm and leg jostled against his. *Hell,* he had to get ahold of himself.

"So, your uncle came to do the postmortem," he deduced.

"Yes, and we sent Connor home," she replied. "He was quite distraught."

Jasper could understand, though his mind was already churning. "How long ago did they part ways?"

"I don't know. Why?"

"If it was my case, I'd look at the men in her life. Strangulation is almost always a murder driven by passion."

She leaned away from him, as if stunned. "You cannot possibly suspect Connor of causing her death!"

"I don't suspect anyone, as it is not my case," he reminded her. "It will be assigned, I'm sure."

Roy Lewis had picked up many of the cases that would have otherwise been assigned to Jasper, and DCI Coughlan had even given the detective sergeant use of Jasper's office these past few months. From what Jasper had heard while at the Yard earlier, Lewis was doing well, solving most of the cases he was assigned with relative swiftness.

Leo turned forward again, her arm once more resting against his. He liked the light touch. It was comfortable, and yet it also made his blood run swiftly.

"I wish you could investigate it," she said.

Though she said nothing more than that, Jasper's instinct sharpened. He knew the way her mind worked.

"Leo," he began, his tone firm. "The police will look into her death. If this woman was murdered, you cannot involve yourself."

"She was wearing a shopgirl's uniform for Gleason's Department Store when she was found," she said, purposefully ignoring him. "Dita has just started working there."

He closed his eyes and swore under his breath. Not softly enough.

"You needn't worry." She reached over to take his hand in hers. "I'm only going to ask Dita if she knew Miss Hailson. It is a harmless question."

"I would much rather you let the investigating detective speak to Miss Brooks," he replied, though he knew it was pointless. Leo was going to do what she wanted to do.

It was yet another reason why he wanted to finish his last few tasks in Liverpool and be back in London, for good.

They rode the rest of the way to Craven Hill in relative quiet, their hands still joined. Bit by bit, Leo's arm leaned more closely against his, and when their cab turned off Park Lane onto Bayswater Road, she dropped her head against his shoulder. Having her nestled there, snug and content, felt entirely right. He wished for more privacy than what the hansom could provide, even if it brought them to that same precarious edge from the night before. However, he settled for the pleasing weight of her body leaning against his as they finished the drive to Francine Stroud's former home.

As expected, the houses along the street were refined and stately structures, established in straight rows along the street. With dusk now gone and night coming in fast, soft gaslight brightened the windows of most of the homes. However, Number 19 was a dark void among them. The driver pulled to a stop along the pavement, and regrettably, Leo sat up straight. Jasper handed her down and paid the driver, asking him to wait. Then, considering how dark the home was and how long it had been unoccupied, he asked the driver if he might borrow the lamp hooked to the side of the cab.

"The gas has likely been turned off," he explained to Leo when he met her at the front door with the lantern. He gave her the key Mr. Corman had given him, and she opened the door.

Stale, cold air greeted them. Their footsteps echoed through the foyer, as did the click of the door as Jasper closed it behind them. Sheets had been draped over the furniture and portraits on the walls in the entry way as well as those inside the rooms to their immediate left and right. Jasper raised the cab lantern, illuminating long stretches of cobwebs reaching out from the arms of a gas chandelier overhead.

"I don't want to stay here any longer than necessary," Leo said, her voice unnaturally loud in the silent, vacant space. "Shall we go upstairs? The letter said the bedroom was—"

Jasper held out his arm, stopping her from taking another step toward the staircase. He'd lowered the lantern, strange markings drawing his eye to the floor. Crouching, he brought the light closer to a mess of muddy boot prints on the white-tiled floor.

"Someone has been here," he said.

Leo followed the prints through the foyer. "They look to be coming from the back of the house."

Jasper stood tall again. "Stay with me," he commanded, his pulse rising. "Whoever made these could still be inside the house."

Leo did not return to his side. Instead, she crouched low, as he had. "Bring the lantern over here, will you?" She waved him down beside her. He saw it right away—a streak of rusty red mixed into the brown mud, as if a boot heel had slipped and skidded to the side.

"Is it blood?" she asked.

Jasper reached for his revolver. "It looks to be. Go outside. Stay there while I search the house."

"Absolutely not." She jumped to her feet. "I'm staying with you."

Of course, she was. He gritted his molars and handed her the lantern. "Fine. At least stay close." He continued toward the stairs, with Leo on his heels. As they climbed the staircase, more traces of mud and blood could be seen on the pale blue carpet. The press of blood into the fibers of the carpet appeared denser as Jasper followed the prints toward an open door at the landing. It was the room, he realized, that Francine Stroud had directed them to in her letter.

Before clearing the threshold into the room, an inkling of what they would find shuddered through him. Sheets draped everything inside this room as well—except for the woman lying in the dark, prone on the floor. A pool of blood underneath her head gleamed in the lantern light. She'd come to rest so that her unseeing eyes were turned toward them.

Leo gasped, though Jasper knew it wasn't a reaction to seeing a dead body. It was because of who it was.

They had found Helen Dalton.

Chapter Seven

Leo noticed several things as Jasper approached the body. While her heart had stuttered at seeing Helen Dalton lying dead on the bedroom floor, the ghastly surprise had not led to panic or fright. Being accustomed to corpses, Leo didn't feel the need to stare at the body. Instead, she peered at a rug on the floor, which had been peeled back and left in a heap. A short plank in the wooden floor, exposed by the lifted rug, had been pried up and set aside.

"It appears Helen knew about the hole in the floor that Francine Stroud described in her letter," Leo said.

And she'd left Cowper Hall in the middle of the night to come here and retrieve the object hidden beneath the floorboard. But how had she known about it, and why would she have rushed to London under the cover of darkness and in a terrible storm, no less? It was just a glass vial, a trinket according to Mrs. Stroud.

"She appears to have been struck on the head," Jasper said, inspecting the body by the light of the cab lantern.

With her blonde hair swept away from her forehead and pinned tightly into a high bun, a profound, bloody depression in her right temple was easy to see. The skull's frontal bone had received a blow too.

Leo wished to see inside the hollow in the floor, but she was more interested to know how long Helen had been dead. She went to the body, careful not to step in the pool of blood. She noticed someone already had done so by the smudging along the outer rim of the pool and the shoeprints marking the person's retreat from the room.

"Let me have a look," she said, removing her gloves. They were soft kid leather, and not only did Leo not wish to stain them, but she could better determine the approximate time of death depending on the corpse's body temperature.

Helen Dalton was cold, of course, and in full rigor. Her head and neck could not be manipulated when Leo attempted to move them, and her arms and legs were equally rigid.

"Helen's been dead at least twelve hours," she estimated.

Jasper made a thoughtful noise in the base of his throat as he calculated the time. "So, she was killed before five o'clock this morning."

Her skin was dreadfully pale and cold, and her clothing was damp too. "She was last seen at Cowper Hall at eleven o'clock last night," Leo said, recalling what her maid had told the solicitor, Mr. Corman. "Without any trains running, she would have needed a carriage or some other conveyance to make the trip. How long do you think it took to travel here by carriage?"

"Two hours, perhaps longer, considering the weather," he replied.

"She must have been drenched when she arrived," Leo said. "The cold house and her lack of body heat have slowed the drying of her clothing."

Jasper braced his elbows on his thighs as he crouched. "Her husband left much earlier than eleven."

"But he was at home this morning," Leo said.

Jasper shook his head. "Not necessarily. All we were told was that Mrs. Dalton had not been seen."

He was correct, now that she recalled the conversation in the breakfast room that morning. Leo had only assumed Mr. Dalton had been at home, as no one had been concerned over his whereabouts as they had been his wife's.

"You think he came here?" she asked.

"Maybe. He needs to account for where he was, that much I know." Jasper stood, but Leo remained low to the floor and took another look at Helen's bloodied head.

The poor woman. She had been nervous last night, and Leo suspected she had known what information her mother's mystery letter contained. But how had she known about the hollow in the floor? And to take a carriage into London alone, at so late an hour, was dangerous. *Obviously*, Leo thought, looking away from the body.

Jasper had left her the lantern to see by, but he'd found something a few feet away on the floor and picked it up.

"There is blood on this," he announced, bringing a brass statue of a peacock into the light. It was about two feet tall, and there were streaks of blood on its tail feathers.

"So, her killer struck her, tossed the makeshift weapon, and ran?" She frowned as she peered again at the rim of the blood pool that had been disturbed by a shoe. "A head wound like this would bleed profusely, but it would have taken at least several minutes for this amount of blood on the floor to accumulate. Either the killer stayed until she stopped bleeding, then tread into the blood, or—"

"A second person arrived afterward, rushed in close to the body, and accidentally stepped in the pool," Jasper finished. It pleased her to know he'd formulated the same theory.

"Yes, exactly." Leo turned now to the hollow in the floor. Taking the lantern, she held it down close to the hollow in the floor. The empty space was about the length of her forearm, and the width of it too. It was empty. Leo lowered her hand and felt around and into the shadowy corners to be certain she missed nothing else that has been stashed there.

"The killer must have taken the vial," she said. "Or the person who entered the room after the murder."

Jasper rubbed his temple. "I need to summon a constable. Will you be all right staying here while I go out? I shouldn't have to go very far."

She nodded, unafraid of being left alone in the house. He didn't take the cab lantern with him but left it for her use, and once Jasper was gone, Leo took a turn around the room, peering at everything. Over her dress, the same one she'd been wearing the previous evening at dinner, Helen wore a coat made of finely spun emerald wool. She hadn't discarded the coat before prying up the floorboard, but a lady's hat lay on the dust-sheet-draped four poster bed along with a handbag and pair of gloves.

Picking up the handbag, Leo noted it wasn't very heavy. When emptied of its contents, she saw that Helen had carried the usual things, like an embroidered, kiss lock change purse, a lace handkerchief, and a small comb. There was one unusual thing among the others, however. A small, folded square of paper.

She unfolded it, and though the inked scrawl had bled into the damp fibers of the paper, the writing was legible: *Meet me at our spot. Wait until midnight.* It wasn't signed.

Helen had been meeting someone, then. She'd placed this note in her purse, where it had become waterlogged during the long ride to London. And then, she had been bludgeoned to death. Had this home on Craven Hill been the designated meeting spot?

There were too many questions, and many more possible answers. It would be best not to speculate too much before Jasper had the chance to speak with Helen's family. He would have to return to Harrow right away. Though the thought of returning so soon to the hall at Cowper Fields made her blood feel as if it was turning to lead, she still wanted to accompany him. However, she knew she could not. There was no valid reason for her to go, and besides, a postmortem would be ordered. Surely, the body would be removed to the Spring Street Morgue, and even though it interested her far less than investigating a case with Jasper, Leo had a job to do with Connor Quinn.

It did not take long for Jasper to find a constable out on his evening circuit, and that constable went directly to the local police station within Hyde Park to summon more officers. Not more than a quarter hour had passed before they arrived, their lanterns brightening the bedroom to an almost garish degree. Leo stood aside as the officers arrived and spoke with Jasper who, upon his return, had read the handwritten note from Helen's purse that Leo handed to him, then tucked it into his trouser pocket. He planned to return to Cowper Hall as soon as Detective Chief Inspector Dermot Coughlan agreed to assign him the case—Jasper was certain that he would, especially since he already had knowledge of the family and the situation.

"I will have to inform Coughlan about Francine Stroud's request," he told Leo as a few officers brought in a long wooden board, which they'd scavenged from the kitchen. They were going to use it to move the body.

"Do you think he will open an investigation into Theodore's death?" she asked.

Jasper grimaced. "I doubt it. Our resources are stretched thin as they are, and he won't be swayed by the contents of Mrs. Stroud's letter. But he will want Helen's murder investigated."

"And I will not be welcome to assist, I imagine," Leo said with frustration.

He sent her a remorseful look but did not disagree. While she understood, it still grated. She'd looked forward to working with Jasper on the inquiry into the boy's fatal fall. Now, a new murder would be his priority.

At that moment, the officers gently rolled the corpse onto its back. The rigidity of Helen's limbs was such that her arms stayed in the same position as they'd been before splayed at the sides of her head in the pool of blood. Now, the viscous blood stained her palms and sleeves. But something else captured Leo's notice as the officers lifted her onto the board.

"Wait a moment," Leo said, stepping forward. Jasper held up a hand, signaling for them to wait, as she'd asked.

"What is it?" he asked.

Helen's coat lapels had fallen aside, exposing the dress she wore. Positioned as she was on her back, the drape of her dress defined a small but discernable abdominal bump. On a larger woman, it might not have been noticeable. But as Helen was quite thin, the bump was evident. Leo turned away from the body and saw Jasper had answered his question himself. He peered at the obvious protuberance with a furrowed brow.

"The postmortem will determine it for certain," Leo said, "however, it looks as though Mrs. Dalton was with child."

Chapter Eight

It was only with a bit of luck that Jasper was able to catch Chief Inspector Coughlan on his way out of Scotland Yard for the evening. By the bristling of the man's ginger mustache, he knew Coughlan was not pleased to be waylaid in the lobby of the building. However, the mention of a murdered woman found inside a stately home near Hyde Park was enough to restore Coughlan's patience and interest. To Jasper's relief, the chief inspector agreed that he could oversee the investigation—at least, the initial phase of it.

"You will, of course, return to Liverpool to finalize the case there," Coughlan decreed firmly. "If you cannot make an arrest here before you are expected back in Liverpool, then the case will be turned over to another detective."

The previous day, Jasper had wired the Liverpool station and alerted his superior officer of his intention to take at least two more days in London. He now regretted not giving himself more time than those two days, but he hadn't anticipated having a murder to investigate. He gathered a few of his trusted men and set out for Harrow right away. Sergeant Warnock and Constable Price had been easy to locate at the Rising Sun public house, and though they were not enthusiastic about the nighttime mission out of London, they knew better than to complain. They downed the rest of their beer and met Jasper in the courtyard out back of headquarters, where he'd arranged for a police carriage to transport them to Anthony Dalton's home at Field's End Manor.

"Anthony Dalton is the murdered woman's husband and is our primary suspect at the moment," he said to Warnock and Price after explaining what had occurred. "But we will question everyone who knew Mrs. Dalton."

The discovery that she was very likely carrying a baby as well as the note Leo had discovered in her handbag led Jasper to wonder if Helen had been having an affair. He highly doubted the message had come from her husband. The man had been staggering drunk, and the two of them had been like oil and water. An affair certainly could have been a reason for Anthony to lash out at his wife—if he'd known. But then, how did the glass vial Francine Stroud had hidden under the floorboard come into play?

There were too many avenues of speculation, and until he could sit down and question Anthony and the others who'd been present at Cowper Hall during their stay, none of them would lead anywhere definitively.

The road north of London toward Harrow wasn't busy, but it was dark. Their carriage lantern shook light over the well-worn dirt, still muddy from the torrential rains the previous night. Debris left over from downed trees and branches littered the road, slowing their progress at times. It was nearly eleven in the evening when their carriage passed the long drive leading up to Cowper Hall, heading instead toward the Daltons' residence next door at Field's End Manor.

In the darkness, and with the sky overrun with clouds that snuffed out any moonlight, the manor was barely visible. Unsurprisingly, the windows were nearly all blackened. Only one room on the second level was still lit, and the glow from it illuminated the limestone exterior nearby, choked with vines.

Jasper descended from the carriage and stretched his aching back. Their approach up the drive hadn't gone unnoticed; a light flared in a ground-floor room. He, Warnock, and Price were met on the front step by a man in a dressing gown and nightcap, his expression one of annoyance at first. But then, at the sight of Jasper's warrant card, it changed to concern. The butler's name was Saunders, and he allowed them into the house and asked them to wait in a front sitting room while he summoned Mr. Dalton.

"I will need all staff members awakened, Mr. Saunders," Jasper said.

The butler frowned, his alarm visibly increasing. "Is that really necessary, Inspector?"

"It is. Please show Sergeant Warnock and Constable Price to the servants' quarters after you've informed Mr. Dalton of my presence."

Saunders nodded, then led the two officers away from the sitting room. Jasper was left to pace for several minutes. He'd had plenty of time on the ride to Harrow to put together his line of questioning for Helen's husband and to brace himself for Anthony Dalton's foul attitude.

He only hoped the man had not imbibed too much liquor this evening and would be clearheaded.

At the sound of fast-approaching footsteps, Jasper turned to greet Mr. Dalton. The man entered the sitting room in his nightrobe and slippers, his dark hair mussed. But he did not look as though he'd been sleeping. On the contrary, he appeared alert and slightly wild-eyed.

"What are you doing here?" he barked, forgoing any polite greeting. Not surprising, really. "Saunders tells me your officers are questioning my staff. What the devil about?"

"Mr. Dalton, I wonder if you can tell me where your wife is," Jasper replied, not yet wanting to reveal her fate.

"Not here," he spat. He ran his fingers through his hair, as though aggrieved. "She's probably in London with the Perrys. The bloody harridan left in the middle of the night yesterday, not telling a single soul where she was off to."

Anthony strode to a table of decanters and poured himself a drink. He did not offer one to Jasper, which was just as well.

"Who are the Perrys?"

"Friends of hers. She stays on with them whenever she's in Town." He tossed back his drink and glared at Jasper again. "Now, bloody well tell me why you are here. Does it have to do with Helen?"

The faintest expression of concern softened Anthony's brow.

"It does, I'm afraid," Jasper answered. "Your wife was found dead at the house on Craven Hill."

He waited a moment to let the news land. Then, as Anthony's shock sent him reeling toward a chair, Jasper continued, "She was murdered, Mr. Dalton. Struck on the head with a heavy object. Scotland Yard has opened an investigation into her death."

Anthony sat down, his gaze flat as he stared across the room into nothing ness. Slowly, he sipped his drink. With more poise than Jasper expected from a man who'd just learned his wife had been killed, he asked, "What was she doing there?"

"That is what we are trying to determine," Jasper answered, unwilling to reveal any details involving the hollow in the floor, which he presumed she'd been there to access. "I'd like to know where you were last night, Mr. Dalton. You left Cowper Hall around ten in the evening."

"I came right here," he replied evenly. "I did not go to London and murder my wife, if that is what you are thinking."

His blasé tone disturbed Jasper as much as his dry-eyed appearance. Other than the need to take a seat, he didn't seem overly affected by the news of his wife's murder. Over the years, Jasper had told many people that their loved one had died. Everyone reacted and grieved differently. But there was a coldness to Anthony's reaction that Jasper did not often see. Had he not loved Helen?

If someone were ever to come to Jasper's door with news of Leo's death, he did not know what he might do. Last summer, when she had been taken hostage by gunmen at a charity dinner, Jasper had spent the next handful of hours believing she would be found dead somewhere, shot just as callously as another woman at the dinner had been. He'd launched a search for her, refusing to give up hope for her return and fighting the paralyzing fear of losing her. Leo had been found safe, but had there been a different outcome, he knew he would not be sitting placidly, drinking a whisky, as Anthony Dalton now was.

"My officers are questioning your staff right now," Jasper said. "If you are telling the truth, it will be verified. When did you learn Helen had left the viscount's home during the night?"

He fidgeted by scrubbing his forehead harshly and tapping his foot. "I don't know. This morning, maybe ten o'clock? I woke up around then, I think, and Saunders told me there was some commotion over her disappearance."

"You didn't worry?"

Anthony waved his hand. "No. She was outraged, and when Helen is upset, she avoids me. I figured she went to see the Perrys in a fit of temper."

"Who did you assume traveled with her into London?" The note in her handbag rose to mind. "It wasn't her maid, as Dora had no idea Mrs. Dalton was gone until this morning."

Again, Anthony waved his hand and shook his head. "To be honest, I didn't give it much thought."

Jasper was incredulous at the man's uncaring attitude. "You didn't worry that your wife seemed to have traveled alone for hours in the night, in a storm, along darkened roads?"

The man did not answer, and his expression remained impassive as he sipped his drink. No. He had not loved his wife. He'd likely only married Helen for her money. She had met with someone last night, though from the wording on the unsigned note currently in Jasper's pocket, it could have been with a friend or a lover—though Jasper leaned toward it being a lover, considering she'd been carrying a child. She had been at least four or five months along, according to Leo's estimation.

Had Anthony discovered she was meeting someone? Or that she was pregnant?

If Anthony was lying about being home last night and had instead gone to London, he would have needed a horse and carriage to get there. If Helen was killed around five in the morning, that would have given Anthony more than enough time to hasten back to Harrow and pretend to have been abed all night. However, his curricle and horse would show signs of use. Jasper would be making a visit to the stables.

"I'm going to need a handwriting sample from you, Mr. Dalton," he said. He'd told Warnock and Price to get handwriting samples from everyone on staff as well.

The man scowled. "Whatever for?"

"I just require it," Jasper replied, his patience thinning. He would not breathe a word about the note until he matched up the writing and knew who had sent it to Helen. Her maid, who might have delivered it to her, might also be aware of the sender's identity.

Anthony grumbled but took his drink to a small writing desk. Using a fountain pen, he scratched something onto a piece of stationary. He slammed the pen down and stalked to Jasper, thrusting the paper at him. "Here. Now, unless you have anything more to ask—"

"I do, thank you," Jasper cut in, taking a cursory glance at what appeared to be a sloppily done signature. He couldn't be sure until he compared the writing side to side, but he didn't think it was a match.

"Were you present in Helen's life when her younger brother, Theodore, died?"

The way he jerked his chin back in surprise, it was evident this wasn't a question Anthony had anticipated. "That was what...ten or so years ago?"

"Twelve."

He scoffed. "I met and married Helen eight years ago. So, the answer is no, Inspector. What has that to do with my wife's murder?"

The remote way Anthony spoke of Helen's demise without so much as a quivering chin or a catch in his throat continued to bother Jasper. He seemed to accept it far too quickly and willingly.

"Eight years," Jasper said. "Did you never want children?"

It was a prying question, however, asking this type of question was what his job was all about. Anthony's cool glare went even more wintry.

"We were never blessed. Is that all, Inspector? I need to inform the viscount."

"I will be doing that, Mr. Dalton, though you are welcome to come with me," Jasper said, hoping Warnock and Price were making good time interviewing the servants. The constable and sergeant had instructions to meet Jasper at Cowper Hall once they'd concluded their inquiries and to bring Helen's maid along with them for additional questioning.

Jasper crossed his arms. "I will wait while you dress." He would not let Anthony Dalton out of his sight just yet.

While the occupant of Field's End Manor showed a distinct lack of shock and sorrow at the news of Helen's death, those under Cowper Hall's roof were appropriately horrified.

Jasper and Anthony arrived past midnight to an utterly dark manor. They'd taken Anthony's curricle, allowing Jasper time to speak with the stable hand, who confirmed his employer had arrived home just past ten o'clock the previous evening. The stable hand had cleaned the mud spattered over the whole of the conveyance and had groomed the horse, which had been equally muddy. The curricle and horse had not left the stables since.

With that assurance, it was looking as if Anthony Dalton had not gone into London during the night after all. It would have been too easy, Jasper supposed, to find Helen's husband responsible for her murder. But he still did not trust Anthony and would not rule him out completely.

It took at least a quarter hour for the viscount's butler, Decamp, to awaken the household and for them to make their way to the main drawing room. Jasper and Anthony spent the time in silence, with Anthony pouring and downing two single malts by the time Viscount Cowper entered the room.

"What is the meaning of this, Inspector?" Lord Cowper asked, his expression twisted not into a look of loathing but into one of fear.

Jasper delivered the somber news, and the older man staggered to an armchair. He put his forehead in his palm and stayed that way. Helen's sister, Nadia, appeared then and, seeing her grandfather in distress, rushed to his side. When he mumbled to her what had happened, she cried out and burst into tears. Their grief seemed genuine to Jasper, and he had seen plenty of crocodile tears in his time. The room devolved into chaos over the next few minutes, as Frederick and his wife arrived and learned of Helen's fate while the shocked butler ordered a tearful maid to wake the housekeeper and return with strong tea and brandy.

Their reactions were unfolding as expected, so Jasper stood back and observed. Anthony continued to drink as he stayed detached from the commotion. Frederick's wife, Millicent, remained dry-eyed as she calmly patted Nadia's shoulder. Frederick sat hunched on the sofa, appearing a little green and holding a clenched fist to his mouth.

Once quiet had descended upon the room again, Jasper began.

"I will need to know all of your movements from after dinner last night through this morning," he said. "My constable and sergeant will be here shortly to speak to your staff as well."

Millicent lowered her hand from Nadia's shoulder. "Our movements? You cannot think that any of us had something to do with Helen's death?"

"She was murdered, Mrs. Cowper, and as I have not yet determined who killed her, everyone associated with Helen is to be questioned."

Millicent shifted uneasily on the sofa, while Nadia nodded her head readily, her eyes glistening with tears.

"Yes, fine, Inspector. After dinner, I…I went to the small sitting room with Helen, Millie, and Miss Spencer. We didn't stay there long. I went to my room afterward and then to bed. This morning, when I joined Grandfather for breakfast, he told me Helen had…gone." She choked out the last word.

Jasper would need to verify her claim against whatever

Warnock and Price learned from Nadia's maid, but he wasn't suspicious of her.

"You already have my alibi," Anthony said as he stared through a window, his back to the others in the room.

Millicent folded her hands in the lap of her thick nightrobe, the collar high and modest. "I left the sitting room before the others and went to my room. My maid drew a bath, and afterward I read a novel for a little while in bed before falling asleep."

Jasper looked to her husband, the Cowper heir. He knew for a fact that Frederick had been in the billiards room around ten thirty, as that was when Jasper had been leaving Leo's room and overheard his terse admonishment of the young maid. "And you, Mr. Cowper?"

He wanted to test him, see if Frederick would tell the truth.

"I think it was just after ten when I left the billiards room. I went to bed and stayed there all night," Frederick answered, his brow taut, his demeanor distracted.

"Can you verify this, Mrs. Cowper?" Jasper asked. He received a subtle scoff and a look of disdain from her.

"Those of our class keep separate rooms, Inspector," she said, making it clear anything else would have been beneath her.

"I see," he said and recalled, belatedly, the penchant upper-class couples had to keep separate bedrooms, often attached by a connecting door or dressing room. Jasper could not see the draw of that; if he had a wife, he'd want her in bed with him every night. The errant thought gave rise to another vision of Leo that had no place being in his mind right at that moment.

"Do you have a valet, Mr. Cowper?" If so, the servant could mark when Frederick was in his room.

"Yes, Winters. But I gave him the night off, so I didn't see him until morning."

"What time in the morning?" Jasper pressed.

"Eight, I believe."

He would check with Winters to verify Frederick's recollection, though Jasper recalled seeing the heir entering the breakfast room at around eight thirty that morning.

The only person remaining to give his whereabouts over the course of the previous night was the viscount. He had not moved from his armchair, nor lifted his head from his hand. His tall, thin frame looked to be sagging in on itself in utter defeat.

Frederick stood up from his cushion on the sofa. "What about that Miss Spencer woman? She was here last night. Shouldn't she be questioned as well?"

Jasper hitched his chin. "She has been." He would not share more than that with them. "Now, it is known that Helen left here sometime during the night after eleven o'clock. She could not have taken a train to Paddington Station, as the tracks were closed, so she would have required a conveyance. Were any missing this morning from the stables here?"

The viscount lifted his head from his hand and spoke with a firmness that straightened every back in the room. "Decamp. Tell him."

The butler cleared his throat. "A pony phaeton and one of the horses, Inspector. They were found to be absent from the stables this morning."

"Did Mrs. Dalton have experience taking the phaeton

out?" The small, sporty conveyance was made for a single passenger, or two passengers squeezed close together.

Everyone—excepting the viscount, whose face was once again buried in his palm—glanced skeptically at one another, as if to seek out the person who might know the answer.

"My wife did not drive often," came Anthony's reply after a pause. "But a phaeton is not so difficult to maneuver."

Perhaps not, but Jasper still wondered if the person who had beckoned Helen to meet them at their "spot" had also driven to London with her. There had been no horse and phaeton parked along Craven Hill earlier that night when he and Leo had found Helen's body, and it appeared the phaeton and horse were still missing.

"I'll have my sergeant take down a description of the horse and phaeton. The Met can launch a search for them in London," he said. "I will also need handwriting samples from all of you." The request elicited the same quizzing looks from them as Anthony had given him earlier. Before anyone could object, Jasper raised his hand to stave off any dissension. "I am requesting samples from everyone here, including the staff. Just sign your name, or whatever you like, on a piece of paper."

As Decamp went to find paper and writing tools, Jasper fielded cold, suspicious glances. It was possible he was making too much of the note; there was the chance it was an old missive, and Helen had simply been storing it in her handbag. When Warnock and Price arrived with Helen's maid, Jasper would see what she knew. If Helen was seeing anyone, and if she'd received a note last evening, the maid would likely be aware of it.

"What was she doing at that house?" Nadia asked as she wrote her name. She handed it to Jasper and met his eyes. "She hated it there. The place is haunted."

He cocked his head, intrigued. "Because of what happened to your brother?"

She blinked, as if surprised he knew about Teddy's death. "Yes."

"It isn't haunted," Millicent said, her tone impatient. "However, Helen did seem upset that the home had been given to you, Inspector, and Miss Spencer. Perhaps she went there to see it one last time."

"In the middle of the night?" Nadia dismissed the idea with a roll of her red, teary eyes. "Helen is sentimental but not reckless. To go all the way to London at that hour, alone… No. She simply wouldn't have done that."

Jasper accepted Millicent's handwriting sample. She wouldn't meet his eyes.

"What do you know so far, Inspector?" Frederick asked as he, too, handed him a writing sample. Jasper collected them but did not look at them, not wanting to be distracted.

"Information is still being gathered," he replied, purposefully vague. He kept his gaze on Frederick. "You could help answer a question, however."

The man's forehead furrowed. "Whatever you need."

"I happened upon you last night," Jasper began. "Just outside the billiards room, you were chastising a maid. Quite harshly, I thought. What was it over?"

The viscount's son hitched his chin. "Hiding in the shadows, were you?"

Jasper smiled thinly. "I didn't want to interrupt."

After a brief glance toward Millicent, as if to check her

reaction—though she was staring straight ahead with pursed lips—Frederick answered, "That was Ursula. A fine enough maid, but she is far too free with her opinions and relishes spreading gossip. I suppose I lost my patience with her last night."

"What did she say?" Jasper asked.

He shifted his footing and then shrugged. "I can't recall the exact wording, but she was weighing in on my sister's choice to give the house on Craven Hill to strangers. She was out of line, and I asked her to mind her tongue."

It matched with what Jasper could recall of the conversation. Frederick had told the maid to mind her own business if she wanted to keep her position at Cowper Hall.

"Oh, Freddie, the poor girl means no harm," Nadia admonished. "She is surely upset over my mother's death." She looked to Jasper and explained, "Ursula was my mother's maid."

He nodded, understanding why Ursula might have felt compelled to give an opinion on Francine's odd choice. And after a trying day, in which Frederick himself had not been welcomed to his older sister's will reading, he might have been feeling bitter and tense.

"It might not have any bearing on the case," Jasper said, eyeing the viscount again. He'd lifted his head from his hand, but he still appeared ashen and morose, and as if hardly listening to the conversation around him. Jasper pressed on, "I would like to know, however, why you, my lord, and you, Mr. Cowper, were not at the will reading."

The viscount's beady glare sharpened. "You are correct, Inspector—it does not have any bearing on my granddaughter's murder."

"I would like to be the one to determine if that is so," Jasper replied. "Were the two of you not invited?"

He knew they would bristle and think him ill-mannered and prying, but that was just the way of things. Jasper did not expect, nor even want, to be liked by the people he was questioning. He wanted them upset, unbalanced, flustered, as that was when the truth most often slipped free.

"There was no reason for my son and me to be there," the viscount answered, his temper flickering higher. "She left her possessions to her children, as she should have. And to you and that morgue worker, although I cannot begin to comprehend why."

Just as quickly as Lord Cowper's temper flared, it ebbed again. His shoulders sank, and he again lowered his head to his hand. Jasper didn't miss how he had not answered the question of whether they had not been invited. But he would leave it for now. Just as he would leave getting the viscount's handwriting sample and his movements the night before. There would be more opportunities to question Lord Cowper, but Jasper did not believe the old man could have rushed to London in a storm, killed his granddaughter, and then made it back to Cowper Hall in time to sit down to breakfast before Jasper had arrived shortly before eight.

"I'll need you, Mr. Dalton, to come to London to formally identify your wife's body," Jasper said, switching tracks.

Anthony's initial reaction was to grimace. Before he could make any reply, Frederick said, "I will accompany him."

At this, Millicent whipped her head around to peer at her husband. “Is that necessary?”

Frederick glowered at her with a visible command for her to hush. She straightened her spine and looked away from him.

“I’ll check in with my constable and sergeant to see how the questioning of your staff is proceeding,” Jasper said, moving toward the drawing room exit. “We’ll leave for London at dawn.”

“We will be ready,” Frederick said, his tone bleak.

Jasper left them to their grief, hoping Warnock and Price had discovered something useful from the viscount’s staff.

Chapter Nine

A miserable pall hung over the morgue the following morning. Leo supposed that to most people, this was what a morgue was supposed to feel like. However, it had never felt like a forbidding and sorrowful place to her before, so the unwieldy quiet between her and Connor stood out as new.

He was still off-balance from his ex-fiancée's body arriving at the morgue the previous day, and she could not fault him for it. As Leo made them tea on the cottage range, Connor sat at the small table they kept in the office. He was reading the postmortem report she'd typed before leaving with Jasper for Craven Hill.

"Asphyxiation," he said in a flat tone.

The bruising around Lydia Hailson's neck had been evidence of strangulation, and Claude had concluded it was the cause of her death.

"A fractured hyoid bone supports my uncle's finding," she said cautiously, as Connor seemed particularly on edge. "There were no other injuries."

Even though Miss Hailson had been shorter and slighter than Leo, her bone structure dainty, and her neck swanlike, it still would have taken some degree of strength to apply enough constant pressure to break the hyoid bone, located just above her larynx, and asphyxiate her.

"Do you know if she had a new beau?" Leo asked, thinking of what Jasper might ask. He'd been immediately suspicious of Connor, which she, of course, knew was absurd, but Leo had to acknowledge that strangulation was, generally, a crime of passion.

He lowered the report to the table and shook his head. "I don't know. We hadn't spoken in some time. Months."

Lydia's corpse was still under a sheet in the post-mortem room, waiting for the funeral service to arrive and collect it. Before Claude had arrived the evening before, Connor had explained that Lydia's only living relative was a grandfather in Wales. She was on her own, and as it would surely take some time to locate her grandfather and decide what was to be done with the body, Connor had decided to take charge of her burial himself.

He placed the report back in the manila folder and pushed it toward Leo's elbow. "Send it along to Mr. Pritchard and to Scotland Yard. I want the inquest and investigation into her death to begin as soon as possible."

Leo did not mention that he would be a suspect himself, given his past relationship with the victim. He was intelligent enough to anticipate that eventuality.

"We have another body in the postmortem room for this morning. I think we should move it to the top of our list," Leo said, wanting to begin the morning's examinations with Helen Dalton.

He drained his tea and stood. "Why is that?"

"Because Jasper and I found the body in the house we now own."

The coroner knocked the backs of his legs into his chair and set down his cup with a rattle. "You found a… What body? What *house*?"

She hadn't wanted to bother Connor with the details of their visit to Harrow yesterday; he'd been bowled over by his own shock and grief. So, as they entered the post-mortem room and made their way to the autopsy table that Helen had been laid upon, she explained everything to him—from the bequest to the letter from Francine Stroud to Helen's disappearance in the night and, finally, to the discovery of her body in the house on Craven Hill.

Once she'd concluded her retelling of events, the hiss of the gasoliers overhead was the only sound in the room for several moments. Connor drew back the sheet covering Helen's corpse, and a frown tugged the corners of his mouth.

"Why do I have the feeling you are about to tell me that you'll be absent from the morgue quite a bit more?" he asked, a brow raised in mock annoyance.

While helping Jasper solve a few cases in the past, she'd kept irregular hours at the morgue. However, that was when she'd been little more than a volunteer. Now, as a paid employee, she would not have the luxury of time off whenever it suited her.

"Inspector Reid doesn't need me for this investigation, I'm sure," Leo said, ignoring a tug of disappointment in her stomach.

Connor merely made a disbelieving grunt in the back of his throat before preparing for the postmortem examination of Helen Dalton. Leo tied on an apron and gathered a pencil and paper to note down his findings. Admittedly, it was discomfiting to observe the autopsy of a woman whom Leo had just been seated across from at dinner a few nights ago. She could still easily recall everything about the dinner, from the details of the room, the table settings, and the décor to what everyone was wearing and how they had behaved. The images of Helen's stiff posture, the nervous darting of her eyes, and the thin seam of her mouth when her husband acted like a drunken buffoon were foremost in Leo's mind as Connor examined the body.

It was not the first postmortem he'd performed on a pregnant woman, nor was it Leo's first time viewing one, but when it became clear that Helen was indeed about four months along in her pregnancy at the time of her death, a respectful dip in conversation marked the acknowledgment of the dual loss of life.

It wasn't impossible that the unborn child had been Anthony Dalton's. However, the note in Helen's handbag, with the instruction to *meet at our spot,* led Leo to believe it was more likely that she'd had a lover.

During the cranial examination, Connor named the cause of death. The strike against her right temporal bone would have been debilitating, while a second, more forceful blow to the frontal bone had been what killed her. As Jasper had already found the brass statue of a peacock with blood on it, Connor agreed after hearing a description of the statue that it sounded a likely match for the murder weapon.

In the process of replacing the skull cap and preparing to suture it closed, something fell from Helen's untidy bun, clinked against the table's edge, and landed on the floor. Her long hair, which had been neatly coiled and pinned into a voluminous topknot, was now in a loosened state, and with good reason, considering all it had endured. But the clattering of the object to the floor near Connor's feet didn't sound like a loose hairpin or comb. It rang hollow instead, like glass.

"Would you mind picking that up, Miss Spencer?" he asked, stepping aside while holding the skull cap in place.

Leo stepped forward and nearly lost her breath. It was a small glass tube about half the length and width of her pinkie finger. At the time of its firing, the clear glass had been swirled with cobalt and amethyst. Though it appeared to be empty, the tube was stoppered with a small wedge of cork. Two holes in the top rim would have accommodated a chain, or a length of ribbon or leather.

Leo stooped to pick it up, holding her breath. This had to be the glass vial Francine Stroud had described in her letter, the one that had been hidden under the bedroom floorboard.

"What in the world is that?" Connor asked as he continued to work. Leo stepped aside, still marveling at the small bottle.

"I think this is what Francine Stroud wanted Jasper and me to find at the house," she said. Quickly, she explained about the small glass vial Francine had found clutched in her dead son's hand after he'd fallen from the roof, and her directions to the specific floorboard that covered a small hollow, where the vial had been hidden.

"Helen must have gone to the house in a rush because she knew we were going to find it," Leo theorized. "And she wanted to get to it first."

"But why put it in her hair?" Connor asked as he sewed.

"To hide it again?" Leo mused, picturing the moment in her mind. Helen had pried up the floorboard—evidenced by the minuscule particles of wood Connor had found underneath her fingernails during the examination. Perhaps she had heard someone coming, quickly grabbed the vial and speared it into her bun to whisk it out of sight. Had she put it into her pocket, whoever had joined her might have easily accessed it.

Connor nodded at that theory. "That would indicate she knew the interloper wanted the trinket as well."

Leo had not considered that yet but agreed it made the most sense. As Connor continued to close the incisions he'd made, she pulled out the tiny cork stopper. A bit of it crumbled under her prying nail, but it came free mostly intact. Putting it to her nose, she inhaled a faint floral fragrance. Perfume.

However, she didn't think the bottle had been intended to be a scent dispenser. She couldn't be certain, but Leo thought it might be what was known as a tear catcher.

Like mourning jewelry and death photography, tear catchers were one of many morbid trends in the death industry. Grieving women would use the little glass tubes to catch their tears. The cork would seal the liquid inside, and purportedly, once it dried up, their mourning could end. It was an overly dramatic and fanciful practice to Leo, not to mention illogical. Grief did not evaporate like water. The fashionable trend was just another way to sell pretty trinkets to anguished people.

Like the tube that Helen had speared into her hair, tear

catchers could be ornate and expensive, or plain and affordable. A pretty one like Helen's would certainly serve well as a perfume dispenser after the initial tears that had filled it were gone.

But why had ten-year-old Teddy Stroud had it in his fist when he'd fallen to his death?

Leo replaced the cork and, after taking another thorough look at the swirled glass, placed the tube in her pocket to give to Jasper when next she saw him. She then assisted Connor in cleaning and dressing the corpse, and Leo even spent a little time tidying Helen's blonde hair with a comb. She styled it afterward to cover the incision on the woman's scalp as well as the two depressions near the front of her skull. The result was satisfactory, though not perfect.

A few hours after they'd begun the postmortem, the bell above the lobby's front door chimed, signaling a visitor to the morgue. As it was nearly ten in the morning, Leo hoped it would be Jasper. He'd gone back to Harrow the previous night to question Anthony Dalton and the rest of Helen's family, a task that could not have been easy, especially as he'd probably needed to rouse them from their beds. Jasper had hoped to return to London before noon today, and sure enough, when Leo entered the lobby, it was to find the detective inspector. He was not alone: Anthony Dalton and Frederick Cowper stood with him, their suits well-pressed and tidy.

Jasper's clothing, on the other hand, was a bit creased, his honey-blond hair unruly as he removed his bowler. Though neatly trimmed, his golden bristle did give him a rumpled appearance. He'd always been handsome, but now that Leo had given herself permission to note it, even just to herself, his attractiveness had seemed to increase. She tried not to smile at him, as smiling was not something one should do when about to discuss the death of a loved one with family members.

"I'll let the coroner know you've arrived for the formal identification," she said, then turned to go back into the postmortem room.

"Must I truly see her?" Mr. Dalton asked, loud and brusque enough to stop her in her tracks. "If you and the inspector are certain it is Helen, then I don't see the point."

He appeared pale and a little sweaty along his forehead. Nerves, she presumed.

"I'm afraid it is protocol," Jasper answered. He nodded for her to continue, and Leo went to inform Connor that Helen's husband and uncle were here for the viewing.

He shed his stained canvas coat and tall, vulcanized rubber boots—neither of which Leo required, as she stood far enough away from the autopsy table during examinations to not risk splatter reaching her—for a more presentable coat and shoes. Together, they wheeled the table bearing Helen into the viewing room.

It was no surprise when Mr. Dalton did not do more than briefly glimpse at Helen once the sheet had been pulled down to reveal her face. Whether it was discomfort or something else wasn't clear to Leo. Frederick Cowper, however, kept a steady, if somber, gaze on his niece. It was still such an odd thing to consider that he was her uncle. But perhaps that was only because Leo's only uncle was Claude, an elderly man.

Connor cleared his throat. "Mr. Dalton, were you aware of your wife's condition?"

Anthony peered at him with narrowed eyes, as if to impart that his question was an annoyance. "Condition? My wife was perfectly healthy."

"Healthy, yes," Connor was quick to say. "However, Mrs. Dalton was carrying a child at the time of her death. About four months along, in fact."

Anthony's face blanched. He shifted his awe-filled eyes to his wife and stared at her, no longer appearing squeamish. Only stunned.

"No. That is… That is not possible. You must be mistaken."

"Mr. Dalton, the coroner is not mistaken," Jasper said. "Why do you claim the impossibility of her condition?"

Anthony hinged his loose jaw, then, with a return of his composure, stalked from the room without answering. Jasper followed, while Frederick slipped his hat back onto his head and sighed.

"They could not have children," he imparted to her and Connor, his voice constrained.

Leo moved into the lobby with Frederick, while Connor began to roll the table back into the postmortem room.

Anthony had gone to the lobby door, as if ready to leave. His hands were locked into fists. "It appears Helen was having an affair after all, Inspector. If she was with child, it was not mine." His attention was fixed on nothing that she could discern, and Leo had the sense that he could not make eye contact with them due to shame. "A riding accident, many years ago, left me unable to…" He glanced at Leo, then away again. "It doesn't matter. She was deceiving me with another man, clearly."

He'd cut himself off, but Leo had an inkling as to what

he'd been about to say. That the accident had made it so that he could be a husband in name only.

"Do you have any idea whom she was seeing?" Jasper asked.

"None at all. She kept to herself most of the time," he answered, sounding petulant again.

"Because you kept her at arm's length," Frederick said.

Anthony spluttered an oath and advanced, fast, but the Cowper heir put his palm against Anthony's chest and shoved. "Oh, stop with your theatrics. If you hadn't pitied yourself so dreadfully, if you'd shown her even a minuscule amount of care, my niece would not have needed to look elsewhere. It was your own doing, Dalton, and everyone in the family will tell you so."

"Perfect, are you?" Anthony spat. "Then why did your sister cut you from her will?"

Flaring tempers in the lobby were nothing new; Leo had seen plenty of scraps and arguments among family members after viewing a dead loved one. Usually, the best way to diffuse the tension was with a bit of guilt.

"The two of you should be ashamed of yourselves," she said. "Show some respect for the dead."

It worked, though only because Anthony winged open the door and disappeared through it. Frederick lowered his chin. "Forgive me, Miss Spencer, that was tactless. It's only that it's been trying to watch Helen all these years, suffering that selfish fool."

Jasper went to the door and shut it, then waited until the chime of the bell fell silent again. "Do you have any idea who the father might be, Mr. Cowper?"

"No," he said with a decisive shake of his head. "Our

lives did not often overlap, and she has always been a quiet sort. I would suggest you speak to Dora, her maid."

"I did attempt to question her on the drive into London," Jasper said, appearing irked at the memory, "but she was in no fit state to speak."

"They were quite close," Frederick said with a grim press of his lips. "Dora will be staying with the Perrys while we are in London. I'm sure she will calm soon and be ready to speak to you."

"Who are the Perrys?" Leo asked.

"Friends of Mrs. Dalton's," Jasper answered, apparently having learned as much earlier while questioning the family in Harrow. "Will you also be at the Perrys?" he asked Frederick.

"No, no, I like to stay at The Great Western Royal while in town," he replied, naming the fine hotel attached to Paddington Station. "Anthony will also have a room there, I'm sure. Now, if you'll excuse me, Inspector, Miss Spencer, I believe I will be the one making funeral arrangements for Helen."

Frederick left the lobby, though he at least closed the door behind him.

As soon as they were alone, Jasper tipped his head back, closed his eyes, and let out a groan. He'd appeared tired before, but now Leo could see the extent of his fatigue. She stepped closer to him and laid her hand on his arm.

"You look dead on your feet," she said, only realizing the inappropriateness of the maxim when he sent her a wry look. Leo bit her lip. "Sorry. Come have some tea."

At his sigh, she knew he was about to refuse. "I can't." He covered her hand with his, and though he lifted it from his sleeve, he continued to hold on. "I'm sorry, but I need to speak to Helen's maid as well as to the Perrys. If anyone knows who the father of the child is, it will be one of them."

"If Helen and her lover met regularly at this *spot* that was mentioned in the note, he must live close to Cowper Fields," Leo said. "And if they met the night of the storm, he might have driven her to London."

The lover could have been the one who came into the bedroom after the blood had pooled. He may have rushed to her side, treading into the blood before then leaving in a rush.

"A horse and phaeton were discovered missing from the viscount's stables that morning," he said, absentmindedly running his fingers over her knuckles. "It hasn't been returned or found."

She tamped down the shiver along her spine that his distracted touching caused her. "Well then," she went on, "if her lover is from Harrow and has fled, he will soon be noticed as missing."

"I hadn't thought of that." He stilled his fingers and grinned. "I'll wire Paddington Division and ask if they've had any reports of a missing person from Harrow."

He lifted her hand and pressed his lips to her knuckles and, with his mouth lingering against her skin, asked, "Anything interesting during the postmortem?"

Leo wanted to laugh at how unromantic the question was. Yet it also pleased her that he wanted to discuss the case.

"Actually, yes. Though, I'll need my hand back." Interest lit his eyes, and when he released her, she reached into her apron pocket.

"Is that…?" Jasper started to say, reaching for the tiny glass vial as she held it up.

"I'm quite sure it is," she replied. "Helen found the vial Francine wrote about in her letter to us and seemingly hid it in her bun before she was killed. The peacock statue struck the temporal and frontal bones of her skull, sparing the crown and back of the head, so the tube hidden in her hair was untouched."

"Her killer wasn't with her originally, then, but entered the house and came upon her in the bedroom." Jasper held the tube up, inspecting it. "It's small enough to fit in a child's hand and in a woman's bun. But why hide it from the person who followed her into the house?"

Leo wondered the same thing, but as she did not know, she didn't speculate and instead explained what she suspected the tube was. He grunted at hearing it was some sort of death trinket; he'd made known his unfavorable opinion of maudlin trends to Leo before.

"Has Mr. Dalton accounted for his whereabouts last night?" Leo asked. "I assume he has, as he isn't under arrest."

"He was at home," Jasper replied, tucking the tear catcher into his coat pocket. "His valet confirmed he was given the night off, but he checked in on Anthony around five o'clock in the morning anyway, only to find the man asleep on the floor. He was so drunk off his face that he hadn't even made it to the bed."

Leo didn't care for Anthony Dalton, but it appeared he was in the clear as a suspect.

The postmortem room door opened, and Connor joined them.

"Inspector Reid," he said urgently. "Have you heard

anything at all about what is being done with Lydia Hailson's murder case?"

As Leo had just sent the postmortem report to Scotland Yard a few hours earlier, the shake of Jasper's head was expected.

"I'm afraid I haven't been at the Yard yet to learn if the case has been assigned," he answered, even as Connor's expression turned stern. "If you inquire with Constable Wiley at the CID, he might be able to tell you something more than I can."

Leo detested the front desk constable at the CID and couldn't suppress her bilious reaction to his name. Jasper witnessed it and sent her an impatient glance.

"I already went there yesterday to report her murder," Connor replied, startling Leo. He hadn't told her that earlier. He must have gone after leaving the morgue, when Claude stepped in to do the postmortem. "The Wiley fellow said there is a backlog of cases, and it might take weeks for this one to be assigned."

Jasper's grimace was one of sympathy. "I understand the victim is someone you cared for. But the Met has too many cases and too few detectives. I'm sure it will be assigned—"

"And meanwhile, Lydia's killer gets to slip away? Cover his tracks?" Connor blurted, crossing his arms over his chest. Leo had never seen him angry before, but she could understand why he was. "Maybe I should hire a private detective. Someone needs to investigate her death, and at least they would take it seriously."

Leo held back her instant urge to defend Jasper and the Yard. She knew full well the police were already disparaged for not solving every murder or suspicious death that came across their desks. The newspapers and public opinion, in general, often called them lazy, bumbling, or even worse, corrupt, only caring to solve crimes committed against the wealthy and influential, while working-class Londoners, orphans, vagrants, and the poor were brushed aside as inconsequential.

While it was true that not every case could be solved, Jasper cared about each one he was assigned. Connor, underneath his anger and heartbreak, knew that as well. He was only lashing out in frustration.

If Jasper took offense, he didn't reveal it. "If that is the route you'd like to take, I'll only advise you to be selective. The Yard has worked with a few private investigators from time to time, but most of them eventually swindle their clients in some way. Stegman and Bishop are a reputable agency."

Connor nodded tightly, accepting the advice. But he wasn't pleased.

Jasper turned to Leo. "I'll call on you tonight," he said softly, then left.

Connor rubbed his forehead. "I'm sorry. I know it isn't Inspector Reid's fault. But I'm impatient to know what happened to Lydia and for the person responsible to pay for what they did."

"I understand," Leo said. "Jasper understands too. He must, since he recommended Stegman and Bishop so confidently. He almost never has nice things to say about private agencies."

They moved back into the postmortem room, where Lydia's body remained on the morgue table. With any hope, the funeral service would arrive soon to take her away. It must have been torturous for Connor to keep having to look over and see her draped figure there. Much had happened since the day before, but Leo couldn't forget the dress Lydia had been wearing: the shopgirl uniform for Gleason's Department Store.

"Did you know that Lydia was working at Gleason's?" she asked Connor. He'd approached the next corpse on the docket for the day, his movements shuffling and distracted rather than confident and prompt as they normally were.

"No, I didn't. Last I knew she was working at a telephone exchange on Coleman Street."

"When was the last time you saw her?"

He rolled his shoulders, as though uncomfortable with having to remember. "The spring. When we...parted ways."

Leo was curious. "Why did you separate?" Then she added, "If you don't mind saying," when he visibly stiffened his back.

After a moment, he relaxed. "She wasn't ready to marry. Like so many young ladies seem to be doing these days, she wanted to work, have some independence." He shrugged and, with a self-deprecating laugh, said, "And I suppose she just didn't love me enough."

It must have pained him to say it; however, Leo suspected that Connor would make a fine husband. He was good-looking, kind, intelligent, and seemed to be progressive in his views on women in the workforce. But Leo wouldn't placate him, as she knew he wouldn't want it.

"I know someone who works at Gleason's," she said instead. "What if I were to ask her if she knew Lydia? Maybe she knows something that would be helpful."

Dita had only been working at the store for a few days, but it was worth the ask.

Connor perked, his attention snagged. But then, he winced. "I don't think so, Miss Spencer. This is a murder. It wouldn't be safe for you to go there asking questions. I will consider Stegman and Bishop." He winced again, and this time, Leo thought she knew why.

"Hiring them will be quite an expense," she said. While Connor's grandfather, Sir Eamon Giles, a knighted barrister and the city's chief coroner, was wealthy, Connor had made a point the last several months to proclaim his independence from his family and live off his own earnings.

"It's hardly dangerous for me to take my friend to a tea shop and ask a few questions," Leo said. Thankfully, Connor's hesitation melted under his desire for answers.

"Very well, but if you do anything more dangerous than visit a tea shop, I insist on accompanying you," he said. "The last thing I want is for Inspector Reid to kick down my door if you get yourself into a spot of trouble."

Leo grinned widely at his agreement, and at that fearful image of a wrathful Jasper. With any hope, Connor would not need to hire the private detective agency at all. She'd helped solve a few murders already. Perhaps she could do so again.

Chapter Ten

Jasper had missed the cramped corridors and offices at Scotland Yard. There was a bustling energy here, an urgent undercurrent that the station in Liverpool didn't have. It had taken him a few weeks to settle in there and begin to know the men he'd be working with. They'd been wary of him at first, a few of them resistant to working under a Scotland Yard detective inspector. But with time, tensions had slackened, and any raised hackles had lowered again.

It felt good to be back among the men with whom he'd worked regularly, even if it was for just a few days. As Jasper made his way through the detective department, he prepared for the awkwardness of entering his office and finding Roy Lewis there, sitting behind Jasper's desk and in his chair. But it had been only right for Chief Inspector Coughlan to shift Lewis into Jasper's unoccupied office to make room for the few new constables that had joined the CID over the last four months.

Jasper knocked on the frame of the open door, the way Lewis always had. The detective sergeant glanced up from a stack of files open upon the desk, seemed to jolt, and hastily stood.

"Guv," he said, as if he'd been caught out at something. "Wasn't sure if you'd be in. Warnock said you and Miss Spencer found a body in your new place. Someone connected to Lord Cowper?"

"His granddaughter, Helen Dalton. She was murdered," he explained. "I've instructed a constable to collect the victim's maid and bring her in for questioning."

It would have been just as easy for Jasper to go to the Perrys' address and question Miss Dora Sweeny there, especially since he would need to speak to them as well. She would be in a familiar setting, amongst people she knew, and perhaps she would have been past the immediate shock of her mistress being found dead. But there had been something contrived in the maid's hysterics on the long drive to London earlier that morning. No doubt she was upset and a bit dazed after receiving the news, but there had been a distinct effort on Miss Sweeny's part to avoid meeting Jasper's eyes in the police carriage.

She'd ridden with him, Frederick Cowper, and Price, while Anthony Dalton had insisted on following in his own carriage. Jasper hadn't argued but had Sergeant Warnock accompany him and his driver to be sure the man arrived in London as expected. If Dalton was guilty of anything, there was every reason to suspect that he might set off toward the coast instead, to flee the country.

All had gone smoothly, however, and with a glance toward the wall clock, Jasper expected Miss Sweeny to arrive at police headquarters at any moment.

"Will you need your office?" Lewis asked, stepping away from the desk as if to vacate the room. Jasper held up his hand to stay him.

"No. It's yours, Lewis," he replied, but added with a wry arch of his brow, "at least until I'm back at the Yard permanently. Christ, I hope Coughlan can scare up another room for you, or else we may be forced to share."

Lewis laughed, but he wrinkled his forehead, as if the idea unsettled him. After the Yard bombing back in May, he and Jasper had been forced to share a desk in the department while Jasper's office was being rebuilt. Neither of them had enjoyed that cramped arrangement.

"I only wanted to stop in and ask if you've received the postmortem report for a recent strangulation. A woman named Lydia Hailson."

He could understand Connor Quinn's frustration; the man had cared for the victim and wanted justice for her. Although he'd suggested hiring a private agency to investigate her death, Jasper didn't trust many of the dozens upon dozens of agencies that had been cropping up across the city. Stegman and Bishop acted with integrity, but their fees were steep, and their waiting list was often backlogged, just as the Yard's was.

Lewis shuffled through a few files on the desk but shook his head. "Sorry, I haven't got it here. I'll ask after it, but it's probably with Burrows or Royce," he said, naming two of the other detectives in the CID. "Why the interest?"

"The victim was known to Mr. Quinn, the coroner," Jasper explained.

Lewis grimaced in sympathy. "I'm sure it'll be assigned if it hasn't been already. We're up to our necks in cases lately. It'll be good to have you back, guv."

He had dark smudges under his eyes, and he appeared more rumpled than usual, supporting what he said about being overworked and undermanned.

"Inspector Reid," a voice called from behind Jasper. Constable Price, who'd gone to the Perrys' Portman Square address, had arrived and was leading Dora Sweeny toward an interview room.

Jasper thanked Lewis for checking on the Lydia Hailson case and followed the constable toward the interview room.

"There is a box of evidence from the murder scene, Inspector. Should I place it inside Sergeant Lewis's office?" Price asked.

"Yes, thank you," he replied. "Is there anything notable?"

"The murder weapon, sir, and the victim's belongings. Also, a glass pane in the back door was smashed," the constable said. "We think that's how the murderer entered the house. Some threads were found attached to the glass left in the door."

Intrigued, Jasper nodded. "I'll have a look."

He then turned into a small room, not much larger than a closet, with a wooden table and unpadded chairs. It wouldn't do to make any suspect in for questioning comfortable. He shut the door, inset with frosted glass, and took the chair across from Miss Sweeny.

The maid looked to be in her early fifties, with gray-streaked black hair pulled into a tight bun at the nape of her neck. She wore a bonnet and a plain, serviceable gown, both black in color, though Jasper did not think it was because she was in mourning. Most women in service whom he'd met wore austere colors, usually with a white pinafore.

Miss Sweeny had held a handkerchief to her nose for much of the drive back to London, though now, she sat with her hands clasped in her lap, her tear-reddened eyes intense with curiosity—and a bit of fear. Good. It was why he'd decided to go out of his way and bring her here, to this spare, intimidating room.

"Miss Sweeny, I have some blunt questions for you," he began, finding he was in no mood for pleasantries. "And I will ask that you answer them truthfully."

She widened her eyes and shifted in her chair. "Of course, Inspector."

"How long have you worked as Mrs. Dalton's maid?"

"Since she was still called Miss Stroud," she answered, her voice quavering somewhat. "I was given the position when she was seventeen. So, thirteen years I've been with her."

The maid's chin trembled, but she exhaled and kept her composure.

"The coroner has confirmed that Mrs. Dalton was about four months pregnant." He watched Miss Sweeny closely for her reaction; she kept her eyes on the scarred wood table, lashes fluttering rapidly. Jasper guessed, "You knew of her condition?"

She gave a single nod.

"And as Mr. Dalton is unable to father children," Jasper went on, "Mrs. Dalton was conducting an affair?"

Miss Sweeny's pursed lips contorted as she again seemed to hold a surge of emotion at bay. But then, she nodded tightly.

"Who is he?"

Whenever Jasper questioned someone who knew an answer, yet did not want to give it up, the person would seem to fold inward. Shoulders hunched, head bowed, eyes down. This was how the maid remained for several moments.

"I require a name, Miss Sweeny, and I know you can provide it."

He didn't want to threaten her with time in a holding cell, but if she insisted on silence, he would do it. Thankfully, after another few seconds, she wilted.

"Mr. Decamp."

Had Jasper been standing, the answer might have driven him back a step. He couldn't believe it. "The viscount's butler? He must be twice her age."

Miss Sweeny gasped and finally looked up at him. "No! Not that Mr. Decamp. Stephen. The butler's son."

"I see," he said. "And does Stephen Decamp also work for the viscount?"

Most often, whole families were in service together, employed by the same titled family.

"He is his lordship's steward," the maid answered. That caught Jasper by surprise. He'd expected him to be a footman or valet.

"That's quite a trusted position," he replied. As his steward, Stephen Decamp would have overseen the viscount's entire estate, his lands and holdings.

Miss Sweeny nodded. "Mr. Decamp was raised alongside Mr. Cowper, I'm told."

Frederick Cowper and Stephen Decamp would have been of two different classes, but that might not have mattered to two boys growing up on the same estate.

"Are they close?"

If they were, he wondered if Frederick would have known about the affair. And if so, why he might have lied to Jasper at the morgue, saying he could not think of who Helen's lover might be.

But the maid frowned. "No, not anymore. They had a falling out."

"When?"

"I don't know exactly. Years back," she said, sounding vexed. "Why do you ask?"

The details surrounding the falling out between Frederick and the younger Decamp intrigued Jasper, but there would be someone more knowledgeable than Dora Sweeny to tell him what had transpired. Nadia, perhaps. Or Millicent Cowper.

"Stephen lives on the estate, I take it?" he asked, moving on.

The maid nodded. "He has a farm. Keeps of few of his lordship's studs there." A gleam of interest shone in her eyes. "You don't believe Mr. Decamp had something to do with my lady's murder, do you?"

"Did Helen receive a message on the night of the storm? Or was it earlier that afternoon?" he asked rather than answer her question.

The permanent pleat between Miss Sweeny's eyebrows deepened. "Why, yes, she did. After the reading of the will, she was quite upset and had me dispatch a note to Mr. Decamp. I usually send her secret notes with Billy, one of Mr. Dalton's stable boys at Field's End. He's a good lad. Always discreet. However, since we weren't at home, there wasn't anyone to trust. I had to take it myself."

Jasper leaned forward, bracing his elbows on the table. "In the storm? Did none of the other servants notice?"

"If they did, they didn't say anything about it when I returned," she answered with a light shrug. "It's possible they assumed I'd gone to Field's End for something Mrs. Dalton required. I brought her Mr. Decamp's reply."

"He wrote his reply?" At her nod, he asked, "Did you read it?"

Offense spread across her expression. "Of course not. I never would have snooped on my lady's private correspondence."

"We found his note," Jasper continued. Because he'd prepared for this, he removed the scrap of paper from his pocket and slid it across the table. He gestured for her to read it. With trembling fingers, she opened it. Her eyes traveled over the words: *Meet me at our spot. Wait until midnight.*

"Do you know what *spot* Mr. Decamp was referring to here?"

"I…" She dropped the note back onto the table, visibly shaken. "I don't know."

Jasper didn't believe that. "The two of them would have needed a place to meet. I don't imagine she brought her lover to the house at Field's End, nor do I think she would go frequently to his farm, where she might have been noticed."

He placed the note back into his pocket and waited. Miss Sweeny finally bobbed her head.

"They would usually meet at night. Upon my word, Inspector, I never did see where they went," she said emphatically. He believed her this time. "She would wait until Mr. Dalton went to bed, or whenever he'd drop unconscious from too much drink. I'd see her occasionally from a window at the house, when the moon was out. She'd be walking out toward the south field."

"Why there?" he asked. "What is in that direction?"

"A barn. An old one, in disrepair," she said sadly. "It's the only place I can think of where they might have met."

"So, Mrs. Dalton received a note from Mr. Decamp, asking her to meet him at their spot. This barn, perhaps," Jasper recapped. "Is it far from Cowper Hall?"

The maid gave a confident shake of her head. "The south field sits between Cowper Hall and Field's End. It would have taken, oh, about fifteen minutes to walk there. But in that storm, and in her condition..." The maid fought another trembling of her chin. "I thought the baby might help to tame her. That she might now have something or someone to devote herself to, rather than living recklessly as she had been."

Reckless was not a word Jasper would have applied to Helen Dalton, or at least to the nervous version of herself that she'd presented at the will reading and later that evening at dinner.

"Reckless how?"

Miss Sweeny exhaled, as if to calm herself. "My lady never had an easy time making the right decisions. I think she always found excitement in doing wrong with men."

The phrasing intrigued Jasper. "Doing wrong in what way?"

"The affair with Mr. Decamp, of course," she replied with a startled shifting in her seat. "She was bound to be caught out."

He sensed the maid was holding back. Had Helen conducted other affairs with men in the past? If Anthony could not perform intimately as a husband was expected to do, it would not be surprising that Helen might have sought the company of men outside her marriage. It might have been wrong, as Miss Sweeny had said, but not completely shocking.

"What other bad decisions did Mrs. Dalton make?"

He thought of Francine Stroud's buried fear that her daughter had been responsible somehow for Teddy's fatal fall. If Helen had shared details of her affair with her trusted maid, she might have also confided in her about other secrets.

But Miss Sweeny shook her head. "None that I know of, Inspector."

He would leave her statement for now. Jasper stood, and as he did, she, too, shot to her feet.

"Is that all, then?" she asked hopefully.

"Yes. Thank you for coming in, Miss Sweeny."

The maid hesitated, as if she expected to be taken into handcuffs at any moment as she left the interview room. Jasper instructed a constable nearby to return her to the Perrys' home, and then he turned toward the telegraph office.

As steward, Stephen Decamp would have had access to the viscount's stables. He could have easily taken the horse and phaeton and driven himself and Helen to London in the middle of the night. The question now was, had he killed her? Or had he been the one to step into her spreading pool of blood after the killer fled?

An older constable in the telegraph office greeted him

as Jasper stepped into the busy room. “Inspector Reid, what can I do for you?”

The discordant clicks and clacks of several telegraph machines filled the air.

“I need to send word to Paddington Division,” he replied. “Instruct them to locate Stephen Decamp of Cowper Fields and bring him into custody.”

Chapter Eleven

Gleason's Department Store rose three imposing stories above Oxford Street near Prince Theatre and occupied nearly half the block. As Leo caught sight of herself in one of the flawlessly clean glass display windows, she came to a stuttering stop on the pavement. A beautiful gown of blush pink silk—a color she would have never considered for herself—was draped upon a dress mannequin, situated an inch or two away from the glass. At street level, as it was, Leo's reflection was aligned perfectly with the dress, so that her head and neck floated right above the ruffled collar. In the reflection, she looked to be wearing the gown. A pretty pink lace parasol lay propped on a silk-covered table beside the mannequin, as were a pair of heeled shoes, silk gloves, and a wide-brimmed Gainsborough hat.

It was a clever display, surely meant to show ladies passing by what a gown like this might look like on them, tempting them to enter the store and seek out a shop clerk. The pink was far too girlish for Leo, but she did appreciate the way the color brought out a similar glow on her usually pale cheeks.

She kept on toward the front doors to the store, the idea of such a gown ridiculously impractical. Where could she possibly wear it? Not to mention, the cost would be enough to drop her jaw.

As a young doorman in smart livery graciously opened the door for her, his eyes flickered disapprovingly over her attire: a sensible cotton twill skirt of dark blue, a matching blue-and-white-pinstriped shirtwaist with a stiff, upright collar, and a black, double-breasted wool coat. The only adornment that might be considered fashionable was her hat, a dark blue trilby adorned with a white silk ribbon bow and a flounce of black tulle. Dita had picked it out for her the previous autumn when Leo had tried to purchase a plain bonnet.

Leo was grateful for the hat now as she entered Gleason's front lobby. The scent of perfume wafted lightly up her nose, though not in an overbearing way. It was pleasant and clean, which was something the regular London air could not hope to offer. The faint strains of a violin playing reached her ears, and though she looked around the space of the ground floor, she could not see the musician.

This first space of the store's ground floor was devoted to home furnishings and decoration, with carefully arranged sitting areas staged to appear like a dining room, a tearoom or a sitting room. Rugs, furniture, fabrics, pillows, trinkets, china and porcelain, glass and silver were all on display here, the styles so modern, Leo couldn't help but feel a pang of longing. The furniture inside her home on Duke Street was decades old, probably purchased secondhand even then, and while it was all well maintained, none of it was fashionable.

She wandered toward a glass case, where lidded urns and shapely vases that looked to be from the Orient were displayed. They were painted with small yellow flowers, or cherry blossoms, or herons with their long beaks and wings.

"May I assist you, madam?"

Leo turned to find a wiry man with a thin face and pencil mustache stepping briskly toward her. His upper body leaned slightly back, as if he wanted to put some distance between them. She was not their usual breed of customer, to be sure, and he would know it.

"I'm looking for the ladies' department," she answered, assuming that was where Dita would have been placed.

He formed a patronizing, close-lipped smile and gestured with his hand toward the main staircase. "That is on the first level. I'm sure one of our shop assistants will help you with…whatever it is you require."

Like the doorman had, he swept her with an assessing glance, though he was not as furtive about it. Most likely, he questioned whether she could afford even a pair of gloves in the ladies' department, but that wasn't for her to concern herself with.

Leo took the stairs and entered a world of feminine delight. There were ready-made dresses of rippling velvet and heavy India silk displayed on dressmaker mannequins in winter hues of crimson, emerald, and sapphire. There were lighter colors and fabrics for the spring too: pale linen, pink lace, vibrant green satin, and robin's-egg blue taffeta. Racks of gloves, shelves upon shelves of hats, and an area of what looked to be women's undergarments filled the airy floor. Several shoppers were roaming the displays and viewing cases, all of whom were being waited on by at least one shop assistant. The young women wore the blue-and-yellow-striped dress Dita had been wearing—and Lydia Hailson too.

"Good afternoon, miss."

Leo nearly jumped as a young woman popped up at her shoulder. A shop assistant, who appeared younger than Dita, turned a welcoming smile on Leo, one much warmer than what she'd received so far.

"May I assist you?" she asked.

Before Leo could respond by asking if she could speak to Miss Nivedita Brooks, she caught sight of her friend in the corner of the shop floor. Dita stood at the ribbons counter, listening intently as an older woman spoke to her.

"I'm here to speak to my friend, and I've just spotted her, thank you," Leo told the assistant, then started toward the ribbons counter.

"You're a friend of Susan?" the assistant asked quickly, sticking to Leo's side and lowering her voice. "You may want to wait a moment if you're here to see her. Mrs. Gleason doesn't like being interrupted."

The older woman must have been Mrs. Gleason, perhaps the owner of the store, and she did appear serious about whatever it was she was discussing. But Leo boggled over why the assistant would have called Dita *Susan*. Had this young woman misremembered her name?

As though able to feel her stare, Dita's dark brown eyes shifted away from Mrs. Gleason and found Leo. Dita startled, and her eyes went wide with panic. Darting her attention back to her employer, Dita nodded obediently to what the woman was saying, and then her shoulders dropped in relief as Mrs. Gleason turned and left the counter.

"There," the shop assistant at Leo's shoulder said. "Now, it should be safe."

Dita motioned impatiently for Leo to approach the ribbons counter, carefully watching the back of her retreating employer.

"What are you doing here?" she whispered harshly the moment Leo reached her. No longer startled, Dita glared at her as if Leo had wronged her somehow.

"I've come to ask you something about a case," she replied, "but I'm more interested in why that other assistant called you *Susan*."

"*Shhh!*" she hissed, throwing another harassed look over Leo's shoulder. "This isn't what you think."

"I'm not sure what I think at all," Leo replied, growing more concerned by the moment. "Are you using a different name here?"

And if so, why in the world would she choose to?

Dita held up her gloved palms. "I promise, I'll explain, but you must go before someone hears you. I have a tea break coming up in fifteen minutes. Go to the shop across the street. I'll meet you there."

As distraught as Dita was, Leo could not do anything but agree. She left, taking the stairs in a whirl of confusion. Had she selected the name Susan because her own name, Nivedita, sounded too foreign? She had, after all, been the only employee who wasn't white. A sinking disappointment filled her as she considered that. It wasn't like Dita to censor herself in any way, least of all her heritage. But as Leo entered the tearoom across the street and was seated at a table near the front window, she ruminated on how nervous her friend had acted. All because of a name?

The pot of Earl Grey tea she'd ordered had just been delivered to the table when Dita hurried across the street, dodging a carriage and a dray. She came through the door, her agitated state even more pronounced.

"I wish you would have told me you were coming," she said as she took the seat across from Leo at their table, shedding her coat and gloves.

"I didn't think it would be so unwelcome," Leo replied, a little stung. "*Susan*."

Dita rubbed her forehead and sighed heavily. "All right. I'll explain. But you must promise that you won't say anything to anyone. Especially to my father."

Leo's intrigue shot skyward, as did her concern. Dita and her father, Sergeant Byron Brooks, had always been close, especially after the death of Dita's mother. If she didn't want her father to know what she was doing, it couldn't be anything he would approve of.

"I'll be discreet," Leo promised.

Dita poured herself a cup of tea, then, cradling it in her palms, whispered, "I'm working undercover."

The few words took too long to make sense. Leo stared at her friend as they came together in her mind. "You're…working for the police?"

Dita gave a sour huff of contempt. "They wouldn't hire a woman, as you well know." She leaned forward and whispered, "I've been hired by Castelan Private Inquiries."

An excited grin curved Dita's lips as she waited for Leo's response. But all Leo could do was gape. At the same time, a greasy spear of envy sank into the pit of her stomach.

"You're working for a private detective agency?"

Dita nodded eagerly. "This is my first assignment."

Leo set down her cup of tea. Private agencies often hired women, as there were some places that only women were able to infiltrate without causing a stir or suspicion. A ladies' clothing department, for instance.

"I had no idea you were interested in being a detective," Leo said, still trying to grasp Dita's new vocation. The unsettled feeling in her stomach disturbed her.

"Oh, I wasn't, not really. When I returned from my aunt's house, I saw a wanted advert for ladies to assist in investigations, and…" She shrugged. "I thought having been a matron at the Yard might help my chances. It seemed it did."

"But you don't think your father will approve?"

Dita scrunched her nose in a doubtful expression. "He doesn't like the idea of private agencies. I doubt he'd be happy with my working for them, so I figure I'll see how this first assignment goes. If I like it, I'll stay on and come clean to my father. If I don't, I'll do something else, and he needn't ever know."

It was very like Dita to be blasé about things and, of course, to have fun. It was good to see her happy again, especially after losing the man she loved back in the spring. But Leo couldn't help but be concerned too.

"What exactly are you supposed to be investigating at Gleason's?" she asked.

Dita looked around—none too casually, either—and leaned closer to whisper, "The owner's wife hired Mr. Castelan. She is convinced her husband is a serial adulterer, and she wants a divorce. But as you know, women cannot get a settlement if they divorce without evidence of wrongdoing on the part of their husbands."

The owner of Gleason's was surely a very wealthy man, and Mrs. Gleason would want her share.

"So, what is your role?" Leo asked. If Dita was to catch him out with his mistress, posing as a shopgirl at Gleason's would not bring results. The man wasn't likely to be conducting an affair on the ladies' floor for his employees to witness.

With a sly arch of her brow and a hitch of her chin, Dita raised her teacup in a dainty pose. "*Susan* is charged with tempting Mr. Gleason into bad behavior."

Leo was grateful she'd yet to pick up her cup again. She would have fumbled it. As it was, her gasp drew looks from a table nearby. She waited until the two women there looked away again before practically mouthing, "You are to seduce him? Dita, you cannot!"

Her friend rolled her eyes and groaned. "No, of course I won't. What kind of woman do you take me for? I am simply to flirt and *lead* him to an attempt. Once he arranges a time and place for us to meet, Mr. Castelan, Mrs. Gleason, and some other third party will interrupt our rendezvous," she explained, though the plan did not allay Leo's worry in the least. Her gaping expression must have said as much. "Leo, don't look at me like that! Nothing untoward will happen. Mr. Castelan has given me his word."

Leo would ask Jasper his opinion on Mr. Castelan and his agency, but she was already not impressed with him.

"Meeting a man for a rendezvous could be dangerous. What if something goes wrong, and the others don't arrive in time to extricate you?" she warned. "You could be compromising yourself."

Dita dismissed the scenario with a *pfft* and a wave of her hand. "I am already compromised."

Leo frowned, more alarmed than before. "Why would you say that?"

"Isn't it obvious?" Dita replied, her tone biting. "I was courting a constable who tried to bomb Scotland Yard. Everyone believes I had to be in on it or at least knew of Lloyd's intention."

"That isn't true. There are plenty of officers who don't believe that. I know Jasper doesn't."

"I don't mean any offense, Leo, but Inspector Reid isn't exactly considered one of the men."

Leo sat back, astonished. "What do you mean by that?"

Guilt flickered in Dita's eyes, but she stayed firm. "You must have heard the whispers. That he is only detective inspector because of his last name?"

Leo had heard the whispers, but she didn't like hearing it so directly from her friend's lips. "That is absurd. Jasper is an excellent detective. He has his position based on merit."

Dita didn't reply but sipped her tea, leaving Leo to wonder whether her friend agreed or disagreed with her.

"Anyhow, this isn't about Jasper or anyone else from the Yard," Leo moved on. "Do you really wish to flirt with Mr. Gleason? It sounds as though Mr. Castelan is simply using you as bait."

Dita's expression hardened, and Leo knew she'd said too much.

"I thought you might be happy for me, since you yourself have been involved in a few of Jasper's cases.

Why is it all right for you to be a lady detective, but not me?"

Leo bit the inside of her cheek, hot with guilt but also with the desire to argue. It wasn't the same thing at all. Jasper had never placed her in a situation he'd known would be dangerous just so that he could secure an arrest. She swallowed the argument, however.

"I'm sorry. I *am* happy for you, Dita, if you are happy. I won't say another word about it." A heavy silence fell upon them. Leo tapped the porcelain of her cup and tried to keep the conversation going. "In fact, your new position might be just the thing that is needed to help Connor Quinn."

Dita's morose glower lifted somewhat toward interest. "Oh? How might that be?"

"Two days ago, a body arrived at the morgue," Leo began. Dita squirmed in her chair, her expression drawn. She deplored any talk of death or dead bodies. "A young woman named Lydia Hailson. She was wearing your same uniform."

Shock descended over Dita, softening her face, her shoulders, and even her back as it rounded. "Lydia Hailson? Oh gracious, how awful. What happened to her?"

"I'm sorry to say she was murdered. Strangled. How well did you know her?" Leo asked.

Dita recovered a little, straightening herself in her chair. "Not well at all. She was only at Gleason's the day I went in for an *interview* with Mrs. Gleason." The emphasis she placed on the word interview must have meant that it was only for show, as the woman had already hired Dita in another capacity. "And then again on my first day on the floor."

"What day would that have been?" Leo asked.

"Tuesday." Dita paused with some alarm. "Now that I think of it, I didn't see her on Wednesday."

Wednesday afternoon, Lydia's body had arrived at the morgue. During his examination, Uncle Claude had determined that she had died late Tuesday night.

"When did you last see her on Tuesday?" Leo asked.

"When the store closed at six o'clock. I have to tell you," Dita said with a hint of urgency, "I suspected Lydia might be having an affair with Mr. Gleason."

Leo sat back in her seat. "Why did you think that?"

"Well, she was jumpy and frazzled all day," she replied. "When she dropped a jar of perfume, I saw Mr. Gleason touch her shoulder and whisper something close to her ear. She blushed at whatever it was he said. So, afterward, I went up to Lydia and made a comment about how handsome Mr. Gleason is. You know, to try and lead her into confessing. And do you know what she said? She bit my nose off, telling me to concentrate on my work and not gossip."

It was certainly a potential lead. Had Lydia Hailson rebuffed the owner's advances, and he'd reacted poorly to her rejection? It seemed a little too obvious and easy a solution, though both Jasper and the late Inspector had often said that most murders were simple, straightforward, and poorly covered up by the assailants.

"I must admit, I didn't like her much after that," Dita said, then sighed. "But it's awful what happened to her. Do you think someone at Gleason's did it?"

The sparkle of excitement in her friend's eyes worried Leo. Dita was working undercover to unveil a cheating husband, not solve a murder. Left to her own devices, however, she might do something rash. It would be better to give Dita something to do.

Goodness, was this how Jasper often felt about *her*?

“Do you think you might be able to find out where Lydia was living? An address?” she asked. “Without being too obvious, of course.”

“I know just who to ask.” Dita sprang from her chair and collected her things. “But you never said how finding out what happened to Lydia would help Mr. Quinn.”

“They were once betrothed,” Leo explained. If anyone could be sympathetic to losing a loved one, it was Dita.

She nodded solemnly. “I’ll see what I can find out.”

Chapter Twelve

With October nearing its end, and the sun slipping below the horizon earlier every evening, Leo arrived home just as shadows began to lengthen along Duke Street. This time of year, sunsets tended to be dull and fast, as if not wanting to give anyone a reason to stay out in the chilly evening air any longer than necessary.

Leo's mind had whirled since leaving Oxford Street, and even more so after stopping in at the morgue to divulge to Connor what she'd learned on her outing to Gleason's. When she'd told him of Dita's suspicion of a liaison between Lydia and Mr. Gleason, he'd been adamant that she would never have engaged in an affair with a married man.

"But perhaps that is why she was so nervous that day," Leo suggested gently. "Maybe she had heard that Mrs. Gleason had hired a private agency to look into her husband's affairs."

But Connor had refused to believe it, and Leo had decided not to push the idea further, especially when he was already so upset. Besides, Dita had only been theorizing; there was no proof of anything. What Leo wanted to do next was see where Lydia had been living and speak to the people she'd known well—outside of Gleason's. Considering she had been killed while still wearing her work uniform, Leo would remain cautious about questioning anyone else at the department store.

Light glowed in the sitting room window inside the small but tidy row house on Duke Street, and as she climbed the front step and let herself inside, Leo looked forward to warming herself by the coal fire that Claude would have stoked. After hanging up her coat and hat and leaving her gloves and handbag on the hall table, she stepped into the front room—and came to an abrupt stop.

Jasper and her uncle stood together in front of the fireplace, each holding a glass of whisky. Claude hardly ever drank, except for a half-pint of ale from time to time, and she most certainly had never seen him having a drink with Jasper. The men were utterly quiet, as if they'd cut off their conversation upon hearing her come in through the front door, and their expressions were furtive.

Leo sensed that she'd interrupted something serious.

"Is something wrong?" she asked, suddenly worried. "Is it Aunt Flora?"

Her uncle startled. "No, no. Your aunt is well. She and Mrs. Zhao are in the kitchen."

It had been one of Claude's days to work at Tate's, she realized, and Mrs. Zhao would have come to stay with Flora.

"In fact, I should go check on them. Mrs. Zhao has made a lovely roast for our supper," her uncle said, setting his untouched glass of whisky on the occasional table.

As he walked toward the door where she still stood, he met Leo's curious gaze. And then winked. She had no idea what to make of it as he left the sitting room.

"How is Quinn?" Jasper asked before she could ask what he and Claude had been discussing. She shook the cold from her skirt as she walked toward the coal fire, then picked up her uncle's abandoned whisky. There was no reason to put it to waste.

"Still upset," she answered, although she had no intention of letting Jasper steer her away from what she wanted to know. "What were you and my uncle speaking about just now?"

"He wanted to know more about the house on Craven Hill." Jasper's answer was too quick, too relaxed, to be believed completely. He was holding something back. But just as she had with Connor earlier, she let it go.

Leo sipped the whisky, and while it wasn't sweet like the Inspector's favorite cherry cordial that they used to share, Jasper's preferred spirits were beginning to grow on her. It might have been because of Jasper himself, and of how the taste reminded her of him. She sat on the sofa, and he took the cushion next to her.

"I haven't really given the house much thought," Leo confessed. "It doesn't feel real yet that it's ours."

He leaned forward, elbows resting on his thighs, and scrubbed a hand over his cheek bristle. "We don't need to think about it just yet. I'd like to arrest someone for Mrs. Dalton's murder first."

"Did you speak with her maid?"

"I did." He sat back against the cushion and shifted toward her. "Helen was having an affair with the viscount's steward, Stephen Decamp."

"Decamp? A relation of the butler's?"

He nodded. "Son. The maid delivered a note from Helen to Stephen the afternoon of the storm, after the reading of the will. He sent along his written reply."

Leo leaned back, drawing her leg up underneath her. "To meet at their spot. So, it was he who took the phaeton and drove them to London. But where is Stephen Decamp now?"

"I sent a wire to Paddington Division for them to take him into custody," Jasper said, taking a sip of his drink. He shook his head. "But I had word before coming here that they couldn't locate him."

"He might have stayed in London." It would explain why the horse and phaeton had not been returned to the stables at Cowper Hall. "If he did kill her, he could have fled the country by now."

"I want Stephen Decamp found so I can question him, but I'm more apt to believe he is the person who came upon Helen after her blood had pooled," Jasper said. "Helen put that glass tube into her hair to hide it quickly. If Stephen drove her to London, she must have told him why she was in such a hurry to get here."

"To find the tear catcher," Leo said, understanding his thinking. "There would be no reason for her to hide it from Stephen."

When he'd found Helen dead, he probably panicked. Knew he'd be accused of her murder if it came out that he'd driven her to London from Harrow in the middle of the night. So, why not drive the phaeton back to Cowper Hall as fast as possible before anyone could notice it missing? Leo posed this question to Jasper, who was considering it when she added, "Unless he didn't think he could make it back in time. Stable hands rise early, often before dawn. A witness seeing him return, with a muddy phaeton and a fatigued horse, would be damning."

The possibility that he'd fled England was now looking more likely.

"I interviewed Mr. and Mrs. Perry, Helen's friends with whom she'd stay whenever she came to the city," he said, his tired eyes drawn to the coal fire. "They didn't see her, of course, and they claim not to have seen Stephen. But they knew about him."

"Did they know about the baby?" Leo asked.

"No, though Mrs. Perry said Helen had recently been talking about taking an extended trip to France or Italy."

To have the child, Leo imagined. Whether she would have given up her infant and returned to her husband afterward was a mystery. And maybe it didn't matter.

"Mr. Dalton seemed genuine in his surprise earlier that his wife was having an affair and that she was pregnant," Leo said. "I don't think he killed her, though he would have had motive to."

"I agree. He didn't care about her enough," Jasper said.

It was a sad thought. "I wonder if he ever did, or if it was only after his riding accident that he stopped loving her."

Mr. Cowper had accused him of pitying himself and thinking nothing of Helen and what she had lost from the riding accident as well. The intimacy of having a husband, the possibility of having a child.

As Leo took another sip of whisky, Jasper leaned his head against the back of the sofa, his eyelids half shuttered. In the soft light of the paraffin lamps and the coal fire, he looked starkly handsome. Somehow, the golden bristle around his mouth accentuated his full lips. At first, she reined in her longing to touch him. But then, recalling their kiss at Cowper Hall, Leo knew it would not be unwelcome. So, she reached for his hand, which was resting on his thigh. He lifted his head and turned his tired eyes onto her, his palm flipping over to grasp her hand more fully.

"Have you slept at all?" she asked, though she suspected the answer. He'd been to Harrow and back during the night and then been bogged down in the investigation all day.

"No," he confirmed. "I'll get a few hours before I leave for Harrow again tomorrow morning."

"Again?"

"I want to search Stephen Decamp's home and interview his father. Depending on how close they are, the butler might know where his son has gone."

Tomorrow would be his last day on leave from Liverpool. Leo didn't know if he would leave straight from Harrow or come back to London first.

"I could come with you," she offered, though she didn't think Connor would appreciate her taking another day off. Already that afternoon, he'd let her leave early so she could visit Dita at Gleason's.

Jasper lifted her hand and brought it to his lips. He kissed it, his beard tickling her skin. "Paddington Division is assisting me."

In case he needed to make an arrest. Of course. She felt a twinge of disappointment but was enjoying the feeling of her hand in his too much to withdraw it.

"I would be vexed if I wasn't already preoccupied with an investigation of my own," she said lightly.

His fingers tensed. "What investigation is this?"

She tried to read Jasper's expression, but as usual, it was inscrutable.

"I'm helping Connor look into Lydia Hailson's murder," she confessed. "I started by speaking to Dita, as I told you I planned to do."

He released her hand and sat forward, skewering her with a wide-awake stare. "I thought Quinn was going to hire a private agency."

His terse voice revealed that he was, indeed, upset. She should have expected as much, though she hadn't really stopped to consider how he'd react.

"He was going to, but we agreed that first, I'd see what I could discover from speaking to Dita," she explained.

It didn't alleviate an ounce of his irritation. He stood and paced away from the sofa, putting a distance between them that she regretted.

"Leo, if the woman was strangled while wearing her shop uniform, the last thing you should be doing is questioning Gleason's staff."

She didn't like him looking down at her, so she got to her feet too. He was still taller, but at least the difference wasn't as browbeating.

"It was only Dita, and besides, there is already a private agency planted inside Gleason's. Castelan Private Inquiries."

Jasper's eyes narrowed. "How do you know that?"

"Because Dita is working for Mr. Castelan," she answered, hopeful that she could hide her envy. She might not wish to have Dita's job of luring Mr. Gleason into a compromising position, but working for a detective agency could be exciting, if she was given the chance to truly investigate.

Briefly, Leo explained Dita's assignment to him, including what her intent was. Jasper's astonishment likely mirrored her own when Dita had first told Leo in the tea shop.

"That is preposterous," he said. "Sergeant Brooks would never condone it."

"You can't tell him," Leo pleaded, belatedly recalling her promise to Dita. "She will reveal her employment there in time, but for right now, she is only trying it out."

Jasper's irritation bordered on anger as he again began to pace. "If Lydia Hailson was killed in connection to Castelan's investigation, luring Gleason into a trap is dangerous for Miss Brooks. And for you, if you keep pressing for answers. It won't go unnoticed."

"There is no evidence that she was killed because of Castelan's agency looking into his adultery," she said. "Dita is finding out where Lydia was living, and I'm going to speak to those whom she knew outside of work."

His glare told her exactly what he thought of that plan. "I spoke to Lewis. He will learn which detective has been assigned to her case. Allow whoever it is to take over from this point forward, Leo."

She set down her whisky and crossed her arms. "I seem to recall you once telling me that I was just as capable, if not more so, than any Scotland Yard officer."

He clenched his jaw, no doubt regretting that compliment now. "You *are* capable. That is not what I worry about. I don't like the idea of you investigating something as serious as a murder by yourself."

"I've been in danger before," she replied, prepared to

list off the handful of times she'd been one foot from death or injury.

He groaned and threw back the rest of his drink in one toss. "I don't need reminding, Leo." Jasper peered at her, wincing in confusion. "I thought you were happy at the morgue, working for Quinn."

"I am," she insisted, though she was surprised by an unexpected prick of guilt. It wasn't a lie. Not exactly. She did enjoy her job at the morgue, especially now that she was being paid. It was a decent wage too, and paired with Claude's income at the funeral service, it was enough to keep them comfortable. And yet, she couldn't remember the last time she'd felt as energized and eager to work at the morgue as she did when she'd gone to visit Gleason's Department Store.

"If you are so content, why have you offered to investigate this woman's murder?" Jasper asked, as though reading her mind. "What is it that you feel you need to prove?"

She pulled back, stung by his assumption that she was helping in order to prove something about herself, rather than to bring Connor information. "I don't have anything to prove to anyone. I enjoy investigating, Jasper, just as you do."

It was something he should have already known.

"Enjoyment shouldn't matter," he replied tersely. "It is about being qualified."

With every new word that tumbled from his mouth, Leo's anger multiplied.

"I may not hold a position at the Yard, but we've worked together to capture murderers and kidnappers and even bombers in the past," she said.

Jasper shook his head. "Those times were different."

"Because *you* were involved?" she presumed. He exhaled loudly and sent her a vexed look.

"You are a morgue assistant, Leo, not a detective."

How many times had she heard those words from him? A dozen? And each time, she would endure them with a grimace because, after all, it *was* true. She wasn't a detective. Nor had she thought she could be one. And yet, now Dita was employed by a detective agency.

"Well, then…" She hesitated only a moment, then jumped off the ledge. "Maybe I will become one."

Warmth climbed her neck toward her cheeks. It had been a bold statement, and she wasn't even sure she meant it or if it was what she wanted. But that wasn't the point right now. Leo braced herself for his reaction. She expected him to shout, or laugh, or roll his eyes. Instead, he held still, and when he spoke, it was with a low, flat timbre: "You cannot do that."

The declaration—or rather, order—lingered between them. Leo's mind whirled, searching for why he would so resolutely refuse the idea. "I'd like to know why not."

He kept his voice measured, his temper restrained. "Because it isn't respectable. The women who are employed by these agencies are not real detectives. They act as bait, as lures, insinuating themselves into disreputable situations, just as Miss Brooks is doing now at the department store. The agencies don't care about these women compromising themselves, and if you were to become one of them, you'd open yourself up to ridicule, not respect."

Earlier that afternoon, she had said these same things

to Dita. Now she understood why her friend had grown so irritated with her.

"Dita would never compromise herself."

"This isn't about her. It is about you, Leo."

"Or is it about you?" The question shot from her mouth before she even knew it had formed.

He narrowed his stare. "Me?"

A notion took shape, one that made her voice shake when she spoke. "Yes, you, and how you might be perceived at the Yard amongst your colleagues if I were to join a private agency. Would it be *you* who is ridiculed, for associating with me?"

His superiors already didn't approve of her, and she wasn't convinced it was only because she'd become involved in some of Jasper's cases. Her work at the morgue was distasteful to many.

He stepped closer to her, still holding himself rigid. "You know as well as I do that the Met cares about the private lives of their officers."

She did know. "Especially of their inspectors," she said.

They were so often in the public eye, representing the entire Metropolitan Police Force, and they had to meet certain standards. It was always a struggle to maintain the public's support and trust, and news reporters were incessantly searching for any reason to disparage officers.

Jasper relented with a nod. "I would be lying if I said I haven't considered what my superiors will think when they learn about you."

"But they already know about me," she said, confused.

He stepped closer to her, the exasperation in his eyes softening to a degree of amusement. "I meant, when they learn I am courting you." More heat built under her skin as he reached for her hand. "If that is what you want."

Leo stared at him, her ears beginning to chime. She took a shallow breath, then another as she held his earnest stare. His hand closed around hers, and the warmth of it fired up her spine.

"Are you asking permission to court me…during an *argument*?"

Had that been what he and Claude were discussing when she'd entered the sitting room?

"I suppose the timing could be better," he admitted, still holding her hand. He brought her palm to his chest; she could feel his steady heartbeat beneath her fingertips. "But yes, I want to court you, Leo. Properly."

A smile formed on her lips, and an answer—*yes*—leapt to the tip of her tongue. But she held it there.

"Jasper, you worry what your superiors will say even now, when I am just a morgue assistant. Let alone if I dare to find employment with a private detective agency."

His chest rose under her palm as he drew in a deep breath. "If the woman I'm courting is compromising herself, then yes, there would be talk. Consequences, even."

Leo tugged her hand out from underneath his and stepped backward. "I would never compromise myself, Jasper. And not just because of how it would reflect upon you at the Yard. I would have thought you trusted me enough to know that."

Regret rushed through her, leaving behind an ache in her chest.

"I've never fit into any conventional role, as you surely

must know," she went on. "I didn't think you cared about that."

"I don't," he insisted. "I wouldn't want you to be anything other than who you are."

Jasper closed the space she'd put between them, and his hand rose to cup her cheek. His woodsy pine scent and the coarseness of his palm warmed her. It compelled her to close her eyes and turn her cheek into his hand, until her lips grazed his skin.

"Leo," he whispered. "Look at me."

She opened her eyes, and though she expected him to kiss her, he only held her gaze. "Do you wish to court me?" he asked softly.

Despite the complication that had just arisen, albeit unexpectedly, her heart knew her answer. "Yes. You know I do."

After an initial twitch of a grin, Jasper's expression clouded. "But?"

"But what if who I am doesn't fall in line with what Scotland Yard wants from one of its finest inspectors?"

From the delay in making his reply, she could see he understood what she was questioning.

"I won't be dictated to," she asserted. "And I won't curtail myself when I feel strongly about something. I *am* going to investigate Lydia's death," she said. "I would like your support, Jasper."

Displeasure filled his eyes. "I cannot agree that you should be investigating a murder on your own."

Though it pained her, Leo slipped from his hold and stepped away. "Then it seems we are at an impasse."

He nodded, his jaw clenched. "It seems we are." After

an awkward moment of silence, he nodded again. "I will collect Mrs. Zhao, and we'll be on our way." Jasper walked to the sitting room door, pausing a moment at the threshold. "Be careful, Leo."

She wilted as he shut the door behind him.

Chapter Thirteen

The low, green hills surrounding Harrow had turned the autumnal shades of golden umber, rusted orange, and vibrant red. The late morning sunshine rippled over swathes of land, and crisp air filled Jasper's lungs as he rode alongside Constable Wiggins. The Metropolitan Police's Paddington Division had sent the gray-whiskered officer to meet Jasper at the Great Western Railway train station, and now they were on their way in an open cart toward Cowper Fields.

"We knocked at Decamp's door and searched his farm yesterday," Wiggins said as he directed the horses along a narrow lane, edged by flat fields. "There weren't no one about."

The constable wasn't happy that Jasper had wired ahead of his morning train, announcing that he would be undertaking a thorough search of Stephen Decamp's home and then interviewing the viscount's butler, the elder Decamp. Wiggins and his sergeant had been unsuccessful in finding their quarry the day before and surely believed the Scotland Yard inspector did not trust they had done their jobs properly.

Had Jasper not been in a black mood that morning, he might have been kind enough to assure Constable Wiggins that he trusted they'd looked thoroughly for Stephen Decamp and that now, he hoped to get some idea of where the man had run off to. However, Jasper *was* in a black mood, and as such, he kept his conversation limited as they rattled along toward Decamp's farm.

He'd slept little the night before, giving up entirely around two in the morning and going to his study for a liberal pour of whisky and a look through his late father's unsolved case files. It was the only thing he could think of to distract himself from thoughts of Leo…though he hadn't been successful.

Jasper had not arrived at her home the evening before with any intention of informing Claude of his wish to court her. But as the two of them had exchanged pleasantries in the front room while awaiting Leo's return, he'd decided it was as good a time as any. They were alone, with Mrs. Zhao occupying Flora in the kitchen, when Jasper asked if he might speak plainly about something.

Claude, his white eyebrows lifting above the rims of his spectacles, had said, "I'll pour us a drink." And while doing that, he'd added, "This is about my niece, I presume?"

The man was old, but he wasn't a fool, and so Claude hadn't been surprised when Jasper confessed that his feelings for Leo were not platonic in the least.

"I wish to court her when I return from Liverpool," he'd said, gripping his crystal glass of brandy with strangely damp hands. He had no reason to be nervous.

He knew Leo's feelings matched his and that Claude, mild mannered and amenable, would not argue against it. Still, this was a stride toward making their relationship official.

"You don't need my permission," he'd said. "Just that of my niece. Which you have, I expect?"

Jasper had grinned and replied, "I think so, yes," while recalling their numerous letters over the last few months, the few instances they had kissed, and Leo's palpable relief when he'd told her that the Liverpool case was solved, and that he would be coming home.

Somehow, though, he'd botched everything.

He'd left the Duke Street residence without a firm answer from Leo and was instead filled with unexpected doubt. There was no question that Leonora Spencer was intelligent, thoughtful, and naturally talented when it came to investigating crime. But when she suggested she might go the same route as her friend and join a private detective agency, he'd been blindsided. And he'd lost his temper.

Nothing he had said was untrue. He'd worked with enough private agencies to know that women like Dita Brooks were mostly employed to do little more than bait criminals and philandering men, or to infiltrate places where only women were permitted. Leo could do far better than subject herself to those sorts of tawdry assignments. Maybe he ought to have said as much last evening; instead, he'd gone and pointed out something else that was true, though unflattering: that she didn't have the necessary experience to single-handedly solve a murder inquiry.

When she'd accused Jasper of caring how it would reflect upon him at the Yard if she were to work for a private agency, his tongue had become leaden. Because she had not been wrong—it would look bad. It might have been selfish of him, but it was true. As much as he despised it, senior detective inspectors had to think about appearances and public opinion. If they had wives, those wives were expected to be conventional. They were expected to remain in the background and take care of the inspector's family and not inspire scandal. They certainly weren't supposed to be stubborn-to-the-marrow morgue assistants or danger-seeking female detectives.

Jasper shifted on the wooden seat of the cart, irritated. With himself, with Leo, with the fact that he could not bloody well get the memory of kissing her in her room at Cowper Hall out of his head. It was always there, waiting for him, reminding him of how much he wanted her. Maybe that was making everything worse. His physical desire for her was tying him up in knots and only adding to his frustration.

"There it is," Constable Wiggins said, severing Jasper's increasingly depraved thoughts. "Up ahead, on the right. Decamp's place."

Grateful for the distraction, Jasper breathed in another lungful of brisk air and got his head on straight. He focused on the stone cottage Wiggins had indicated. It was a rambling sort of home, constructed of fieldstone and covered with a mossy slate roof. Green vines, changing in color to autumnal fire red, clung to the exterior, and set close to the main house was a large stone barn and two smaller cowsheds.

Several muddied pigs gathered frantically near the fence of a paddock near the cowshed, as if seeking attention, and a black sheepdog with a white muzzle barked incessantly from where it had been tied to a hitching post next to the barn. The barn doors were open, and just inside, Jasper saw an unhitched gig.

"Was that gig here when you came by yesterday?" he asked Wiggins, gesturing toward the two-seater conveyance.

The constable was eyeing the dog warily. "No, Inspector. Though I heard the dog. It were inside the house, barking."

"What time were you here?"

"Not long after the wire from Scotland Yard came in. I'd say two in the afternoon. Maybe half two."

So, Decamp had returned two days after Helen's murder. Had he shuttered the dog inside the house the night of the storm with the notion that he would be returning before morning? And now, the dog was tied up outside and agitated.

Jasper decided to leave the dog where it was for the moment. Its frenzied barking had marked his and Wiggins's arrival, and he expected to see Stephen Decamp exiting his home or one of the sheds to seek out the cause of such a disturbance. But Jasper and Wiggins had made it to the flagstone step at the front door and brought down the knocker, and there was still no sign of the home's owner.

A foreboding crawled along Jasper's spine and shuttled out along his nerves. Something was wrong. He reached for the door's handle. It was unlocked.

"Mr. Decamp?" he called as he opened the door a few inches. He raised his voice. "Stephen Decamp, are you in?"

No answer came.

Jasper held up his hand. "Constable, go around to the back. Make sure he doesn't do a runner."

It was possible Decamp was waiting to escape out a back door as soon as Jasper entered the home. But as Wiggins left to go around the house, and Jasper stepped inside, the silence that met him was ominous, not tense.

The front hall was cluttered with boots, jackets, hats, and other detritus. Everything belonged to a man, and as Jasper slowly moved toward the narrow set of darkened stairs, he noted the distinct lack of feminine touches. Things were tidy enough but spare. Dust motes floated through the air, illuminated by some rays of sunlight entering through a window at the top of the stairs.

"Decamp," Jasper called one more time. Nothing.

Outside, the yips of the dog were muffled but still grating. There was a dreary sitting room to the right; Jasper poked his head inside. The stove was cold. A pile of blankets near the hearth looked to be where the dog would bed down. And on the seat of a shabby armchair was an uncorked, empty liquor bottle.

Down the short hall from the front door, there was another room to the left. Jasper anticipated that it would be a dining room and, when he turned inside, saw that he was correct. He also discovered what his intuition had been alerting him to: A man sat slumped in the chair at the head of the table, and he was clearly dead.

Sunlight came through the two windows in the room, brightening the space enough for Jasper to see blood spatter on the wall behind the body, a pool of blood puddled beneath the chair, and that the man had been shot in the left temple. From Jasper's limited view of the right side of the man's skull, it looked to be a ruined mess.

Jasper walked forward cautiously, his eyes on the floor to be sure he didn't disturb anything. No muddy or blood-rimmed footprints like there had been in the house on Craven Hill. No items dropped to the floor. He was glad Wiggins was still outside; it gave Jasper time to take in the rest of the room without interruption.

The man was likely in his late thirties. Stephen Decamp, Jasper presumed. The body was slumped back in the chair, but the man's head wasn't thrown back to match. Instead, his chin was tucked, his head drooping forward. In the dead man's left hand was a loosely gripped snub-nosed revolver. It, and his hand, had come to rest limply in his lap.

Jasper stared at this for several moments, trying to picture what had happened. Decamp had lifted the gun to his temple, pulled the trigger, and then…his hand and the weapon had flopped down into his lap?

There wasn't much of a fetid odor that met Jasper's nose, just the faint tang of blood, and the unmistakable sour stench of gin. Without any fires burning, the stone craftsmanship of the home had kept the interior cold, slowing the decay of the body. Much like a morgue. The thought brought Leo to mind. If she were here, she'd be able to estimate the approximate time of death. Jasper would simply have to do his best on his own.

The congealed blood no longer appeared shiny or wet. And when he reached for the man's arm, trying to lift it, he found it was stiff. Likewise, the man's foot, when Jasper crouched and tried to lift it from the carpet, was difficult to move. Based on what Leo had explained in the past about the increasing rigidity of a corpse, the man had been dead for some time. Perhaps half a day or more.

By all appearances, it looked to be a suicide.

On the table in front of the body, another uncorked, empty liquor bottle lay on its side. There was no label, indicating it was some homemade concoction. And underneath the bottle was a slip of paper.

"Inspector?" Constable Wiggins's voice emanated from the back of the house.

"In here," Jasper called, reaching for the paper.

The constable arrived a moment later. His coloring paled at the sight that met him.

"Oh, good Lord," Wiggins said.

"It is Stephen Decamp?"

The constable nodded, still a bit ashen-faced. Jasper read the few words written on the piece of paper. The handwriting was practiced, slanted, and a bit rushed.

I cannot live with what I've done.

It wasn't signed, but it was clearly meant to be Stephen Decamp's explanation for having shot himself.

The note found in Helen Dalton's possession was back at Scotland Yard. Jasper would compare the two handwriting samples when he had the chance. But the slanted script seemed, at least from his memory, to be a match.

"Have you ever come upon a person who has taken their own life?" Jasper asked as he crouched yet again next to the chair. This time he was looking at the hand limply holding the gun.

"No, Inspector," was Wiggins's reply. "Not in all my years."

Jasper had found suicide victims before, and more than once. None had ever been as neat a scene as this. Still seated upright in the chair, head lowered, hand in his lap… There was something not quite right about it.

"I'm not entirely sure you have now," he told the constable.

"Sir?"

Jasper straightened up. "Do you know of anyone in this area who could photograph the scene?"

Wiggins balked at him. "Why would you want to go and do something like that?"

"I know a coroner in London," Jasper said, thinking of Connor Quinn. "I'd like him to see the body, as it has come to rest. I'm not convinced this was self-inflicted by Stephen Decamp."

"Looks like it to me," Wiggins said.

As the man had just admitted to never having come upon a suicide, Jasper did not give his opinion much weight. "A photographer," he repeated, standing tall. "Is there one?"

The constable shook his head. "None I can think of."

Jasper sighed. Of course, there wasn't. He would have to commit every detail to memory, it seemed. *If only Leo was here,* he thought for the second time.

"Arrange for the removal of the body, Wiggins, if you would," Jasper instructed. "Meanwhile, I'll search the home and grounds."

He would start with the gig in the barn.

Wiggins hurried off, eager to be gone, it seemed, and Jasper went out into the yard again. The dog, its shaggy neck looped with a rope and tied to a hitching post ring, had tired of barking. Its bright eyes were alert as Jasper approached.

"Who put you out here?" he mused aloud as he extended a hand to its snout. He hadn't much experience with dogs. Mrs. Zhao disliked them, as they caused nothing but messes, so Jasper and his father had never brought one into the house. Oliver had a couple of hounds he used for hunts, but they were happy to ignore anyone who wasn't their master. However, Jasper knew to allow the dog to scent him before getting any closer.

The dog did so and, deciding it had nothing to fear from him, started to whine for freedom. Jasper worked at the knot around its neck, loosening it enough to release the animal. The dog yipped and pranced away from the hitching post but didn't go far. It was too interested in following Jasper into the barn, where he took a closer look at the unhitched gig.

The compact carriage would have been a light and fast option for a midnight ride to London. Most gigs didn't have hoods, but this one did, and it was currently raised into position. It would only have protected Stephen and Helen so much from the rain, which would account for the state of Helen's damp clothing and hair, even so many hours after her death. The black-painted wood of the dashboard and the two shafts that would have attached to the harnessed horse, were covered in dried mud. Some clumps had flaked off into a mess on the ground underneath the conveyance, but it was obvious the gig had been out along muddy roads.

It had not rained since the night Helen was killed, and by yesterday, the roads would have been mostly dry. The mud still clinging to the gig indicated that Stephen had taken it out during or immediately after the storm.

A pair of horses, one tan and the other a darker chestnut color, occupied two nearby stalls. With a quick look inside each stall, Jasper saw the tan horse had not been groomed. Its hooves and fetlocks were caked with dried mud, and its coat needed a good brushing. By all appearances, when Stephen Decamp arrived home yesterday afternoon, he'd seen to the bare minimum of unhitching his horse. He'd then downed a few bottles of gin. Presumably, in his drunken state of grief and guilt, he'd tied his dog up outside before going back into his house, writing the short note, and killing himself.

Jasper searched the gig for anything that might indicate that Helen had been a passenger. There was nothing. However, he was convinced Stephen had driven it to London with Helen, especially now that he knew Stephen had summoned her to their meeting spot the night of the storm.

If his theory was correct, why then would the viscount's stables be missing a phaeton and horse? Unless Helen parted ways with Stephen after they met at their spot, then took the phaeton and pony on her own to London. Might Stephen have followed her there? Had they quarreled?

There were too many questions, and now, the only person left who might have been able to answer them was dead.

Chapter Fourteen

From its exterior, the boardinghouse on Brewer Street, just north of Picadilly Circus, appeared to be a modest and respectable place for Lydia Hailson to have let a room. It was a well-kept house, surrounded by a church, shops, and homes that also looked well cared for.

Last night, shortly after Jasper and Mrs. Zhao left, a knocking had come at the front door. Leo had, momentarily, wondered if he had returned. Part of her had hoped it was Jasper, and yet when she'd seen Dita standing on the front step, Leo had exhaled in relief. The argument with Jasper had left her shaky and disappointed, and she knew deep down that if he'd come back right then, they would have only argued more.

Joining a detective agency wasn't what she wanted in the least. She'd only used it as an example—and perhaps out of anger, to provoke him. But she didn't want to be told what she could and could not do as a detective inspector's potential wife.

That word set her heart aflutter each time she thought

of it. Visions came, unbidden, of waking next to Jasper every morning, and of falling asleep in his arms every night. Of living under the same roof, sharing their evenings, and setting off each morning for work, arm in arm.

However, that was where a swirl of frustration set in—over the rules and expectations that would come with marrying a Scotland Yard detective inspector. Would she be expected to stay home? Would she be forced to give up her work at the morgue?

Leo cared deeply for Jasper, and her attraction to him was overwhelming to the point of distraction. But how could she accept his courtship if it meant she would need to restrict herself from doing what she wanted to do?

Last evening, she'd allowed Dita inside and invited her to stay for dinner. Mrs. Zhao's roast was plenty big enough to feed them all for a few days. But Dita had only been stopping by on her way home to deliver the information that Leo had requested.

"On my first day at the department store, I saw Mrs. Gleason place *Susan Clark*'s employee information in a file cabinet drawer," Dita said, emphasizing her false name and arching a brow. "So, I waited until she and Mr. Gleason left for the evening, then dashed into her office and found Lydia's file."

Leo was both impressed with Dita's daring and irritated by it, though her frustration was more likely a remnant from her argument with Jasper.

Dita had jotted down Lydia's address before returning the file to the drawer and escaping the office, unnoticed.

"I could ask Evelyn, another shopgirl, about Lydia, if

you want," Dita said as she handed Leo the scrap of paper with the address on it.

"No, don't bring her up. I don't want you to appear interested in her at all. It could be dangerous."

After Dita's answering sigh, Leo realized how much like Jasper she'd just sounded.

After rising earlier than usual the following morning, she set out for Brewer Street on foot, hoping to arrive around the time the landlady at the boardinghouse would be providing breakfast to her lodgers. Leo wanted the chance to speak to the other women who lived there, if possible. She anticipated that the landlady would allow Leo inside when she announced that she brought news of her missing lodger.

Mrs. Ferland, a middle-aged woman who offered rooms to working-class women, invited Leo inside and led her to a small but cozy sitting room. It was empty, though the voices of her lodgers drifted in from another room, alongside the clatter of cutlery and china.

"You said you bring news of Miss Hailson?" the landlady asked, her concern evident by her fraught, imploring stare. "I went to the police station on Vine Street yesterday when she didn't return for a second night. They suggested that she'd taken off. But that isn't like Lydia. Not that they listened any."

Not all police stations were staffed with good officers, as Leo well knew. She wasn't surprised that Mrs. Ferland's worry for her lodger had been dismissed.

"I'm sorry to have to report to you, Mrs. Ferland," Leo began, "but Miss Hailson is dead."

The landlady's eyes scrunched shut, and her chapped hand came up to cover her mouth. "Oh no. Oh, how awful." She sat down in the nearest chair. "What…what happened to the poor girl?"

Leo had not known what to expect from Lydia's landlady—if she would be caring, or cold and businesslike—but this reaction of sorrow heartened her. She took a seat on the chair adjacent to Mrs. Ferland.

"She was strangled," Leo provided, which caused the woman even more visible horror. "I am assisting a man who knew Miss Hailson and would like her murder investigated."

Teary-eyed, the landlady lowered her hand. "Are the police not doing that?"

"Not just yet."

After the way she'd been treated at the local station, Mrs. Ferland only pursed her lips and gave a shake of her head.

"Mrs. Ferland," Leo began, her questions many, and her time short. She imagined the woman also needed to see to her lodgers. "How long had Lydia been living here as your lodger?"

"About four months," she answered. "She were a good lodger. Kind and respectful."

"Did she have family or friends, or perhaps a beau?"

"No, none of that. A few of the other girls here invited her to join them on an evening out from time to time, but she always said she were too busy."

"Doing what?" Leo asked.

"Working," the landlady said readily.

Leo blinked, confused. "But how could she work in the evenings? She was employed at Gleason's Department Store."

The store closed its doors in the early evening.

Mrs. Ferland dabbed at the corner of her eye and sniffed. "I saw that dress she were wearing lately and knew she were off to that store each day, but that weren't her real work."

Intrigued, Leo leaned forward. "What was her real work?"

Agitation gripped the woman, and she sniffled again as she stood up, arms crossed. "I knew it were too risky. Worried something might happen, and now... *Oh.*" Her chin quivered as she tried to stem the flow of new tears.

Leo got to her feet and asked again, "Mrs. Ferland, what was Lydia's real work?"

The landlady composed herself and answered, "She were a writer. A reporter, though no paper would hire her on permanently, of course, seeing how she were a woman. But she published stories wherever she could sell them. Did well enough to pay her rent on time every week."

A thrill vibrated through Leo, opening a whole new avenue of inquiry. If Lydia had been a reporter, did that mean she had been working at Gleason's for a story?

When she asked Mrs. Ferland this question, the woman bobbed her head. "That's right, undercover, she said. It were a big story, she claimed. One that were sure to get her onto the payroll of a newspaper."

Or one that would get her killed. Leo's skin prickled with gooseflesh.

"Did she tell you what the story was about?"

Mrs. Ferland shook her head. "She wouldn't say. Got the impression it were dangerous since in the past, she'd told me about her other articles. Didn't breathe a word about this one, though. I told her to be careful. I told her…" She shook her head and lifted her apron hem to dab at her eyes and nose again.

"May I look at her room?" Leo asked. If Lydia had been working at Gleason's undercover and writing a story, it was possible she'd have notes or drafts of her article stashed there.

Mrs. Ferland agreed and led Leo to the second floor. Voice quavering, she said she'd checked Lydia's room each evening, hopeful that she had returned at some point during the day, but with no luck.

The room was small—no larger than Leo's own cramped Duke Street bedroom. It was much tidier than Leo's room, however. The bed was neatly made, there were no articles of clothing left lying about, and a narrow stand of shelves was organized with Lydia's few possessions. Even the small writing desk near the single window overlooking the street was orderly and clean, with a Remington typewriter, some books, fountain pens, and a box of typewriter paper.

She walked to the desk, hopeful that there would be some typing on the paper in the box, but the pages were blank. Opening the desk drawer, she saw that it was empty.

"Have you tidied the room recently?" Leo asked.

"No, this is how Lydia likes to keep her space," she answered. Then after a pause, she added, "*Liked*, I mean."

Downstairs, another lodger called for Mrs. Ferland. The landlady excused herself for a moment. Leo twitched the curtains, looking out over the street, thinking. If Lydia was a reporter, why wouldn't she have anything she'd written on her desk, or in it? There were no pages on the stand of shelves, and no closet to put anything in. Just a bureau where, Leo discovered after a quick search, was filled with clothing and undergarments.

Leo got down on all fours and peered underneath the bed. Some boots and shoes were lined up, though nothing else had been stored there. Before pushing back onto her feet, she considered a hiding space that she had used in the past herself, after Aunt Flora had found and read the letters Leo had written to her dead family shortly after she and Claude had taken her in. She'd been a child, still raw with anguish, and spoiling for a fight too. Leo had liked living with the Inspector in his big house with the kindly Mrs. Zhao who made delicious food. Even Jasper, the tall, quiet, unsmiling boy off the streets hadn't been too awful. The truth was, Leo hadn't wanted to live with her aged aunt and uncle, whom she did not know at all. In her letters to her dead family, she had written honestly, perhaps even cruelly, about her discontent. She knew her family would never be able to read her letters, but Leo had wanted to talk to them. Writing letters had seemed like the best way to get out her thoughts.

Flora had called her an ungrateful little girl and then tossed the letters into the kitchen stove. Her aunt had been crying as she did so, Leo recalled, and now she understood Flora, too, had been in anguish. She'd lost her sister to inexplicable violence. After reading her aunt's letters to her mother, Leo realized that Flora must have felt guilt or frustration, or both. She'd known the family was in danger, but she hadn't been able to stop it.

After watching the letters to her dead family burn, Leo kept anything that was remotely private under her mattress. Flora did not change the bedlinens, for that was Leo's chore, and so her private things were safe there.

Leo lifted Lydia's mattress and grinned as she pulled free a thick manila folio, toggled with string. She sat on the edge of the bed and began to go through the papers. There were several newspaper clippings, all of them advertisements for Gleason's, and some typed pages riddled with edits and notes scribbled in the margins. Leo quickly read the first few lines on one of the pages, and it appeared to be the beginning of an article on stolen goods being sold in one of London's most fashionable department stores.

With her pulse beginning to kick, Leo pulled a slim, leather-bound journal from the folio. The pages inside were covered in handwriting. Her eyes skimmed over the pages, in which Lydia had chronicled the names and descriptions of the shop assistants she worked with, as well as others in different departments. She noted people's schedules and habits, as if she were compiling information on everything related to Gleason's employees. Then, there were notes on products being sold, like urns, vases, statuary, and decorative home items such as pillows and clocks.

Just as Mrs. Ferland's returning footfalls sounded in the corridor, she turned a page in Lydia's journal and read a word, which had been underlined twice: *Opium?*

She stood up from the bed a moment before the landlady came back into Lydia's room.

"Forgive me if I were too long away. The other lodgers were quite upset to hear about poor Miss Hailson." She saw the folio lying on the bed. "Did you find anything helpful?"

Leo stuffed the papers and the journal back inside the folio and tied the toggle. "It was under her mattress. I'm quite sure it details what she was working on at Gleason's."

If opium and stolen items were involved, whatever Lydia had been investigating had been dangerous. She'd also, obviously, been caught.

"I will need to take this with me to share with a detective from Scotland Yard," Leo said, thinking first of Jasper, but then, as he would be leaving for Liverpool—perhaps even before she had the chance to see him again—of Roy Lewis. "If they know she was onto something dangerous and illegal, the police will have every reason to open a case to investigate her murder."

At least, that is what she hoped.

Mrs. Ferland nodded avidly. "Of course, take it, if you think it will help. I still can't believe she's dead. It just isn't fair. She were so certain this story would be the start of her career..."

The landlady didn't have to finish her thought. She was right. It wasn't fair at all. Murder hardly ever was, but the bite of some cases was felt more sharply than others. What Lydia thought would start her career had very likely ended her life.

After thanking Mrs. Ferland again and promising her that she would be in contact, Leo left the boardinghouse. She had the folio tight under her arm as she walked along the pavement toward an omnibus stand at the end of the road, near Picadilly Circus. She'd come on foot, but she was too eager to return to the morgue and share Lydia's trove of notes with Connor. Or perhaps she should instead go straight to Scotland Yard. Jasper would not be there; he would be traveling to Harrow. But Roy Lewis might listen to what she had learned about Lydia's precarious position at Gleason's.

Leo approached the omni stand, where three men in business suits and a woman wearing a large, fussy hat waited for an omni. Another man, tall and wide set, stepped up onto the pavement a few strides in front of Leo and walked toward her. He didn't move aside to allow her to pass, and when she tried to move around him, he slid to block her path again.

"Excuse me, sir," she said, her patience wearing thin.

But he did not move. Just then, a black-and-maroon-painted carriage came to a stop next to her in the street. The tall man standing before her raised his arm, gesturing toward the carriage. The door opened, and Leo saw a familiar face looking out at her.

"Good day, Miss Spencer." It was Eddie Bloom, the proprietor of Striker's Wharf and the leader of a criminal racket out of Lambeth's wharves. "I think you should join me."

Leo held still where she was, alarm coursing through her. "No, thank you, Mr. Bloom," she said, a bubble of air trapped in her throat. "I have an omni to catch."

The man blocking her on the pavement didn't budge.

"That wasn't a request, Miss Spencer," Eddie said, his tone a shade less polite. "Get in. You have something I want."

Chapter Fifteen

The inside of Eddie Bloom's carriage was as posh as his nightclub across the river, on the Lambeth wharves. Scarlet plush benches, black and gold silk walls, and gold brocade curtains in the windows gave the impression of wealth—and a suggestion of sin. The curtains were open, keeping the busy street and pavements within view as Leo sat across from Mr. Bloom. Had they been drawn closed, it would have felt even more like climbing into the mouth of a predator.

"What is the meaning of this, Mr. Bloom?" She kept her back straight and the folio tight underneath her arm.

It had been several months since she'd last encountered the crime lord. In the spring, Leo had gone to his club alone and asked him what he knew about her father, Leonard Spencer, who had been working for the East Rips as an accountant. She'd wanted to know what had motivated the slaughter of her family and believed that Eddie Bloom would have more information about the bloody events that had transpired sixteen years before.

But he had warned her off, telling her that if she were to poke around for answers, she would be risking herself, even now, since there were some among the Carter family who viewed her as a loose thread to be eradicated. Drawing attention to herself would also draw attention to Detective Inspector Jasper Reid—and other members of the Carter family, besides Andrew, might recognize his true identity. So, to protect herself and Jasper, Leo had let the matter go.

Seated on the backward-facing bench, his palms resting on his thighs, Mr. Bloom smiled affably. "We need to have a talk about what you were doing at that boardinghouse." His eyes slipped to the folio. "And what you have there."

The man, somewhere in his mid- to late forties, had a distinct charm about him and smiled often. However, those grins held a cunning edge and were accompanied by a menacing gleam in his dark eyes. The effect, Leo knew, was to make the recipient of those smiles feel willing to do anything to appease the man.

Leo felt a little of that same yearning to cooperate now, although she also knew Mr. Bloom appreciated a challenge.

"How are you concerned?" she asked, her mind spinning furiously as she tried to understand his interest.

He kept his slightly amused stare on Leo as the carriage joined traffic. "I could ask you the same question. How did you come to be in Miss Hailson's boardinghouse and in her room, at that?"

Leo startled, wondering how he could have known that detail. But then, she remembered she'd gone to the window and looked outside.

"You're having Miss Hailson's boardinghouse watched."

His white smile flashed, as if to reward her for her correct guess. "My boys saw you apply at the front door with the landlady, and they sent word to me."

"Why would they do that?" she asked. "How do you know Miss Hailson?"

"How do you?" he countered.

Leo sighed, tiring of this dance around direct answers. It was possible that Eddie Bloom had played a role in Lydia's death. Why then would he be having her lodgings watched?

"Miss Hailson's body arrived at the Spring Street Morgue two days ago," she replied. If she were straightforward in her answers, perhaps Mr. Bloom would be too. "She'd been strangled."

His expression lost any trace of amusement or lightness, and his stare hardened. He shifted his attention out the window, as if in thought.

"I wondered if she was dead," he said. "It's why I had eyes on her place."

"Tell me how you knew her." Leo heard how commanding her tone was just as Mr. Bloom turned his eyes back on her in surprise—or annoyance. He kept his lips sealed, and she knew he was waiting for her to explain her own interest first.

"She was known well to a friend of mine, and he asked me to investigate her murder."

He cocked his head. "The bobbies aren't interested in doing that?"

"Her case hadn't been assigned the last I knew," she replied. "Now, please tell me how you and Lydia were acquainted…and if it has anything to do with the article she was writing."

Leo had tacked that last bit on to see if he would react, and it worked. He lifted his chin but didn't respond.

"Mr. Bloom," she said, growing impatient. "I am aware that Lydia was working at Gleason's Department Store to gather details about stolen items being sold to their customers. I'm going to presume you knew this as well."

He nodded. "I knew."

"And do these stolen goods have anything to do with you?"

"They belong to me." The answer baffled Leo, and he noticed. "I didn't have anything to do with her murder, Miss Spencer. In fact, I'm the one who planted her at Gleason's."

Leo stared at him, flummoxed. "Why would you have done that?"

"Because she was a bloody good reporter, and I wanted to find out who had stolen from me."

She frowned as the underlined word in Lydia's journal came forward: *Opium.*

Jasper had told her that Eddie Bloom was small beer compared to other criminal rackets like the East Rips and Spitalfields Angels, but that he was still dangerous. Not very long ago, opium was readily available to anyone who wanted it, especially in its most common form of laudanum. But now, the sale of opium was restricted to chemists and apothecary shops, which were required to record every sale, the amount, and the identity of the buyer. It was still sold on the black market, however, and Leo imagined men like Mr. Bloom and other criminal syndicates were primarily responsible for that.

"When was your opium stolen?" Leo asked.

He frowned and clenched his jaw, as if he did not like her knowing the item stolen was opium. But he didn't ask how she'd determined that. "Two months ago, I received a shipment. The crates were unloaded at night and placed under guard at one of my warehouses. The following morning, the guards were dead, and my crates were empty."

Gracious. Leo wondered how much opium had been stolen.

"Then, I started hearing whispers about pills being sold to toffs up in Mayfair and Bloomsbury," he went on with an arch of his brow.

"You believe it was your stolen product," Leo said as the carriage traveled along Regent Street. He seemed to be taking her back toward Westminster. "But I don't understand. Why would you need Lydia Hailson to find out who stole from you? You are Eddie Bloom. Could you not hunt down the thieves yourself?"

She hadn't meant to sound so contemptuous, but she wouldn't apologize for it. The man was dealing in illegal opium, and it was starting to look as though his involving Lydia in his inquiry had resulted in her murder.

"Believe it or not, Miss Spencer, I'm a pragmatic man," he replied, unfazed by her question or tone. "Shows of brute force aren't my style. They also tend to attract unwanted attention from the bobbies. I have no intention of letting the people who stole from me go unpunished. I just have a shrewder, less obvious notion of how to take them down."

"By hiring a reporter to investigate and expose the

illegal opium operation the thieves were running with your pilfered product?" she presumed.

He grinned and gave a nod.

Eddie Bloom's name would not be attached to the opium, though the names of the thieves would be. They would be arrested and prosecuted, and although Eddie would not recover the opium that he'd lost, he would have the satisfaction of knowing the thieves were being punished and eliminated from the market.

"How did you narrow in on Gleason's?" Leo asked.

"Miss Hailson found that a few shops up in that posh area were dealing pills in a clandestine manner, but as Gleason's was the only one hiring women, that's where she went."

"And how did you know Miss Hailson would work with you, without exposing your part in the plan?"

Another one of his sly grins formed. "Her articles in *The Illustrated Police News* were top notch. I must say, even better than those articles that described you so well."

The articles he was referring to were short profile pieces that ran last winter, much to Leo's chagrin. Constable Elias Murray of the *Police Gazette* had written them anonymously, hoping to get his foot in the door at the popular weekly newspaper. They had detailed her tragic past and her current occupation at the morgue, soliciting shock among readers.

"She was a regular at Striker's Wharf," he continued when Leo did not react to his goading remark. "I was doing her a favor. This article would've been a spectacle, big enough to make her name known. And besides, Miss Hailson was too smart to cross me."

The carriage was now trundling toward Trafalgar Square.

"I am certain she was quite smart," Leo said. "But unfortunately, she wasn't careful enough to go unnoticed. She was wearing her uniform when she was found dead. She must have been caught snooping."

Again, Mr. Bloom's square jaw shifted, exhibiting frustration. Or perhaps it was remorse. Then again, maybe she was being too generous.

"She was due at the club," Mr. Bloom said. "When she didn't show, and no word came, I suspected something had gone amiss."

As the carriage diverged from traffic and came along Spring Street, his attention dropped to the folio still clutched tightly under her arm. "You found that in her room? Is it what she was writing?"

"I am not giving it to you just yet, Mr. Bloom," she stated. "I've yet to read her papers and notes thoroughly. So, considering we have a mutual interest in finding Miss Hailson's killer, I propose you allow me until the morning to go through them. After that, they are yours."

He laughed, and the sound of it was just prickly enough for Leo to wonder if she had pushed too far. But he sighed and said, "You have until ten o'clock tonight. I'll send someone to your home to collect the papers then. No tricks, Miss Spencer. This is a fair deal."

The carriage came to a stop in front of the morgue's front door. She would have plenty of time to commit Lydia's papers and notes to memory.

"All right," she said, and though she didn't like the idea of Eddie Bloom's man coming to her door at that late hour, she gave the nightclub owner her address. He grinned, and something about it said that he'd already known where to find her.

The carriage door opened, and the tall man who had blocked her path near the omnibus stand earlier was there to extend his hand. Reluctantly, Leo took it.

"Be careful, Miss Spencer," Mr. Bloom warned as she stepped down. Before the door closed, he added, "Or at the very least, be more careful than Miss Hailson proved to be."

Chapter Sixteen

An agitated hush had fallen over the servants' quarters at Cowper Hall. Jasper had arrived at the viscount's front door about a quarter hour earlier, and when he'd informed the butler, Decamp, that he needed to speak to him privately, the man's firm chin had quivered with worry.

He'd led Jasper belowstairs to his office in the butler's pantry. Along the way, he'd chatted nervously, informing Jasper that Mr. Cowper and Mr. Dalton had not yet returned from London, and that the viscount had been prescribed a sleeping draught as he had not been doing well since receiving news of his granddaughter's death.

Once they reached the pantry, where Decamp guarded the family's silver, china, and crystal, all polished to an otherworldly gleam for when they were laid out upon the dining room table, the butler had run out of things to say.

Informing the older man about the death of his son had unfolded as Jasper predicted: The announcement that he brought bad news had forewarned Decamp, and the older man had braced himself. But he had still staggered to a chair and collapsed into it when Jasper explained what he'd found at Stephen's farm.

When Decamp remained speechless, his head in his hands and tears falling freely, Jasper stepped out to summon a passing maid. It was the same young woman whom he'd overheard being chastised by Frederick Cowper on the night of the storm, outside the billiards room. He asked her—Ursula, he recalled—to bring tea, which she did within a minute.

"Stephen is dead," the butler told her, his voice raspy. "The inspector found his…his body…"

Ursula gasped and then pressed the cup and saucer into Decamp's shaking hands. She added another cube of sugar, perhaps to help balance out the shock that must have been surging through the man.

"Mr. Decamp," Jasper began. "I understand this is a very difficult moment, but I do have questions for you regarding your son's movements over the last few days. Specifically, since the reading of Mrs. Stroud's last will and testament."

The butler nodded, though it was with obvious effort and sorrow.

"I'll stay with you, Mr. Decamp," the maid offered. She glanced at Jasper. "If that is all right."

"It is," he assured her.

Before he could begin, the click and scratch of paws on wood floors sounded from the corridor, gaining speed and proximity. Two enormous wolfhounds scurried into the small pantry, the head of each dog reaching nearly to Jasper's hip. The same dogs had been at Nadia Stroud's side at dinner the night of the storm. They circled and sniffed about the room for only a moment before Nadia herself appeared in the doorway.

"Porthos, Aramis," she called, snapping her fingers. The wolfhounds obediently rounded up next to her and sat. Then, Nadia turned her intense focus onto Jasper, as if wishing she could snap her fingers at him to make him disappear. "I heard you were here, Inspector, and were speaking to our butler. It seems you are unaware that it is bad form to question an employee without first speaking to their employer."

Jasper took the reprimand with gritted teeth. "As my business is with Mr. Decamp, I saw no reason to ask permission to speak to him."

"The Inspector has brought terrible news, Miss Stroud," Ursula said, her voice high and tinny, more like that of a young girl than of a young woman.

Nadia crossed her arms. She wore a riding habit and, by her dusty boots and skirt hem, looked to have just come in. "What terrible news is this? Is it about Helen?"

"No," Jasper answered. "I've just found Stephen Decamp at his farm, dead."

The peevish attitude Nadia arrived with fled instantly, and the dogs next to her whined, as if they, too, understood the announcement.

Nadia turned her concern toward the butler. "Decamp, I am so very sorry." She went to him quickly and laid a hand upon his shoulder, then looked to Jasper. "Inspector, what happened?"

With a glimpse toward the butler, he revealed, "At this time, it appears he took his own life."

"No." Decamp shot up from his chair, dislodging Nadia's hand and forgetting that he held a teacup and saucer. They fell to the floor with the telltale sound of porcelain breaking. "No, my son would never. He wouldn't!"

As Nadia tried to calm him, and Ursula crouched to mop up the tea with a rag and collect the broken pieces of cup and saucer, Jasper waited. It was common for family members of suicide victims to reject the finding, to make the claim that their loved one would never end their own life, even when the evidence was ample that they had. No one wanted the memory or the legacy of their loved one to be tainted by the scandal of suicide. The elder Decamp would be no different in this regard.

However, Jasper admitted that there had been something not quite right about the scene in Stephen's dining room.

Once Decamp had collapsed back into his chair, and Ursula had gone to fetch another teacup and saucer, Jasper related, "There was evidence he'd been drinking heavily. In his distraught state, he might have been driven to an extreme decision. Especially after Helen's murder."

Decamp blinked and tightened his jaw but stayed quiet.

"Did you know of their affair?" Jasper asked. The butler certainly looked guilty with knowledge of it. Nadia, too, seemed to draw up her shoulders as though bracing for something unpleasant. Their silence lengthened.

"Did you know she was carrying a child?" Jasper asked next.

The bite of their eyes as they each stared at Jasper, dumbfounded, told him they had not. Nadia's lips parted, distress pulling her brow taut.

"A child? My God. She never said." She closed her eyes

to compose herself. "I knew what Helen was doing. I think we all did."

"Not Anthony," Jasper interjected.

"He would have known, had he not been pickled all the time," Nadia replied, her dislike for her brother-in-law evident in the way she fought the rolling of her eyes.

"How long had they been having an affair?" Jasper asked.

Decamp, his dejection causing his head to hang and his shoulders to droop forward, appeared utterly defeated. And why shouldn't he, given what he'd lost?

"Several months, that I know of," Nadia replied. "But they were in love long ago too. Before she married Anthony."

Jasper cocked his head, his interest piqued at this new bit of information.

"For what reason did Stephen and Helen part ways?"

"It was inevitable, wasn't it? Grandfather would never have approved of their match, and I told her so," Nadia said abrasively. Angrily, even. With a flicker of remorse, she glanced at Decamp. "I mean no disrespect, but you understand, Decamp. It is the way of things."

He nodded morosely. "I do understand, Miss Nadia. So did Stephen...eventually."

"He took the rejection hard?" Jasper asked.

"Yes. She broke things off after Master Teddy's fall," the butler replied. Sighing, he then added, "The boy's death broke the whole house. The family, the staff, everyone. Stephen was heartbroken, but so was everyone else."

Jasper was surprised to hear Teddy's name, and the connection drawn to his death.

"Why after the young master's fall?" he asked.

"Helen and I went away," Nadia provided. "We spent several months with friends in southern France, while our mother was in Wales at a…retreat," she said. The uneasy tone of her voice and a furtive glance in Jasper's direction revealed that the *retreat* had likely been an asylum of some kind.

"And Stephen?" he asked.

"He returned here, to Cowper Fields," Decamp provided.

"Do you mean to say he was at the Craven Hill residence at the time of Theodore's death?"

"Yes, working as a groomsman," Decamp provided. He raked his fingers through his thinning silver hair. "Inspector, do you truly believe my son took his own life?"

Jasper did not feel confident enough in his answer, so he skirted it with another question of his own. "After I reported Helen had been murdered, did you go to your son's home? Did you try to tell him what had happened?"

Decamp stiffened in his seat and tensed his jaw. "I did."

"He wasn't home, I take it?" Jasper asked. At the answering shake of the butler's head, he followed with, "What about his gig? Had he taken it somewhere?"

Decamp held up his palms in surrender. "I know I should have said something. But with Mrs. Dalton dead in London and my son missing, his carriage and horse gone… It looked bad for him."

Nadia's incisive glare settled on the butler. "It *looked* as if he had taken my sister to Craven Hill and killed her. And yet you kept this to yourself?"

Decamp lowered his head, his palm rising to cover his eyes.

"It appears Stephen and Helen did travel to London

together the night of the storm and that he did not return to Harrow until late yesterday. Is there somewhere in the city where he might have stayed overnight before coming home? Friends he might have approached?" Jasper asked.

The stench of spirits on his person, the empty liquor bottles, and the delay in arriving home, all pointed toward a stretch of time spent wallowing in either grief or guilt.

"No, he didn't often go to London. He didn't like it. Too dirty, he said, and congested." Emotion slackened Decamp's face again. But he rallied in the next moment. "He had a farmhand a few years back, a boy by the name of Everton. Sam Everton. He bought a patch of land in Sudbury. Stephen would check in on him from time to time. They were friends."

As Sudbury wasn't far from Harrow, it would be worth a visit.

Ursula returned to the butler's pantry with another cup and saucer. She went to the pot of tea to pour for Decamp.

"The servants are asking questions about the inspector's visit, Miss Stroud," she said.

Nadia rubbed her temple. "Tell Mrs. Renwick that I will address them soon."

"Should I ask his lordship's valet to wake the viscount?"

"No, no, not yet. Let him rest." Nadia glanced at Jasper. "My grandfather has been taking a draught to calm himself. He'll be better once Frederick is home from London."

Ursula, handing the filled teacup and saucer to Decamp, nearly made a hash of it as her hands and wrists shook violently, rattling the porcelain. "So sorry," she squeaked before stepping back and clasping her hands behind her.

Jasper wondered if it had been the mention of Frederick that had flustered her. He had, after all, reprimanded her harshly outside the billiards room a few nights ago.

"Ursula, I overheard a terse conversation on the night of the storm between yourself and Mr. Cowper. He told you to mind your own business if you'd like to keep your position here," Jasper said, and at the instant draining of color from her already wan cheeks, he was glad he'd brought it up. He'd asked Frederick about the encounter, but not her. "What was he referring to?"

Frederick had been vague about it, saying it was some gossip and trouble the maid was prone to stirring up. But as Ursula's wide-eyed terror flicked between Nadia and Decamp, he found himself wanting more specifics.

"Ursula." Nadia's tone was sharp enough to make the maid jump. "Answer the inspector's question."

"I'm so sorry, miss," she said, her eyes beginning to fill. "I made a mistake. An awful one, and I feel terrible about it. I thought for certain Mr. Cowper was going to sack me then and there. I fear he still might."

Jasper held up his hand. "Slow down, Ursula. What mistake was this?"

She was now twisting her fingers together before her, looking nauseous. "It was when Mrs. Stroud was ill. I found her in bed, asleep, but she'd been writing a letter on the breakfast tray in her lap. I gathered the tray and was putting the papers and pen back on her writing desk, and…well…I couldn't help but read some of the lines." The maid winced. "I shouldn't have done it, I know I shouldn't have, but before I knew it, I'd read several more."

Jasper had an inkling as to what letter the maid had seen. "Who was this letter addressed to?"

"The envelope was addressed to you, Inspector. And Miss Spencer," she answered, her chin quivering.

Nadia stared at the maid. "You read the private letter my mother gave to her solicitor for Inspector Reid and Miss Spencer?"

Ursula emitted a little whine of desperation. "Not all of it! Just a few sentences. As soon as I came to my senses, I stopped and put it away. I swear! I didn't realize how important the letter was, not until after the will reading."

"Its importance doesn't matter. You should not have been reading your lady's private correspondence at all," Decamp said with the typical sternness of a butler.

"What happened after the reading, Ursula?" Jasper asked to stave off another reprimand from Nadia.

The maid quailed but answered, "I was bringing fresh towels to Mrs. Dalton's room. It was before dinner, and she was telling Dora about the secret letter to the inspector and Miss Spencer, and how everyone was in an uproar. I remembered the letter I'd seen, and I didn't mean to say anything, but I did. I said, '*That* letter?' And when Mrs. Dalton asked me what I knew of it… Well, I'm an awful liar. So, I confessed."

"Did you tell Mrs. Dalton what you'd read?" Jasper asked, and when she nodded, he continued, "What, exactly, did you tell her?"

Depending on how far into Francine Stroud's letter she'd read, Helen might have learned that her mother had suspected her of having a hand in Teddy's death. It might have spurred her on to leave for London and the Craven Hill residence in the middle of the night.

"First, she sent Dora from the room," Ursula said. "Then, I told her what I could remember. That Mrs. Stroud had asked you and Miss Spencer to find justice for her son, Teddy."

"What?" Nadia exclaimed. "Why would Teddy need justice? His fall was an accident."

"I just know what I read, Miss Stroud," Ursula said, quivering in fear. "Something about a glass vial belonging to Helen—Mrs. Dalton, I mean—and that someone who possessed it was on the roof with Teddy that night." Here, the maid cast her terrified eyes to the floor, her cheeks heating under Nadia's flaying glare. "Mrs. Stroud wrote that she'd hidden it under a floorboard in the old house. That's where I stopped reading, I swear it. I don't know anything more than that."

Christ. It at least answered how Helen had known to get to London as soon as possible. She must have dashed off a note to Stephen immediately, setting her plan in motion to leave Cowper Fields that night. She'd wanted to get to the vial first.

But why? Jasper and Leo already knew about the vial clutched in Teddy's hand. A tear catcher that had traces of floral perfume inside. Taking possession of the vial itself seemed unnecessary. Francine Stroud had mentioned in her letter that recently, she'd started to doubt her suspicion of Helen and wished for the vial to be returned to her. However, that revelation had come at the close of the letter, a part which Ursula had apparently not read.

"Someone was on the roof with Teddy when he fell?"

Nadia asked as she moved toward her two dogs, both of which were still sitting obediently.

"Possibly," Jasper confirmed. "Your mother found the glass vial clutched in his hand when she came upon his body. And before she was killed, Helen succeeded in finding it under the floorboard."

"But…why did my mother never say anything about it?" Nadia asked.

Grateful he'd thought to keep the vial in his pocket, Jasper brought it out, holding the slim glass tube between his thumb and forefinger.

Nadia stormed up to him, her eyes hinged on the vial. "That is Helen's tear catcher."

"You recognize it?"

"Of course, I do. Our mother gave them to us when Aunt Emmaline and our cousins died," she said, referring to Gregory Reid's wife and two children who'd drowned eighteen years ago. At the time, Nadia would have been quite young, perhaps nine or ten. Helen, perhaps a few years older than that.

Nadia reached for the tear catcher, and Jasper let her hold it. She gazed at the pretty twist of amethyst and cobalt glass. "I'll confess; I didn't know my cousins or aunt well, so I filled mine with a few drops of water instead of tears. I remember feeling guilty for it, even though I shouldn't have—Helen filled hers with perfume." She shook her head as she handed the tear catcher back to him. "We wore them for over a year, as necklace pendants, before our fake tears dried up inside. But they were so pretty we kept wearing them, and I filled mine with perfume too. It's so odd. I hadn't thought of these tear catchers in years, and now, this is the second time in just a few months."

Jasper pocketed the tear catcher, intrigued. "When was the first time?"

She peered at him. "Is it important?"

"It could be."

Nadia crossed the small butler's pantry toward Decamp. He and Ursula had been listening quietly, the maid riveted, and the butler, his eyes damp and probing.

"Very well, then," she said. "I was going through my jewelry boxes, setting things aside that I no longer wanted, and happened to find my tear catcher. I showed it to Helen and asked what had ever happened to hers. Her cheeks went tomato red. She was utterly flustered and didn't want to speak about it. Of course, I wanted to know why, so I needled her, and eventually she shouted that she'd given it to someone."

"Who?" Jasper asked.

Nadia arched a brow. "A man. I attacked her with questions, but she wouldn't say more, just that it was someone she wished to forget all about. She was so upset, she nearly cried."

Jasper's mind began to whirl with everything Nadia was saying. He forced it to slow. "Did you believe her? That she'd given it to a man?"

Nadia furrowed her brow in thought. "I know my sister well." She paused. "*Knew* my sister. I always knew when she was lying. Her nostrils would flare, and she'd blink too much. But when she said she'd given the tear catcher to someone else, there was none of that. I only saw humiliation, oddly. So, yes, I believed her."

"And when you had this conversation with Helen

about the tear catchers, was your mother present?" he asked next.

"Yes. Come to think of it, she was. She was upset by our little tiff and went to lay down."

Jasper unclenched his hands, which he'd balled into fists at his sides. He exhaled, finally understanding. After hearing her daughters' argument, Francine had learned the little vial might not have been in Helen's possession at the time of Teddy's death. That it may have already been given to a mysterious young man.

"Inspector," Decamp said. "If Mrs. Dalton gave that tear catcher to someone else, how was it found in Master Teddy's hand?"

"I believe that is what Mrs. Stroud wanted Miss Spencer and me to discover," he replied. "If Theodore was pushed, and he ripped the trinket free from around his attacker's neck, where it was being worn..."

"It may have been the man Helen gave it to," Nadia provided.

"Why would that man, whoever it was, have been on the roof with Master Teddy?" Ursula asked. But then, she covered her mouth and hunched back. "Forgive me, it's none of my business."

At the maid's question, however, Nadia did not appear irritated. Instead, she blanched. "Oh no."

"What is it, Miss Stroud?" Jasper asked.

"Stephen," she whispered. Decamp stood up on unsteady legs.

"What about my son?"

"He and Helen would...well, they would often meet on the roof of the house on Craven Hill to be alone," Nadia whispered, her eyes blinking rapidly.

Jasper thought of Helen's relationship with Stephen. It had ended right after Teddy's death. If *Stephen* had been the man to whom Helen had given the tear catcher, he might have worn it as a sentimental trinket. Had Teddy come upon the lovers on the roof?

He might have pushed the boy from the roof, and Teddy's hand might have closed around the tear catcher, ripping it free from Stephen's neck.

When Nadia had brought up the tear catchers shortly before their mother's death, Helen might have panicked with the memory of what had happened that night, of what she'd participated in. Perhaps that is why she and Stephen had traveled together to London—to retrieve the tear catcher. But again, the vial alone was not evidence of any foul play. And if Stephen had pushed Teddy off the roof, even accidentally, why would Helen have conducted an affair with him now, all these years later?

It made no sense.

Jasper rolled his neck and shoulders, frustrated by the circles he kept traversing with this case.

"Stephen never would have harmed Master Teddy," Decamp said, though his voice shook.

"Of course not, Decamp," Nadia said quickly. "I just remembered that they would sometimes rendezvous there. I'm sure I'm wrong about the night of Teddy's death."

An awkward quiet fell over the room. Wishing to change the subject, Jasper focused on the maid again.

"Ursula, you've explained your transgression of reading Mrs. Stroud's letter, but you still have yet to explain how Frederick Cowper learned of it and knew to reprimand you for it."

The maid's coloring flooded back into her cheeks, and she again appeared timorous.

"I went to the billiards room to bank the fire for the night," she began. "Mr. Cowper was there alone, and he commented that Mrs. Dalton had seemed distressed at dinner. He asked me to bring her something for her nerves. I'd been so upset all day, I just started to cry. He made me tell him why, and when I explained about reading the letter, he was furious."

"As he should have been," Nadia murmured, her dislike of the maid plain.

"Thank you for explaining, Ursula," Jasper said, frowning. Frederick had said the maid had been gossiping about Francine's decision to give up the Craven Hill home to strangers. He hadn't mentioned anything about knowing the contents of the letter. Jasper wished to know why.

He checked his watch. If he was going to visit Sam Everton in Sudbury on his way back to London, he needed to leave now.

"Constable Wiggins will be by shortly with Stephen's body," he said as gently as possible to Decamp. "Given the circumstances surrounding your son's death, an inquest will be standard. I believe the viscount is a magistrate, so I will leave it to him to organize."

With the evidence as it was, there was little doubt it would be quickly ruled a suicide. Although there was still a niggling sense that there was more to it than that, Jasper had nothing firm to stand on, other than a feeling of the scene being just a little too neat.

He started for the door but recalled something. "Someone should collect the dog. It was tied up and barking when I arrived. I've turned it loose, but I'm sure it's still hanging about the farm."

"Beau was tied up?" Decamp shifted in his seat to peer at Jasper, his expression one of confusion.

"If Beau is the collie I saw, then yes," he replied.

Decamp continued to frown. "How peculiar. Stephen never tied up Beau. The dog has the run of the place. One of the best herding dogs there is."

The sense of foreboding Jasper felt upon arriving at the farm and seeing the barking collie tethered to a post returned. If Stephen had been planning to kill himself, it made sense for him to have wanted to close the front door to his house to keep the dog outside. But to tie him up as well didn't seem to have much purpose.

"Are you certain he would not have restrained the dog?" Jasper asked.

"I suppose he might have, if he had company that didn't care for dogs," Decamp said with a shrug, but then rubbed his face again, his heavy anguish palpable.

If his company didn't care for dogs. Not liking dogs was a phrase Jasper had heard recently. His mind sought where he'd heard it and from whom. Grasping the answer felt like grabbing hold of a live electrical wire.

"Excuse me," he said, his pulse quickening as he unceremoniously left the butler's pantry. He needed to be on the next train to London.

Chapter Seventeen

The first time Leo visited Gleason's Department Store, she had felt supremely out of place and unfashionable. The salesclerks, trained to spot those with wealth and those who were merely browsing with dreamy-eyed hope, had quite obviously dismissed her as one of the latter. However, this time, she arrived better prepared, in one of her nicest ensembles—a green-and-black-striped silk bodice and skirt, complete with a small bustle beneath to give her figure a voguish S-shape.

Leo rarely bothered with such sartorial details; even when she and Jasper had gone out to dine before he left for Liverpool, she hadn't worn the uncomfortable bustle. But for this new turn in her investigation into Lydia Hailson's murder, she'd decided she could not arrive at Gleason's as the usual Leonora Spencer.

"Are you quite sure about this?" Connor Quinn held Leo's arm stiffly as they strolled onto the housewares floor.

"Not entirely, but I think we stand a good chance of

success," she answered softly, then pasted on a bright smile as the same housewares clerk from the other day approached her. If he remembered her at all, he did not show it. But unlike the last time when he'd given her a once-over and found her lacking, he simpered and sketched a small bow in greeting.

"Good afternoon, and welcome to Gleason's. How may I be of service?"

The clerk looked to Connor for a reply, but disconcerted as he was by this spontaneous undercover ploy Leo had cooked up within the last few hours, he remained silent.

Leo could understand Connor's ruffled state. She had felt the same agitation after leaving Eddie Bloom's carriage earlier that day. Once inside the morgue, she'd walked past Connor, who was already at work on the first postmortem of the day, and gone straight to her desk in the office. There, she sat down and opened Lydia's folio. Mr. Bloom had given Leo until later that evening before one of his men came to reclaim the materials, but she would not need that much time. One thorough read-through of everything, and it would be firmly ingrained in her memory.

Connor had followed her into the office, both concerned and curious as to what she had found at the lodging house. He'd been shocked to learn that his former betrothed, who had worked as a switchboard operator, had become a reporter. He'd been even more dismayed that she had been working undercover at the department store at the time of her murder.

Together, they'd gone through the folio, reading Lydia's

notes and a partial first draft of her article. As Mr. Bloom had said, there was no mention of his name anywhere among her writings. It seemed she had respected their agreement to keep him out of the limelight. Lydia's disjointed notes had proved that she'd not imagined anyone but herself would ever read them, and the partial draft of her article was riddled with lines of ink scratching out words and messy notes made in the margins. In her journal, fragmented sentences and thoughts had been jotted down, alongside sketches of people and of items. Vases and snuffboxes, pots of creams and cosmetics were drawn without explanation. One sketch on the final page of notes in her journal was of a fleur-de-lis symbol.

After setting aside the folio and joining Connor to continue the postmortem he'd already begun, the fleur-de-lis had kept niggling at the back of Leo's mind. At last, just as Connor was investigating the abdominal cavity of the poor man who had died while traveling to Picadilly Circus on an omnibus, the reason why it was bothering her lit through her.

Now, as the housewares clerk waited for either the gentleman or the lady that had entered his floor space to speak, Leo noted he was as one of the several people Lydia had sketched.

"My husband and I are here to peruse some of your housewares for our new home," Leo replied to the clerk, her arm squeezing Connor's a little more intensely. Suggesting the ruse that they would present themselves as a married couple had made the assistant coroner blush, but she had assured him it was the most practical way to gain the clerk's trust.

The beak-nosed man simpered again. "Ah, excellent. I believe you will be very pleased with our selection."

"A dear friend of ours assured us of the same thing, didn't he, darling?" Leo said, looking toward Connor. "What was it he said? That Gleason's had superior stock?"

Connor cleared his throat. "Quite right, my dear," he replied. "Superior."

Leo watched the clerk's expression and gave Connor's arm another squeeze when it transformed with awareness. It had worked.

Among Lydia's last pages of notes had been a few lines about customers commenting to certain clerks about looking for *superior stock*. It seemed to be a signal of sorts or a code, Lydia had written. On the same page of notes, the fleur-de-lis symbol had been sketched a handful of times.

The symbol was one Leo had seen marked on a few items the first time she'd visited Gleason's, when she'd been peering inside cases in the housewares section. As she was there to see Dita, and the prices written in pencil on the manila price tags had been far too dear, she'd paid no attention to the small symbol of the French monarchy. It wasn't until the sketch in Lydia's notes had tugged at a memory that the image of where she'd seen the symbol had shuffled its way to the forefront of her mind.

With a knowing arch of the clerk's brow, he canted his head and grinned. "Your friend was correct." He began to walk toward the same display case of vases and urns that Leo had approached previously. "May I suggest one of these urns, direct from the Orient?"

He opened the case and removed a dual handled jade urn etched with herons. Holding the urn, he presented it to Connor, who lifted the manila tag to read the price. As if the paper had burned him, he let it drop.

"Is there a problem, sir?" the clerk asked.

"No, no, I'm just not certain it is our...preferred style," Conner replied, though he sounded a trifle nervous. Seeing the price must have set him back on his heels. When the clerk turned to set the urn back into the display case, Leo tugged Connor to the side.

"We aren't truly buying it," she said, mouthing the words hardly above a whisper.

"I know, I am stalling for time," he mouthed back, though he had not yet finished before the clerk turned back to them. He caught their private exchange and raised his brow again, though this time with skepticism.

"I do hope your friend explained that our superior stock comes at an elevated cost?"

"Of course," Leo said brightly. "Perhaps we could see another item?"

She had every intention of stalling, just as Connor had.

Before leaving for Gleason's, Leo had sent a message to Roy Lewis at Scotland Yard, telling him of her potential discovery and requesting that he meet her and Connor at the store. Of course, there was every chance Sergeant Lewis hadn't been in the detective department when the note arrived and had yet to read it. It was a risk. But if she'd gone to the Yard in person to ask for his assistance, the sergeant would have never allowed her and Connor to carry out their ruse at Gleason's. At least this way, she would have a hand in the operation.

The clerk hesitated, then looked over his shoulder. "Why don't you come with me, Mr. and Mrs. ...?" He waited for their surname.

Leo, caught by surprise and not having planned to give a name to the clerk at all, stumbled for one now. "Reid," was the first surname that popped into her mind, and she blurted it out.

The clerk gestured for them to fall into step behind him and started across the department floor. Leo met Connor's amused, raised brow as they followed the clerk. Her cheeks heated in embarrassment as they passed a few displays and two other women being helped by another sales assistant, this one a woman in the standard-issue Gleason's uniform.

Leo wondered where the salesclerk might be leading them as they passed the sales counter and till, toward a closed door. There might be a back room with other products marked with the fleur-de-lis tags, but when the clerk opened the door and stepped aside to allow them entry, she saw that it was an office, with a large desk, leather chairs, and a parlor safe set prominently in the corner.

"Do wait here a moment, and someone will be right with you," the clerk said, then shut the door as he left.

Leo released Connor's arm, and he shook it out. "You have quite a grip for a woman, Mrs. *Reid*."

She groaned. "Don't tease me, it was the first name I could think of that wasn't either of our own."

"The Inspector is foremost in your mind, I see," he said, then cocked his head and laughed. "What now?"

He walked toward the desk and chairs. It was a masculine space with its abundance of leather and heavy, dark wood paneling. Perhaps it was the manager's office. Leo wondered if Mr. Gleason himself would join them. If opium was being funneled into London via his shop, surely, he must be the one behind it.

"I'm worried you've spooked the clerk," Leo said.

"Forgive me my reaction, but did you see that price tag?" he asked defensively. "One silly urn costs more than I earn in a month. It's absurd."

It was obscene, Leo agreed, and as she didn't wish to criticize Connor's inability to think on his feet, she let it go.

"He will no doubt send someone in to speak to us," she said. "Let me do the talking. I'll think of something."

Connor whipped off his bowler, agitated. "Sergeant Lewis likely has no idea what we are doing. We're going to have to extricate ourselves. My God, what was Lydia thinking, going undercover for a story this dangerous. Better yet, what are *we* thinking?"

He was panicking. But while Leo considered the current situation risky, she didn't imagine someone would come in here and strangle them as had happened to Lydia. However, she was beginning to sense that their hasty plan to pose as husband and wife trying to purchase opium might be falling apart.

She was about to suggest to Connor that they leave when a door Leo had not noticed on the back wall, papered over with the same dark floral wallpaper, opened. A tall woman with greying blonde hair, upswept in a fashionable twist, and wearing a ruffled dark blue skirt and bodice entered. It was the same woman who had been speaking to Dita the other day, Mrs. Gleason.

She shut the door behind her. "My floor manager advised me that I should come speak with you. It seems there is some concern over our superior stock?" Her blue eyes, edged by fine lines, narrowed on Leo. They flashed with recognition. "I know you. You were here yesterday. You spoke to Miss Clark in ladies' fashions."

Leo was surprised the woman remembered her. She'd hoped she would be forgettable.

"Yes, I believe I was at the ribbon counter," she confirmed, thinking it better not to lie. "I was impressed by what I saw of the store and thought I'd bring my darling husband. We have a new home to fill, after all."

Connor had come back toward her upon Mrs. Gleason's arrival, but his bearing was tense and protective, as if he suspected the woman of something.

"Is that so?" Mrs. Gleason replied, cutting Connor a suspicious glance, then, settling it back on Leo. There was a shift in the air, and Leo knew their ruse was over.

"Miss Clark is working for a detective agency," the woman said, her stare now hard and businesslike. "Are you as well?"

Leo wasn't quite ready to give up and, hoping their cover could be salvaged, laughed. "Detective agency? How amusing. You cannot be serious, though. Can you?"

Mrs. Gleason didn't so much as blink. "How did you hear of our exclusive stock?"

Now, it was Connor who attempted a laugh. "Is it not on view in every display case?"

If possible, her glare would have cut him in half. "Do not play coy. I will ask you once more, how do you know of it?"

Again, Connor began to deny that he knew about what she was speaking, but Leo rested her hand on his arm. She tried to think what Jasper would do in this situation. Intuitively, she suspected he would stop playing games.

"Lydia Hailson told me," Leo said. And when the tension around Mrs. Gleason's eyes smoothed with her astonishment, she continued, "Or rather, her article on the drug smuggling operation you are running here did."

"That is impossible." Mrs. Gleason looked ill, and her fingers gathered the sides of her skirt, as if preparing to run. "Miss Hailson can't have published any article."

"Why not?" Connor asked, no longer sounding nervous over their subterfuge. "Because she is dead?"

Mrs. Gleason sealed her lips into a thin line at his angry question, the revelation that her employee was dead not startling her in the least.

"You know she was murdered," Leo said. "What did you have to do with it, Mrs. Gleason?"

"Nothing," she hissed. "I don't know of what you speak." She hastened to the door leading out to the department floor. "I demand that you both leave. *Now.* Before I send for the police."

Leo stayed where she was. "Scotland Yard is already on their way." At least, she hoped that Roy Lewis was.

Mrs. Gleason tripped to a stop, her hand already reaching for the doorknob. She lowered it back to her side and then started for the papered-over one. She moved in a panic, starting slow but then picking up speed.

"You cannot escape, Mrs. Gleason," Leo said. "The police are aware of your *superior stock,* so to speak."

The warning did not convince her to stop. As she tore open the door, Leo shook her head. "Connor, go out to the street and summon a constable. Go!"

"What are you doing?" he asked as Leo rushed after Mrs. Gleason. "Wait! Leonora!"

She entered a narrow hall and found her quarry dashing away. Leo set off after her.

"I have all of Lydia Hailson's research!" she shouted as she hurried to keep the woman in sight. "She knew what you were doing."

Mrs. Gleason turned at the bend in the corridor, and Leo picked up her pace.

"You found out, I presume," she called. "And that was why Lydia had to die."

As she came around the bend, she nearly collided with a man carrying a mannequin's torso. His eyes were wide with alarm, and he was looking after the scurrying Mrs. Gleason, who was several paces ahead. She'd arrived in a large storage room, packed with crates and racks of clothing, striped boxes stamped with the department store's logo, and display mannequins, not to mention a handful of men who looked to be laborers. Mrs. Gleason wove through the storage room, paying no mind to the men, but throwing increasingly agitated looks over her shoulder at Leo.

"But it wasn't you who strangled Lydia, was it?" she said, knowing somehow to keep needling the woman and not let up. "No, the bruising on her neck wouldn't match your smaller hands. It was from a man's grip. Your husband's?"

Mrs. Gleason had reached another door, this one leading into a delivery yard behind the store. She swung around for a mere second to throw Leo a foul glare. "That fool?" she hissed, spitting the words out.

But then, as though reconsidering her need to keep moving, Mrs. Gleason turned and continued down a set of stone steps into the yard. Leo recalled Dita's undercover mission: to lure Mr. Gleason into a compromising situation, so that his wife could successfully challenge him in court for a divorce. If she despised her husband, Leo questioned if she would have even bothered involving him in this opium scheme.

Leo kept up the pursuit, even though her heart was racing and she had no plan for what to do if she did manage to overtake the woman.

"It was you who was foolish. You left Lydia's body to be found still dressed in Gleason's uniform," Leo said loudly as she skipped down the stone steps and continued following the fleeing woman through the yard. "I imagine the person who strangled Lydia was the criminal you are procuring the opium from. He wouldn't have wanted her discovery to make it into the newspapers."

Mrs. Gleason threw another panicked glance over her shoulder as she turned into an alleyway and disappeared from view.

Leo raised her voice. "Where do you think you can go, Mrs. Gleason?"

The alley only led out to Oxford Street. Though tired of the chase, Leo kept onward without pause, entering the alley. Her feet were beginning to ache in the fashionable shoes she'd put on earlier, and when she nearly stumbled over a pile of loose bricks, she wished she was wearing her more sensible boots.

"There is no point in—" Leo swallowed the rest of her sentence as a hand gripped her wrist and tugged hard.

Mrs. Gleason, having ducked behind some scaffolding in the alley, now shoved Leo hard against the brick wall. The back of her head struck the surface, and pain fogged her vision for a crucial moment. When it cleared, Leo forced her senses to sharpen; Mrs. Gleason held a brick, poised high to come down onto her head.

The woman held it steady, her teeth bared in frustration as she pinned Leo in place using her free arm. "You are just as meddlesome as that girl was."

"You didn't kill Lydia, and you won't kill me," Leo declared, though she wasn't at all confident in that last bit.

"I'm warning you to leave off, just as I did her." Mrs. Gleason's hand trembled as it held the brick high. "But she was relentless. She wouldn't listen, and once they knew what she was doing, it was out of my control."

"Who?" Leo asked. "Who found out what she was doing?"

A bead of sweat shone on Mrs. Gleason's brow. "No one goes up against the Angels. Not me, and especially not young, interfering nobodies like you and Miss Hailson!"

"Stop! Drop the brick and step away!" From the head of the alley at Oxford Street, a pair of men approached: Constable Drake and Detective Sergeant Lewis.

When Mrs. Gleason craned her neck to look down the alley, Leo lifted her foot and kicked the woman's shin as hard as she could. Mrs. Gleason staggered back, and her arm swept down at the same time. The brick glanced off Leo's shoulder before she could move out of the way, but in the next moment, Mrs. Gleason had dropped the improvised weapon and started running back toward the cobbled yard behind the store. Connor, however, appeared at the other end of the alleyway and blocked her retreat.

"Mrs. Gleason, stop!" Sergeant Lewis had hastened down the alley, and now his command was met with compliance. The woman closed her eyes with a pained expression of defeat.

"Are you all right, Miss Spencer?" the sergeant asked.

Leo rubbed her smarting shoulder, grateful the brick had hit her there and not on the head.

"I'll be fine," she answered. "I'm relieved you got my note."

"From the looks of how we found you, so am I," he said with a chastising raise of his eyebrow.

"I don't know what this woman has told you, but I am innocent," Mrs. Gleason stated, eyeing Constable Drake with wariness as he stood ready to apprehend her.

"She is selling opium to her customers in marked vases, urns, and other housewares," Connor explained. "Her former employee, Lydia Hailson, discovered the operation, and when she did, she was killed."

"Mrs. Gleason knows who killed her—a Spitalfields Angel," Leo added.

There were many members of that particular criminal gang in London, and Leo's experience with them so far had been harrowing. Months ago, Jasper had been severely beaten by a group of Angels as a warning to him to stop investigating the bombing outside Scotland Yard that had killed Police Constable John Lloyd. But Mr. Bloom had wanted to know who had stolen his product and killed his men, and now, he would have his answer.

However, as Lydia had, Leo kept Eddie Bloom's name to herself.

"That is a ridiculous accusation." Mrs. Gleason tried to force a laugh, but it was strained and shrill.

"Then why did I find you just now, prepared to bludgeon Miss Spencer?" Sergeant Lewis asked.

The woman scoffed and stammered the beginnings of an excuse. But another uniformed constable, this one unfamiliar to Leo, joined Connor in the yard. In one hand, he held the same jade urn that the salesclerk had tried to sell them earlier, and in his other was a small, brown-paper-wrapped parcel.

"Sir, it's as you said," the constable announced. "Found this under a false bottom inside the urn."

He handed the parcel to Sergeant Lewis, who tore at the brown paper to reveal a tin with a hinged lid. Opening it revealed at least a dozen small, white-coated pills. He closed the lid again.

"Mrs. Gleason, you'll come with me to Scotland Yard. I have questions for you," the sergeant said, then gestured to Constable Drake to cuff her wrists. He ordered the second constable to go through the store and find all the other items tagged with a fleur-de-lis.

By then, a handful of employees, both storeroom laborers and uniformed sales assistants, had gathered in the yard. Mr. Gleason joined them, his shock apparent as he saw his wife in handcuffs.

"What is the meaning of this, officers? Clara, what are they accusing you of?"

Mrs. Gleason did not answer her husband or even look at him as Constable Drake led her down the alley toward Oxford Street. It would be a spectacle to be led out onto such a popular street in handcuffs and then placed into a police wagon.

"Officer! I demand to know what is happening," Mr. Gleason shouted at Sergeant Lewis. But Lewis let him stew a moment.

"Miss Spencer," he said as he passed her on his way to

meet the store owner. "Good work. I'll take things from here but do come to the Yard to give a full account as soon as you can."

She caught the twitch of a smile as he went to meet the red-faced Mr. Gleason. Leo rubbed her shoulder lightly. Pleased as she was by the sergeant's praise, it was difficult for her to be too upset by the small injury.

"Are you badly hurt?" Connor asked as he reached her, but he wasn't so much concerned as he was indignant. "You should not have chased after Mrs. Gleason the way you did. It was reckless. What if I hadn't come across the sergeant and his constable as soon as I reached the front doors of the store?"

"I don't really think she would have bludgeoned me," she replied, trying to soothe him. "She's complicit, but she isn't a murderer."

"Leo!" Dita elbowed her way through the gathering employees in the yard, her jaw loose with shock as she stared down the alley. "Tell me you haven't had Mrs. Gleason *arrested*?"

"I'm sorry, Dita," she said. "I know she is your client, but she's involved in drug smuggling and with Lydia Hailson's murder."

Dita groaned as she joined Leo and Connor. "I suppose those things are somewhat more important than adultery," she conceded, then sighed heavily. "Mr. Castelan is going to be livid."

Connor blinked in surprise as he stared at Dita. Leo realized the two had not yet met and introduced them. "Connor, this is my good friend, Nivedita Brooks. She's working for Castelan Private Inquiries. Dita, this is Mr. Connor Quinn, the assistant coroner at the morgue."

Dita's disappointment in the sudden end to her undercover work transformed to regret, her dark brown eyes filling with sympathy. "You had been Miss Hailson's beau. Leo told me. I hope you don't mind."

Connor, with his bowler in hand, raked his fingers through his already mussed strands of dark hair. "Not at all, Miss Brooks. Still, I can't help but feel it's all so meaningless and pitiful. Lydia was truly killed over a drug smuggling operation?"

Leo understood his grappling sense of futility. Lydia ought to have had decades more to live. Resting a hand gently on his shoulder, Leo replied, "It appears that way. I'm sorry, Connor."

He nodded. "At least now, we know."

After another moment, in which none of them knew what more to say, Dita untied the knot at the back of her pinafore. She slipped it off and tossed it on a nearby crate. "I don't know about you two, but I think I need a pint before I return to Mr. Castelan and update him. And it looks like I'm out of a job at Gleason's anyhow."

The relief Leo felt that Dita would no longer be attempting to lure Mr. Gleason into some sordid rendezvous nearly had her agreeing. But she did want to get to the Yard to give her account of the events, and she wished to see if Jasper had returned from Harrow. They had left off on a sour note the night before, and the more time that passed before they addressed it, the more difficult she worried it would be.

Leo apologized for having to turn down Dita's invitation, but to her surprise, Connor felt differently. He held out his elbow to Dita.

"I think I could do with a drink too," he said, "if you wouldn't mind my company?"

She gave him the once-over again, as if inspecting him for some fault, but Leo had seen that same glint in her eyes many times before.

"I suppose that remains to be seen," she teased before taking his arm.

The pair of them waved goodbye to Leo as they set off down the alley, already absorbed in the beginnings of a conversation. She was suddenly relieved that she'd begged off, rather than sit with the pair of them as they became better acquainted.

"Oh, and Leonora," Connor called as he seemed to remember something and turned around. "I won't forget your fee."

"We didn't discuss a fee," she said.

He grinned mischievously, then, his arm still hooked with Dita's, turned and kept walking.

Chapter Eighteen

It was unsettling to be inside Jasper's office at the CID now that it no longer belonged to him. It was Sergeant Lewis's hat and coat hanging on the stand, and his half-eaten lunch languishing on the desk. Boxes of casework and evidence had piled up next to the desk, as well as in the chair that Jasper had always kept empty. As Leo paced the small office, she noted another stack of papers on the mirrored stand that Jasper had often used to shave or tidy himself up when he'd been out all night and couldn't make it home before the next workday began.

While she knew Sergeant Lewis had only been placed into this office temporarily while Jasper was in Liverpool, she did wonder how the sergeant would feel when he was shuffled back to his desk on the department floor—if he even had a desk to return to. When Leo arrived, there had been a few new faces in the department, all of whom were younger men who peered at her quizzically as Constable Wiley reluctantly led her to Lewis's office.

The front desk officer had not missed her over the last few months, if his curling lip when she'd first approached was any indication. He'd closed her in the office and told her to wait. At least fifteen minutes had passed since then, and Leo began to question if the constable had even told Sergeant Lewis of her arrival. Or perhaps the constable was having a good chuckle at her expense and hoping she'd come storming out in a fit of temper.

Well, she wouldn't give him that.

Leo continued to pace the office, impatient and bored. Outside, evening was falling faster than usual, thanks to a sleety rain. It *tinked* against the window, the sound assuring her that she would become drenched on her walk back to Duke Street. It only darkened her mood and heightened her restlessness.

As she passed the desk, she peered at the side of a box where a small, metal-framed window held a paper placard. The name *Giles Beatty* had been written in ink. It was an evidence box, she knew, and she couldn't help but be curious as to who Giles Beatty was and what he'd done… or what had been done to him.

She started to lift the lid to peek inside but then grimaced and stopped. If Jasper found her peering into an evidence box, he'd be annoyed. If Sergeant Lewis found her doing so, however, his reaction could very well be to throw her out of Scotland Yard for good. Not that she really thought he would go to that extreme…but the truth was, she didn't know the sergeant well enough. It was better for her to be cautious and restrained until she did.

Leo walked around to the chair in front of the desk, where another box and some papers had been stashed. She bent at the hip to read that case placard, but when she did, she immediately forgot the promise she'd just made to herself to behave.

The box of evidence was labeled with Helen Dalton's name.

Leo didn't stop herself from lifting the lid off this box, reasoning that it was *Jasper's* case, not Sergeant Lewis's. Inside, she found several items relating to the case, including those from the scene of Helen's murder. Helen's personal belongings that Leo had set aside at the morgue, including her clothing, boots, and handbag, were tucked next to the peacock statue, which was the suspected murder weapon.

The door to the office opened, but instead of Sergeant Lewis, it was Constable Wiley who entered. He wasn't alone. Frederick Cowper followed him into the office, his hat in his hand and his greatcoat glistening with rain. Wiley screwed his face up in contempt.

"What do you think you're doing? That's off-limits to you."

Quickly, Leo replaced the lid. Not because the constable had reprimanded her, but because Mr. Cowper's attention had gone straight to the open evidence box. The visual reminders of his niece's murder weren't anything he needed to see.

"Mr. Cowper," she said. "I didn't realize you were still in London."

"Miss Spencer," he replied, greeting her with a distracted nod. "I was waiting for the funeral service to complete the casket I commissioned for Helen. I thought my father would appreciate the Cowper family seal upon the lid." He grimaced at the sorry thought. "My train is due to depart soon, but I wanted to see if I could claim some of Helen's belongings before I leave. The constable thought it would be fine."

Leo slid a disappointed look at Wiley and laid a hand on the lid of the evidence box. "I am sure Inspector Reid will have Mrs. Dalton's possessions sent to Harrow as soon as the case is closed. But as the investigation is still ongoing—"

"I'll ask you not to interfere with official police business, Miss Spencer," Wiley interjected.

She set her shoulders. "I think it is premature to release evidence, Constable Wiley."

His cutting glare was as good as a command for her to shut her mouth.

Mr. Cowper, discomfited by their tense exchange, raised his hands. "If it will be too troublesome, I'll simply wait."

But Wiley wasn't willing to give up, especially if it meant allowing Leo to win this round.

"I'll speak to the Chief Inspector and see what he has to say on the matter," he announced, then left the room in a fine pique of temper.

Mr. Cowper arched a brow in what appeared to be amusement. "I don't think that man is very fond of you."

She sighed heavily. "The feeling is mutual."

He came toward the chair, gesturing toward the evidence box with his hat in his hand. "I was hoping that Helen's brooch might be in there. It's a family piece, and I know Nadia will wish to have it."

"Helen wasn't wearing a brooch," Leo said.

There had been no brooch when she'd viewed the body, nor when she'd done a quick perusal of the items inside the box. Mr. Cowper, however, didn't appear convinced.

"Are you certain? She always wore it."

"Quite certain. I have a very good memory."

Intrigue brightened his eyes. "Ah yes, I remember now. Nadia mentioned it at dinner, didn't she? A photographic memory."

Leo didn't like to talk about her perfect memory. She never wanted to appear too proud or too strange, and strange was certainly how she'd felt when Nadia Stroud had commented on it at dinner.

"Do you truly remember everything?" Mr. Cowper asked, cocking his head with interest.

"It's difficult to explain," she said, squirming a little. "But for the most part, yes, I remember what I see and read, and much of the time, what I hear. Everything is… just there, in my mind, waiting for me. Like I said, difficult to explain."

Hoping to avoid any further questions, Leo opened the box to perform a search. "I'll look, just in case," she said but hesitated when lifting the lid. "There is blood on some of the items, if you would rather not look in."

He gave a solemn shake of his head. "I'll be fine, Miss Spencer, but thank you for such thoughtfulness."

With him at her side, Leo removed the lid. She checked the neck and bodice of Helen's dress for the brooch, though she already knew it would not be there. She also pushed aside a small stack of handwriting samples, tied together with string, and then Helen's mud-encrusted boots. Every item had been pinned with a small tag, upon which a description had been written.

"I don't see a brooch," Leo said as she moved the dress

to cover the murder weapon, thinking it better that he not view it. Doing so revealed something at the very bottom of the box. A small, ripped scrap of fabric that Leo had not seen before.

She took it up, and her fingers rubbed the soft material, dyed a dark burgundy.

"What do you have there?" Mr. Cowper asked.

"I'm not sure," she murmured. The strip of fabric was narrow, so much so that the small tag pinned to it was nearly equal in size. Leo read the card's writing. "Snagged on broken glass, back door."

As Helen had possessed a key to the house in her handbag, it was left to reason that the killer had smashed some glass in the back door to gain entrance.

Holding the plush fabric between her fingers, her memory worked to remember where she had seen this color and fabric before. The tug of recognition was there. She only needed to concentrate. She closed her eyes.

"What is it you are doing?" Mr. Cowper asked.

Leo opened her eyes and lowered the fabric. "Trying to place where I've seen this material before."

"With your extraordinary memory?" he asked, grin forming. "Any luck?"

"Nothing yet." She placed the fabric back into the box. With some focus, she might be able to come upon an answer, but she was too unsettled by Mr. Cowper's interest in her memory to do so right then. "It will come to me."

Constable Wiley returned then, his usually pale cheeks tinted pink.

"Mr. Cowper, it seems to be the opinion of the Chief Inspector that it would be best for Inspector Reid to send the victim's belongings after the case is closed." He spoke swiftly and quietly, and though he tried, he could not avoid glimpsing Leo's smug grin.

"Constable, thank you. I'm sure that is the best course of action," Mr. Cowper replied.

"And you, Miss Spencer," Wiley said harshly. "You are to return tomorrow to give your accounting of today's events. Chief Inspector's orders."

That was just fine by her. Leo was growing tired of waiting and of Wiley's presence, anyhow.

As Mr. Cowper and Leo left the detective department, he said, "May I escort you to wherever it is you are going?"

"I'm only walking a short distance," she assured him as they passed Constable Woodhouse at the front desk in the lobby. She smiled at the friendly constable, bidding him a good evening, and then she and Mr. Cowper stepped outside into the rain.

"If you are quite certain?" he asked as he signaled a hansom.

"Entirely. Besides, you must need to get to your train."

He tipped the brim of his hat and closed himself into the hansom.

Leo put down her head and started for the morgue. The sleety rain pelted her, and she wished she was not wearing her finest gown and shoes. At least she had a hooded cloak, which she pulled up now to protect herself from the rain.

As she walked swiftly, Leo began to pull up images from the day and night she and Jasper had spent at Cowper Hall. From the first moments of entering the large Tudor home and seeing the Viscount Cowper standing ominously above them at the balustrade, to the will reading in the library, and those who were present. More images flipped forward, each one vivid and detailed, as if she were standing inside each memory again.

The scrap of fabric in the evidence box was small, no larger than the length of her thumb, and no wider either. The soft, plush material was most likely velvet, and the color continued to trouble her. She *knew* she had seen it before. But where?

As she approached the back lane to the morgue, she went through what each member of the Cowper family, as well as the solicitor Mr. Corman, had been wearing at the reading of the will, then later at dinner. The vivid memories shuttled into the front of her mind, distracting her from the poor weather, and Leo saw again each person seated around the dining room table the evening of the destructive storm that had kept her and Jasper from departing Cowper Hall as planned.

Her feet came to a stumbling halt. She took a short, gasping breath as her mind's eye lingered on the picture-perfect memory that had arisen, providing an answer—though little comfort.

Oh, good Lord.

She hurried for the back door to the morgue, her pulse at a full gallop as she realized the enormity of the mistake she'd just made.

Leo was opening the door to the back office when she felt a presence behind her. Before she could turn, a hand shoved hard between her shoulder blades, thrusting her into the darkened morgue.

Chapter Nineteen

The sun had slipped beneath the London skyline, and a cold rain had started to trickle down by the time Jasper left the Perry residence. He'd come into Paddington Station on the afternoon train from Harrow and immediately set out for Portman Square, where Helen Dalton would stay whenever she visited town. He'd wondered if he might meet Sergeant Warnock there, or perhaps Roy Lewis, or whoever had been available when he'd wired the Yard from Harrow Constabulary earlier. But when Jasper arrived on the Perrys' doorstep, he was informed that a sergeant and pair of constables had already come and gone with their quarry.

After a brief conversation with Mr. and Mrs. Perry, Jasper had set out for Scotland Yard. A coating of sleet had started to accumulate on the cobblestones by the time he arrived at Met headquarters wet, cold, and hungry, but he merely doffed his damp hat and overcoat and tossed them onto a chair as he entered the CID. He stalked past Constable Wiley, who'd stood and started to say something, but didn't finish before Jasper went straight into his old office. Lewis wasn't there, but all he needed was an item in the evidence box stored on one of the chairs. He found it and, giving it a cursory look, grinned. It was what he'd hoped for.

He went to meet Detective Sergeant Warnock, who'd stood from his desk when Jasper arrived. The young officer was now waiting by the office door.

"I put the suspect in the interview room. She tried to run, sir, but she didn't get far."

Hearing that she'd tried to escape only bolstered Jasper's good mood. He was now certain of the woman's guilt.

Thanking Warnock, Jasper went to the interview room, which was being guarded by a uniformed constable. Inside, Dora Sweeny sat in a chair, her cuffed wrists resting on the small table. Helen Dalton's maid hitched her chin when she saw him enter and drew her hands into her lap.

He closed the door and looked the woman over. The last time she'd been in that chair, she'd been weeping, her eyes red and swollen in stark anguish. Now, she wore an expression Jasper often saw upon the faces of guilty suspects—defiant righteousness.

"I've been to see the Perrys," he began. "They cannot account for your whereabouts yesterday afternoon and evening. It seems you were out running errands and helping with the arrangements for Mrs. Dalton's return to Harrow until nearly nine o'clock in the evening."

He stayed on his feet, too restless to sit. Miss Sweeny made no reply.

"However, I don't need to question Mr. Dalton or Mr.

Cowper about the help you provided during those hours, because I know that was a lie. You see, Miss Sweeny, as large as the station in Harrow is, and as busy as the stationmaster is there, he is remarkably adept at keeping an eye on who comes and goes from his terminus. You arrived on yesterday's 3:25 train."

The maid stayed stonelike, except for the rapid fluttering of her lashes.

"I presume that after leaving Scotland Yard, you started to think about Stephen Decamp's note to Helen that I showed you earlier, the one asking her to meet at their spot after midnight. You knew they must have gone to London together, and with my interest in Stephen, you must have put together what he'd done. He had every reason to kill your mistress. Every motive, especially with Helen now carrying his baby. Their affair was about to become known to Mr. Dalton, and to the viscount himself. Stephen was sure to lose his position."

Miss Sweeny pressed her lips together tightly, her defiant expression beginning to falter.

"When you arrived at his farm yesterday, you found him soused," Jasper said.

He now knew Stephen had been at Sam Everton's farm the day after Helen's murder, drinking himself into oblivion. The stop in Sudbury along the rail route had set Jasper back more than an hour, but he had a clearer picture of where Stephen had been, and what state he'd been in.

Devastated was the word his former farmhand had used to describe him. And the more Stephen imbibed, the looser his tongue became.

"He welcomed you in. Even tied up his collie for you, because he knew you were afraid of dogs."

Without Nadia Stroud's comment at the uneasy dinner the night of the storm, about Helen's maid being afraid of dogs, Jasper would not have known to connect Miss Sweeny to the tied-up collie.

"What then, Miss Sweeny? Did you encourage Stephen to have a seat at the dining room table, while you poured him another drink?" Jasper had turned over numerous possibilities as he'd traveled from Harrow. "I'm curious, though. Did he already have his revolver with him? In his devastation, maybe he was already leaning toward ending it all."

The maid finally met Jasper's stare. "He shot himself."

"No, he didn't. Perhaps he would have, but you couldn't risk that he'd back down, could you?" He pulled from his coat pocket the note that had been left on Stephen's table, in front of his body. Then, he laid out the note Stephen had sent to Helen the night of the storm.

"I'll have a graphologist compare these writing samples, of course, but have a look," he urged, taking the seat across from her. He touched the tips of the two Ws in the suicide note.

"There is a slight, fanciful tilt of the middle arch of the Ws in this note. *I cannot live with what I've done.*" He then tapped the W in the note delivered to Helen the night of the storm, asking her to *wait until midnight*. "There is no such tilt of the middle arch here."

She huffed a sound that Jasper took for amusement. "People do not always form their letters the same way every time, especially when someone is drunk as a wheelbarrow."

He took from his pocket the handwriting sample Dora herself had given just after Helen's body was found and set that one out for her as well. He tapped the W in her surname and allowed her a moment to see the same fanciful tilt of the middle arch. Her false bravado crashed.

"I believe a graphologist would agree that you authored the suicide note, Miss Sweeny. So, stop wasting my time, and let's get to the reason why you did it."

He waited as she visibly calculated what to do next. She had been seen in Harrow the day of Stephen's death, and she'd lied about her whereabouts. The handwriting samples would only be another strike against her in a court of law. Murder was murder, and if she confessed, she would either be imprisoned for a great many years, or she would face execution. Though clemency was more often granted to women than it was to men.

"Cooperate, Miss Sweeny, and I will do what I can to see that you do not hang."

At the flaring of her eyes, he knew he had her.

"She trusted him," the maid said softly. As she kept speaking, her voice began to climb. "My lady, she trusted him, and he killed her. He killed the babe inside her too. And he lied. All these years, he lied and tricked her into thinking he was a good man, but Stephen Decamp was nothing but a *murderer*."

"He lied and tricked her all these years?" Jasper's attention caught on that phrasing. "How do you mean?"

Miss Sweeny's chin lifted, and she looked to be reconsidering her decision to speak.

"Cooperation is your best chance, Miss Sweeny," he reminded her. "How did he lie and trick Helen all these years?"

The maid sighed in resignation. "The tear catcher."

Jasper braced his arms on the table. "What do you know of it?"

He'd made no mention of the trinket found in Helen's hair to the maid. But then, he remembered what Ursula had said earlier in the butler's pantry at Cowper Hall. "You were dismissed from Helen's room when Ursula brought up the letter from Mrs. Stroud to myself and Miss Spencer. But you listened at your mistress's door, didn't you? You heard Ursula tell Helen about the small glass vial found in Theodore's hand after his death."

But there had been no mention of it being a tear catcher.

Which meant Dora Sweeny had already known of it.

"You were Helen's maid before she married. Nadia informed me that Helen had given it to someone. A man. Did Helen tell you that she'd given it to Stephen?"

"She never said his name, but I knew it was him," the maid answered. "My lady always wore the necklace strung with that little tear catcher, and when it disappeared from her jewelry box, I feared I'd be accused of taking it. But then she told me she'd given it away."

"How do you know she gave it to Stephen?"

Miss Sweeny lifted a shoulder. "She said she'd given it to a man she shouldn't have. A man that society would never approve of."

The viscount certainly wouldn't have approved of Stephen. Society, too, would have put Helen and the butler's son through the wringer.

"And when you heard Theodore was found with the tear catcher in his hand, you presumed *Stephen* was involved," Jasper said.

The maid was solemn, but there was also an undercurrent of anger she couldn't suppress. "Stephen would meet my lady on the roof of the Craven Hill house," she said, echoing what Nadia had revealed earlier in the butler's pantry at Cowper Hall. "I don't know how he and Master Teddy found themselves on the roof that night, but if Stephen had the tear catcher, and they struggled…"

"The boy might have grappled with Stephen and grabbed hold of the tear catcher before being pushed," Jasper finished theorizing for her. But that was all it was. A theory. And one the maid had not properly thought out.

"Explain to me then, why Helen would have asked Stephen to take her to London. If she suspected the small glass tube her mother wrote about was her old tear catcher, and Helen knew Stephen was the last one to possess it, why would she involve him?"

Miss Sweeny blinked. "Maybe she didn't tell him what it was she was after. I don't know, and neither do I care. Stephen killed her when she found out he'd pushed Master Teddy. He took my lady and her babe from me, and he deserved what he got!"

Jasper sat back in his chair and crossed his arms, contemplating the maid's version of events. Clearly, she'd been devoted to Helen. So much so that she would commit murder to avenge her. He wondered if Helen would have done the same for her, had their roles been reversed, and found he could not believe she would have.

"Did Stephen confess before you shot him?"

This question seemed to startle her, and the maid scowled. "He said it was his fault. He kept mumbling about her body and all the blood, and how he just left her there. It was a confession."

"Or you jumped to the wrong conclusion without proper evidence," Jasper said. "Helen told you she gave away her tear catcher, but she never named Stephen specifically. I'm sorry, Miss Sweeny, but if she held any suspicion at all that he might have had a role in Theodore's death, it simply doesn't add up that she would have arranged to meet him the night of the storm, let alone go with him to the Craven Hill house."

Jasper got to his feet as another theory took shape. "However, if she'd given the tear catcher to another man, and she learned *that* man might have grappled with Theodore before his fall..." He paced toward the door, his mind working quickly as he mused aloud, "What if she wasn't rushing to London to beat Leo and me to the hidden trinket, but someone else? Someone who knew that trinket would connect them to the boy's fall."

Miss Sweeny slammed her iron-cuffed wrists against the table. "No! It was Stephen. It had to have been. Before she married, my lady wasn't out in society enough to have met any other unsuitable men. She stayed at home, she and Miss Stroud and Mr. Cowper and Stephen."

"You said Stephen and Frederick Cowper had a falling out," Jasper reminded her.

"They did," she said.

"When?"

She lifted her chained hands and rubbed her temples in frustration. "I don't know exactly. Everything unraveled between everyone after Master Teddy died. I think it was around that same time."

Jasper had paced to the door. Now, he held still. The missing phaeton and horse from Cowper Hall had plagued him, especially after finding Stephen's muddied gig and horse at his farm. Sam Everton had confirmed Stephen had taken Helen to London, too.

So that meant someone else had taken the phaeton and horse from the viscount's stables. Someone who would have had ready access to them. Someone who would have wanted to reach that little glass tube hidden under a floorboard before anyone else.

Someone who had known about Francine Stroud's letter and what she'd found in Teddy's hand.

"Inspector?" the maid queried. He'd been silent too long.

Her voice snapped him out of his trancelike focus, and he wrenched the door open. Sergeant Warnock was still at his desk, though the rest of the department had thinned out. Constable Wiley remained, along with Price and another newer constable that must have been hired while Jasper was in Liverpool.

"Where is Lewis?" he asked sharply.

Warnock grimaced and shot a glance toward Chief Inspector Coughlan's office. The door was closed, but the Irishman's grumbling voice could still be heard.

"He's in with the chief," Warnock said. "Coughlan's none too pleased to hear Miss Spencer was involved in another arrest."

Jasper stilled. "What arrest?"

The sergeant's lips gaped like a landed fish. "I thought you knew, sir. Mrs. Gleason from Gleason's Department Store. Some kind of opium smuggling ring."

"*Opium?*" Christ. What in hell had happened since the previous evening? He held up his hand. "Never mind. Warnock, Price," he said. "You're both with me. Wiley, charge Miss Sweeny with the murder of Stephen Decamp. She has confessed."

Wiley hoisted himself up from his chair, looking peeved to be given an order this late in the evening. Especially as there would be paperwork to complete and arrangements to be made to hold the prisoner for the night.

Warnock and Price, however, jumped to their feet, and each reached for their coat and hat.

"Where are we going, sir?" Price asked.

"To the hotel at Paddington Station," Jasper replied, reaching for his own still-damp coat and bowler. "If Frederick Cowper is still there, I need to speak to him."

"Cowper?" Wiley asked, pausing from his walk toward the interview room. "He was here earlier."

Jasper's heels dragged to a stop as he was putting on his coat. "When? What did he want?"

"A half hour ago, or so. He was leaving London and wanted some things belonging to his cousin, the Dalton victim."

"What things?"

"Didn't say. Of course, I told him we couldn't release any evidence until the case is closed," he said, puffing up his chest with a look of superiority. "And I told Miss Spencer to quit going through the box, too."

Jasper had started away again, but at the mention of Leo, he stopped and stared at the constable. "Miss Spencer was here as well?"

Wiley snorted derisively. "Aye, she said she was here to give her report to Sergeant Lewis about the arrest of that department store owner. But instead, Mr. Cowper and I found her going through the evidence box for the Dalton murder. Can't keep her bloody beak out of police business, that woman."

Jasper clenched his hands into fists at his side. "When did she leave?"

"Same time as Mr. Cowper."

His pulse skipped. "They left together?"

At Wiley's nod, he turned and started for the corridor. On the face of it, Leo and Frederick's departure together might have meant nothing. But if Frederick had been looking for a piece of evidence, and he'd found Leo going through the box… Jasper's worry might have been unfounded, but by the time he reached Constable Woodhouse, he knew he couldn't set it aside.

"Woodhouse," he said, approaching the reception desk. The constable was donning his boiled wool coat as he prepared to leave for the evening. "Did you see Miss Spencer go out?"

"Not long before you arrived, Inspector," he answered with a nod.

"And was a man with her?"

Another nod. "A gent. He offered to escort her to where she was going. She declined, saying it was but a short walk."

Again, on its surface, the overheard exchange didn't sound overtly alarming. But Frederick Cowper was the only other person who had known about Francine's letter. Ursula had confessed to him in the billiards room, stoking his anger…or had it been panic?

"Did she say where she was going?" Jasper asked. At the shake of the constable's head, indecision stole through him. Her home on Duke Street was a short walk from the Yard. But so was the morgue.

As he, Warnock, and Price exited through the back door into the courtyard behind headquarters, he tried to determine where Leo might have gone.

"Sir?" Warnock said. "Shall I get a cab for us?"

Jasper knew he should go to Paddington Station, on the chance that Frederick's train had not yet left. But he could not shake the suspicion that Leo was in trouble.

"Yes," Jasper said, making his decision. "Take Price and go to Paddington Station. If you find Mr. Cowper, take him into custody and bring him back here."

Warnock accepted the task with alacrity, and he and Price set off toward the line of carriages for hire.

Jasper pulled the brim of his hat down against the rain and set off in the direction he hoped Leo had gone.

Chapter Twenty

It was pure good fortune that Leo did not topple to the office floor when she was shoved from behind. Had she fallen, she had little doubt that her attacker would have pounced. Instead, she caught herself by grasping the corner of a low bookshelf next to the door and whirled to the side, out of reach.

The back door slammed shut, severing the minuscule amount of light that had been coming in from outside. Connor had not yet returned from his pint with Dita, and so, not a single bracket gasolier or lamp was lit, leaving the office drenched in darkness.

But even blind, Leo knew who had shoved her from behind.

"You recognized the fabric, didn't you, Mr. Cowper?" she said, chilled air filling her lungs as she dragged in breath.

She backed up toward her desk, where she knew she would find a paper knife in the drawer. Besides the scalpels stored safely away in the postmortem room, it was the sharpest object she could think of.

Ahead of her, she saw the barest slip of movement through the dark.

"You did not notice the tear along your jacket's cuff when you arrived to breakfast the morning after the storm," she said. Even Leo had not noticed it at the time, but she'd been able to peruse the details her memory had stored of their momentary meeting.

In that one image, she had noticed things she'd not paid attention to previously: a footman, lifting a silver cloche cover to reveal a plate of sausages for the viscount; the scowl upon the viscount's lips when he saw Jasper and Leo leaving the dining room; and the way Frederick had been straightening the cuffs of his jacket when he'd nearly collided with them in the doorway.

"My guess is that you didn't realize you'd torn your cuff at all until I picked up that scrap of fabric in the evidence box," she added. Belatedly, she realized the look that had filled Frederick's eyes when he'd seen it had not been one of confusion, but fear.

Her hip brushed the edge of the desk, and her hand fumbled toward the knob of the center drawer.

"This gives me no pleasure, Miss Spencer," the viscount's heir replied, and with a rush of alarm skittering through her limbs, Leo realized he'd nearly reached the desk, too. "I wish you did not possess the sort of memory you do."

She certainly wished that Nadia had kept her mouth shut about it.

Leo opened the desk drawer and, knowing precisely where the paper knife was, gripped its ebony handle. She held it before her, wishing her vision would hurry up and adjust to the dark.

"*You* put your fist through the pane of glass at the Craven Hill house," she said, backing up again, the blade she used to open letters poised before her. "You found Helen in the upstairs bedroom, and you killed her."

But why? And what could he have possibly wanted with Helen's tear catcher?

"Except for you, no one can place me there," he said, his voice oddly calm.

"When matched to your torn sleeve, that scrap of fabric will," she replied.

"Not if the jacket burns as soon as I return to Harrow." A shape moved to her right—and Leo's skin jumped as the loud, yowling hiss of a cat rent the air.

Mr. Cowper had trodden upon Tibia's tail in the dark, she realized. Using the moment of distraction, Leo rushed for the door to the back lane. She flung it open and was one foot outside when a hand grabbed her arm and hauled her back into the office. This time, Mr. Cowper's thrust succeeded in throwing her to the floor, but when Leo rolled onto her back and saw the black stamp of his figure looming over her, she didn't hesitate—she plunged the paper knife's blade into the body part closest to her: his calf.

He cried out and staggered away, while Leo bounded to her feet and ran again, this time toward the postmortem room door. She punted it open, but the wretched man again caught her, slamming into her back and wrapping his arms around her. He propelled them both into an unoccupied autopsy table. With the wheels locked, the table only screeched across the floor, but the edge of it rammed painfully into Leo's ribs.

She'd kept hold of the paper knife, rather than leave it lodged in his leg, but now, Frederick's hand smashed hers against the table once, twice, until pain radiated through the bones of her wrist and caused her fingers to open involuntarily. He wrenched the paper knife from her and, pinning her arms with his, brought the flat side of the blade against her collarbone. The pointed tip aligned with the base of her neck.

Frederick held her in a merciless squeeze, and suddenly, they were both still. His heaving breaths gusted against her ear, his face cradled by the curve of her neck.

"I didn't expect Helen to be there," he huffed, his breath hot against her skin. Leo's stomach swirled with both disgust and fear. He aimed to kill her, just as he'd killed Helen.

"You both wanted the tear catcher," she said, her own breaths fast and panicked. "But why?"

How had Frederick known where it was? And why would he have rushed there, just as Helen had, to find it?

"Because it would implicate him in Theodore Stroud's murder."

The stalwart voice emanated from across the post-mortem room, and an overwhelming surge of relief throbbed through Leo, from her chest to her limbs.

Tears pricked her eyes as the gasoliers overhead rushed with flames. The sudden light brought the room—and Jasper—into view. He stood within the office entrance, his police-issued revolver in his hand, though not raised. He would not aim his weapon at her, she knew. His eyes assessed Leo, his mouth taut with fury as he saw the paper knife's blade at her throat.

"When I asked why you had scolded Ursula outside the billiards room, you claimed that she was being a gossip," he began. "But it was more than that, wasn't it? The maid had confessed what she'd read in Francine Stroud's letter. That Theodore was found dead with a glass vial clutched in his hand." Jasper took slow strides into the room, his grip on his revolver firm. "Ursula explained that she'd told Helen of the letter's contents, and so you knew that your niece would suspect the trinket was, in fact, her tear catcher." Jasper held still. "The very one she had given to you shortly before her brother's fall."

Over her pounding heart and racing pulse, Leo tried to follow what Jasper was saying. Helen's tear catcher had been in *Frederick's* possession at the time of Teddy Stroud's death.

"You pushed Teddy," Leo said, her voice a rasp thanks to the man's grasp around her ribs.

"You were on the roof the night of his fall," Jasper added. "You were wearing the tear catcher, and in your struggle with him, he ripped it free from your neck."

Leo's ribs already ached from Frederick's clamped arms, but now he constricted them tighter. It forced even more air from her lungs and an involuntary yelp from her throat.

"Release her," Jasper ordered, his eyes bobbing to the paper knife. "There is no reason to silence Miss Spencer any longer, Mr. Cowper. You've been found out."

Frederick didn't obey and, instead, dragged Leo back several steps toward the lobby.

"Why were you on the roof that night?" Jasper asked, stalking toward them. "What did Theodore see?"

"He shouldn't have been up there." Frederick's blunt voice rumbled against Leo's eardrum.

"The roof was where Helen and Stephen Decamp would meet," Jasper said. "You knew as much, I presume. It was why you were there. To spy on them."

Though the postmortem room was icebox-cold, a fine perspiration had built up on Leo's chest and back. Her breathing turned ragged as she tried to wriggle free from Frederick's hold. The tip of the paper knife poked her skin, and she went still again.

"I couldn't be with her," Frederick whispered, the words a strident whine, as though squeezed by emotion. "But Stephen could. I knew it was wrong, but it was the closest I could come to having her for myself."

He'd wanted to watch Helen and Stephen together. Leo's stomach pitched.

"Helen knew how you felt," Jasper said. "She'd given you her tear catcher as a token of sorts."

"She felt the same," he said, shaking now. With Leo's back sealed against his body, the tremors vibrated through her as if they were her own. She swallowed, the blade pressing harder against her skin now, aligning with her trachea.

They'd been so close in age, more like cousins or friends than uncle and niece. Understanding seeped through Leo, oily and cold, at what must have happened on that roof.

"Teddy found you watching them," she surmised.

"He couldn't understand," Frederick admitted. "And he

wouldn't shut up. He was whispering question after question, but he was getting louder and…"

"And you had to silence him, so he wouldn't give you away," Jasper said. "And when Helen learned her mother had found a glass vial that had belonged to her in Theodore's dead clasp, she went to Craven Hill, to the spot where her mother had hidden it, to reclaim it."

Jasper took another step toward them, but Frederick dragged Leo closer to the lobby door. She took a shaking breath as Jasper held his free hand up, palm shown, as if to calm Frederick.

"Had I or Miss Spencer found the trinket, as Francine wanted, we'd surely ask questions," he said. "Helen had been on the roof that night, as had Stephen, and yet neither of them had ever admitted to being there. She knew we would suspect them. Telling us that she'd given you the tear catcher would sound desperate, and besides, you could have easily denied it."

"But you couldn't allow Helen to even try to accuse you," Leo said, her peripheral vision focusing on an autopsy table they were nearing, topped by the corpse of a sheeted man. "So, you took the phaeton and horse from your father's stables and went to London, not knowing Helen would already be there."

And when she confronted him, he'd silenced her, just as he had Teddy.

"Enough," he hissed in her ear. "I'm taking Miss Spencer with me. Don't follow, Inspector, or you know what will happen."

"You are going to release her now," Jasper replied. "And I will give you a ten-second head start. It is a generous offer, Mr. Cowper; I suggest you take it."

With ten seconds to flee before being pursued, Frederick could disappear into the bustle of Trafalgar Square. At night and in the rain, the poor light would make it difficult for Jasper to hunt him. He might never return to Harrow and his family; he might be lost forever.

Leo knew what she risked, but she also felt braver with Jasper so close.

As Frederick dragged them closer to the lobby door, the occupied autopsy table she'd been eyeing came within reach—of her legs, at least. Burying her fear, Leo raised her right leg, planted her foot against the table's leg, and shoved hard against it. The sudden motion drove her back, even harder against Frederick's torso, and as it caught him off guard, it also unbalanced him.

The postmortem room erupted with sound as the autopsy table clattered to the floor, and Frederick roughly tossed Leo to the side. She landed on the floor, breath driven from her lungs and her vision whirling. But she still saw Frederick tearing through the lobby door as he fled.

Jasper was crouching at her side in a blink. "Are you injured? Christ, Leo." He touched her chin to lift it, and pain flared along the left side of her neck. "You're bleeding."

She reached for the spot and felt the unmistakable viscosity of blood. There wasn't a profuse amount, however, and Frederick was getting away.

She waved Jasper off. "It isn't dire. Go, hurry!"

He straightened and disappeared through the lobby door without another moment's hesitation. Leo's vision swam as she got to her feet and followed Jasper, her legs feeling more like two columns of warmed jelly than anything made of bone, muscle, and tendon. She opened a linen cupboard in the postmortem room and, with trembling hands, snatched out a clean towel. Pressing it to her wound to staunch the bleeding, she hurried into the lobby. The door to Spring Street was wide-open, and outside, Jasper's shouts for Frederick to stop echoed. She reached the front step in time to see their two darkened figures rushing toward Trafalgar Square.

"Leo, what is happening?"

She spun around at the sound of Dita's voice and, in the dim light streaming from lampposts, saw her friend and Connor Quinn approaching the morgue.

Connor increased his pace when he saw the linen she held pressed to her neck. "Have you been hurt?"

"I don't think the cut is very deep," Leo answered. "Can you summon a constable? Jasper is—"

"Watch out!" The bellowing cry came from the terminus of Spring Street, toward which Frederick Cowper and Jasper had been running.

Leo spun back around in time to see a fast-moving, horse-drawn carriage collide with a man in the street. Her heart stuttered to a stop as the viscount's son disappeared beneath the carriage's wheels.

Chapter Twenty-One

A cacophony of shouting, whinnying horses, and the stricken cries of onlookers swirled around Jasper as he crouched to see beneath the carriage where Frederick now lay, sprawled on the cobblestones. The next minute was a blur of commotion as Jasper directed the driver to carefully pull forward so that they could access Frederick's body.

He hoped like hell the man wasn't dead. He wanted to arrest the bastard, not see him put in the ground before a conviction could be levied.

"Stand back, now, all of you!" A few constables on foot patrol had run to the scene and now held out their arms to keep back a surging crowd of gawkers.

Once he was able, Jasper knelt next to Frederick's unmoving body and pressed his fingers against his neck. He closed his eyes and concentrated, desperate to feel a pulse. *There it was*—a weak, thready throb against the pads of his fingertips.

"Oh, good heavens!" a familiar voice cried out.

Jasper glanced over his shoulder to find Nivedita Brooks being blocked by a constable's outstretched arm.

"Let her through," Jasper commanded. "Constable, fetch a wagon to transport this man to St. Thomas's Hospital. Hurry!"

The officer darted away toward the bustling Trafalgar Square, blowing sharply on his police whistle. Jasper stood straight to meet Miss Brooks as she inched forward hesitantly. She turned her face away from the broken angles of the viscount's son's legs and the bloody mess of his head.

"Where is Leo?" Jasper asked, his concern mounting. He'd expected her to join him shortly after he'd gone in pursuit of Frederick.

"She's with Mr. Quinn," Miss Brooks answered. "He brought her into the morgue to look at the wound on her neck. He wanted to be sure a vein hadn't been nicked."

"A *vein?*" Jasper had seen the blood dribbling from the slice to Leo's neck, but she'd assured him she was fine. He started away from Frederick's sprawled form, only wanting to be at Leo's side.

Miss Brooks held up her hands to stop him. "Leo says she will meet you at the hospital. If—" Her lashes fluttered rapidly as she tried to look toward Frederick Cowper but couldn't quite succeed. "If he is still alive?"

"He is, though barely." *And probably not for much longer.* Jasper cursed under his breath. As the viscount's heir had confessed to two murders, Jasper had a duty to stay with him, even if he lay half dead in the street.

"Fine," Jasper finally relented. "Just make sure Quinn takes care of her. If he doesn't, he'll have me to answer to."

With a nod, Miss Brooks turned to scurry away from the gruesome scene.

A paraffin lamp guttered in the corridor outside a surgery theatre at St. Thomas's Hospital. Jasper paced the tiled floor, his impatience—and trepidation—climbing. Frederick Cowper had been rushed inside more than a half hour ago. Since then, a few nurses had come out of the surgery, blood smeared over their pinafores, but none had answered his inquiries as to whether the patient would live or die.

Jasper took his watch from his waistcoat pocket, and when he read the time, his nerves crackled. Where the devil was Leo? She was supposed to have met him here. Unless something had happened. Had Quinn met with some complication while assessing her neck wound? Jasper whisked off his hat and raked his hand roughly through his hair.

Footsteps echoed down the corridor. He whirled away from the closed surgery doors, only wanting to see one person.

"Inspector Reid." Jasper masked his disappointment at finding Sergeant Warnock before him. "A reply telegram has come from Harrow. Viscount Cowper is on his way."

Jasper had directed a constable to Scotland Yard earlier, to send word to Cowper Fields about Frederick's accident. He did not look forward to explaining to Lord Cowper what had happened to his heir, or what Frederick had done to his own nephew and niece. But then, it was possible the viscount may have already suspected.

Francine Stroud may have as well, considering she had not welcomed either her father or her brother to the reading of the will.

"Thank you, Warnock," Jasper replied. "Have you heard anything regarding Miss Spencer?"

The young sergeant crinkled his forehead. "I just saw Mr. Quinn in the lobby. He informed me that Miss Spencer is with a surgeon."

"A surgeon?" Ice, followed by heat, flushed through Jasper's limbs.

"Yes, sir, that is what he said—"

"Stay here," Jasper ordered and then started at full speed toward the doors at the end of the surgery corridor. He burst through them into another corridor, where he stopped the first doctor he saw.

"Leonora Spencer," he barked. "She is here seeing a surgeon. Where can I find her?"

The startled doctor adjusted his spectacles. "I do not know, sir. You'll have to inquire with the admitting nurse."

The doctor continued on his way, and with escalating irritation, Jasper stopped three more nurses before he finally got an answer: Leonora Spencer was in Room 12 on the next floor up. He dashed there, heart racing, and when he finally came upon the closed, white-painted door, he didn't bother to knock.

He burst into the pocket-sized room, and Leo, reclining in the narrow hospital bed, vaulted upright.

"Jasper!" She clutched at her chest. "You startled me. Whatever is the matter?"

He took in the sight of her—her neck wrapped in linen gauze, the collar of her white blouse stained with blood—

as he strode to the bedside.

"Warnock told me you were in with a surgeon," he said, his thudding pulse still sounding in his ears.

"I was," she replied. "Connor wanted a second opinion on the sutures he'd placed in the wound to be sure all was well. I told him it wasn't necessary, but when Dita relayed your warning, he was quite intimidated."

"My warning?"

Leo smirked. "The one in which you threatened that should anything happen to me he would have to answer to you."

"Ah. That warning." He felt a bit sheepish now, but seeing her smile melted some of the tension from his body. Jasper sat in the wooden chair next to the bed. "So, you're going to be all right?"

She leaned forward and reached for his hand. "I am. The cut from the paper knife was deep enough to require several sutures, but Connor said it missed the external jugular vein by a good two millimeters."

Hell. "That's a fraction of an inch, Leo."

"I know what two millimeters is," she replied tartly.

"It was too close."

She didn't argue with him, likely because she knew he was correct.

Thank God he'd listened to his intuition earlier. Had he not decided to check in at the morgue rather than go to Duke Street, or even Paddington Station with Warnock and Price, Leo would have been killed. Frederick Cowper had likely been but a few moments away from slitting her throat with that paper knife when Jasper had come upon the open back door to the morgue. The tumult inside had reached his ears, and he'd drawn his Webley. But of course, he had been unable to use it with the bastard using Leo as a shield.

His thumb brushed over her knuckles, her palm dry and cool in his.

"Tell me what you need," he said. "Are you in any pain? I'll fetch the doctor."

Leo tensed her fingers around his. "I'm perfectly fine. I'm only waiting for the doctor to officially discharge me."

It wasn't often that Jasper was overcome with emotion, but in that moment, he let go of restraint. He gathered her hand and lifted it to his mouth, pressing his lips against her knuckles. His eyes locked on hers, as he whispered against her skin, "I keep picturing Frederick with that knife to your throat. You shouldn't have been in that position. I cannot lose you, Leo."

She took a breath, her lips quivering and eyes softening. "You aren't going to."

He nodded, though he knew neither of them had any control over such a thing. Fortune and circumstance too often outmaneuvered intention. But to dwell on it wouldn't do either of them any good.

"How is Mr. Cowper?" she asked hesitantly.

Jasper lowered her hand but kept it in his. "He was taken into surgery, but his condition is grim."

"He won't live?"

"If he does, it will only be to hang," Jasper replied, knowing he sounded harsh but also not caring at all. The man was a murderer, not to mention his twisted feelings for his own blood relation.

"Mr. Cowper must have taken the phaeton and horse from the stables that night," Leo said. It brought Jasper a bit of comfort to hear her discussing the case. It was a bit of normalcy and proof that she was, as she claimed, perfectly fine.

"He was back by breakfast," Jasper nodded. "But by then, the stable hands were awake. He hadn't wanted to give away that he'd been out overnight."

"You think he stashed the horse and phaeton on the property somewhere?" Leo asked. Then, her eyes opening wider with zeal, she added, "One of the unused outbuildings, like the barn where Helen and Stephen Decamp would meet."

Jasper had considered that too and would have Constable Wiggins conduct a search. "He might have turned the horse loose or, if he was smart, exchanged it for another either in London or on the road back to Harrow."

There were any number of livery stables along the route where he might have done so.

"Has Stephen Decamp been found yet?" Leo asked.

Jasper frowned and explained what he'd discovered at Stephen's home, as well as the person he'd placed under arrest for the crime.

"Helen's maid staged it to appear to be a suicide?" Leo asked.

"Not very well. The crime scene looked off," he said, thinking of how he'd questioned the positioning of the body at the table. "It would have been good to have you there to lend your opinion on the matter."

Although pleasure lit her eyes, she shrugged lightly. "You didn't need my opinion. You figured it out."

"Yes, that is true," Jasper assented. "But I found that I missed figuring it out with you by my side. If that makes any sense."

A bashful grin bowed Leo's lips and grew until it was a full, unabashed smile. "It does. And in a way, we did solve Teddy and Helen's murders together during the confrontation with Mr. Cowper at the morgue."

The memory of that scene would not leave him any time soon, unfortunately.

"Why did Frederick come after you there?" Jasper asked. "Constable Wiley said the two of you were in my office, going through Helen's evidence box. Did you find something?"

"A piece of fabric that had been collected by constables at the Craven Hill house, snagged on the broken glass in the back door," Leo said. "When I saw it in the box, I knew I'd seen the fabric before. I couldn't place it, not right away. But I was a fool and assured Mr. Cowper that my memory would give me the answer."

She exhaled and looked genuinely mortified.

"It did, on my way to the morgue," she went on. "He was wearing a coat made of burgundy velvet at dinner that night and was still wearing it the following morning when Helen was discovered missing. He entered the breakfast room in it, and at the time, I didn't notice his torn sleeve. But when I was going back over my memories, I saw it."

Knowing Leo's perfect memory would sink him, Frederick Cowper had decided, as he had with Teddy and Helen, to silence her.

"I will have his coat collected, if it is still among his possessions at Cowper Hall," Jasper said. If Frederick defied the odds and recovered from his injuries, he would stand trial. The courts would demand irrefutable proof of his guilt.

Leo's eyes shuttered for several moments. Jasper sat straighter, alert.

"Is it your wound? Is something wrong?"

"No, no. I'm just tired. It's to be expected after losing a little blood," she replied, though she did so with her eyes still shut. Jasper grinned at her stubbornness. Giving in to the need to touch her, he gently swept his fingertips over her bandaged neck. She opened her eyes and held his gaze.

"Do you think Mr. Cowper was telling the truth?" Leo asked in a hushed voice. "Did Helen feel the same for him as he did for her?"

Dora Sweeny had told Jasper that her lady had always chosen men who were wrong for her. Stephen had been below her in station, Anthony Dalton had been selfish and unkind, and then, Frederick had been a blood relation.

"I think so," he answered. "She did give him her tear catcher."

"But what significance could that have held?"

A lock of Leo's hair, loose around her shoulders, drew his attention. He reached for it, curling the tress around his finger.

"Your scent," he said. "The perfume you wear. What is it?"

Her lips broke into a bewildered grin. "It's just cheap scent. I hardly ever wear it."

"Honeysuckle and lemon," he said, knowing it even though there was no trace of it now in the air. "It doesn't matter if it is inexpensive. It's what you smell like. And it affects me."

He let the silky curl of her hair unwind from his

finger, and reluctantly, he sat back in the chair as color blossomed in her cheeks.

"Helen's tear catcher was filled with her perfume," she said, understanding. "It...affected him."

Frederick had likely been hidden on the roof, watching and listening to Helen and Stephen make love. As he'd breathed in Helen's scent from the spout of the tear catcher, he must have imagined himself close enough to take Stephen's place. He may even have been taking himself in hand when Teddy Stroud had happened upon him. A greasy wash flooded Jasper's stomach when he thought of the boy's fate. All because one man lusted after a young woman he could not, and should not, ever have.

Silence took over for several moments, until, growing predictably restless, Leo swung her legs over the side of the bed. "Let's find the doctor so I can go home. Claude will be worried about where I am." Jasper rose from the chair as she stood—and caught her by the shoulders as she swayed.

"By any chance, did Quinn give you laudanum before he placed those sutures?" Jasper asked.

Leo pressed her hand to her cheek. "I forgot about the laudanum drops. I wondered why I felt so lightheaded. I thought it was due to some blood loss, not opium."

Jasper hooked her arm firmly in his, happy to have her slight weight leaning against him.

"Speaking of opium, I hear you were involved in an arrest today at Gleason's Department Store. Care to tell me what happened?"

She looked up at him with an expression of innocence. "You might become angry, and I'm not sure I could bear it in my weakened state."

He could only chuckle at her obvious attempt to avoid his question. "I heard it was an opium smuggling operation for their wealthier patrons."

"Yes, and when Lydia Hailson discovered it during the course of her own investigation, she was killed."

"Why was she investigating?" Jasper asked.

Leo pinned her lips together with a distinct expression of guilt. "You'll be angry."

"As you've already said."

"Can I tell you tomorrow?"

He dragged in a long breath, impatient to know what she was hiding. And yet, he also did not want to become angry with her right then. Despite her injury, and the fact that they were in a hospital room, there was a cozy bubble of peace surrounding them that he didn't wish to pierce.

Jasper nodded. "Very well. Tomorrow."

Chapter Twenty-Two

Fourteen typed death certificates sat at Leo's elbow, and the fifteenth was nearly complete. The backlog had grown over the three days she had been forced to stay home and recuperate from her neck wound, and now, over a week later, she was just barely catching up. Jasper, Claude, Dita, and Connor had all banded together to keep her from returning to work. Had the slice from the paper knife been anywhere near fatal, Leo might have understood her need to stay at home to ensure a complete recovery. But as it had only been a minor wound, their overly cautious handling of her had turned Leo into a wretched, belligerent patient.

Bound to the confines of her home, Leo had grown increasingly restless to resume her duties at the Spring Street Morgue. Her worry that Connor couldn't possibly work as swiftly or smoothly without her was dashed when Dita visited on the second day and informed her that a medical student had come to assist him in her absence. But the news agitated Leo and instilled a different worry—this time, of being replaced.

When, on the third day, she entered the kitchen and told her uncle that she was taking herself to the morgue, Claude had merely sighed and asked her to be careful. Walking the short distance to Spring Street had been as uneventful as she'd expected, and Leo had arrived to find that Connor had dismissed the medical student for being sluggish and disorganized. The news had lifted her spirits. As had the letter from Jasper, posted from Liverpool.

He'd left London the morning after the confrontation with Frederick Cowper, and now, in the final stages of wrapping up the counterfeiting case, which included mounds of paperwork and preliminary court appearances for those who'd been arrested and were to stand trial, Jasper wrote that he would be home—for good this time—within a week.

Helen Dalton's murder case would not be as painstaking to conclude, considering the man who had confessed to the crime was no longer able to stand trial or receive punishment from the Crown. By dawn of the morning after the carriage accident on Spring Street, Frederick Cowper had succumbed to his injuries. Since Jasper was leaving for Liverpool once again, Chief Coughlan handed the case over to Sergeant Warnock, but not before Viscount Cowper had managed to corner Jasper outside the morgue at St. Thomas's Hospital.

Cowper was a broken man, Jasper had told Leo afterward, desperate to blame his son's death on Jasper. However, when he was made aware of the full extent of Frederick's crimes, the viscount had paled and gone silent. He'd then turned on his heel and left. The viscount retreated to his Harrow estate, and Frederick's wife, Millicent, reportedly left for her ancestral home in northern England before the funeral had even taken place. What she'd known about her husband's actions was not clear, and Leo supposed, in the end, it didn't matter. Nothing would change the fact that he'd killed Helen and Teddy, that he'd confessed to it, and that Leo had narrowly escaped becoming another of his victims.

The missing phaeton was found stashed in an unused barn at Cowper Fields, and when word of the scandal lit Harrow like a flame to dry kindling, Constable Wiggins heard quickly from a local farmer about the handsome horse he'd found in one of his fields the morning after Helen's murder. He'd presumed the animal had spooked and jumped a paddock fence during the wild thunderstorm the night before, but when none of his neighbors recognized the horse, he'd shrugged and seen it as good fortune.

And when a livery owner near Craven Hill confirmed that he'd been awakened from his slumber around four in the morning for an exchange of horses that same stormy night by a man fitting Frederick Cowper's description, there was no longer any doubt what his movements had been.

These details Leo had gleaned from Detective Sergeant Roy Lewis when he'd paid her a visit at home a day after her injury. Leo had shown him into the front sitting room, and while Claude was gone, making tea and opening a tin of biscuits, Sergeant Lewis had discussed how Warnock was wrapping up the case. He'd then set in with questions about the arrest of Mrs. Gleason and the opium smuggling ring Leo had somehow uncovered. She'd merely relayed that Connor Quinn had asked her to look into the murder of Lydia Hailson, and in the course of her investigation, she'd discovered Lydia's writings, which had detailed the operation.

"She took too large a risk, working undercover like that," Sergeant Lewis said with a sad shake of his head.

Leo didn't refute his comment. Perhaps, if Lydia had not been working entirely alone, if she had instead trusted another person with what she was doing, she would have had someone to watch her back.

Although Lewis had not specifically mentioned anything about Leo having conducted her own inquiry without help, she had acknowledged it to herself. She'd missed discussing elements of the case with Jasper, and although Connor had been with her at the department store during her confrontation with Mrs. Gleason, it hadn't been quite the same as having Jasper at her side.

Leo made no mention of Eddie Bloom or his interest in the stolen opium to Sergeant Lewis during the brief interview over tea and biscuits. She wasn't at all keen on making an enemy of Mr. Bloom. Already, she had failed to give him the materials she'd taken from Lydia's lodging house—and not only because she had been at St. Thomas's at the appointed hour.

To make any charges against Mrs. Gleason stand required proof, and Lydia's notebook, her writings, and sketches were what Sergeant Lewis would need to do just that. So, she had decided to give the folio to him, despite the risk that doing so would incur Eddie Bloom's wrath.

Somehow, Mr. Bloom had learned of her injury and had given her a day of reprieve. His hired man arrived soon after Sergeant Lewis's visit, and Leo had permitted Mr. Bloom's muscle into the foyer. If the man felt any compassion for her at the sight of her bandaged neck, he didn't show it.

"Mr. Bloom won't be happy you don't have the folio," he warned when she explained she had given it to the police.

"I have something better for him," she'd replied. "A name."

Sergeant Lewis, it turned out, had been all too happy to divulge over tea and biscuits that Tricky Mills, one of the higher-ups in the Spitalfields Angels, had been taken into custody for trafficking opium into Gleason's. Mrs. Gleason had not given up her contact within the criminal gang—she was too wise to do so. But her sales associate, the one who had tried to sell the jade urn to Leo and Connor, had not been sufficiently afraid of the Angels and gave up the name. Whether the associate, a Mr. Alistair Findlay, would survive his reduced prison term remained to be seen.

Mr. Bloom's man had accepted the name with a nod and left. And Leo had exhaled as she shut and locked the door behind him, her body trembling from pent-up nerves.

Now, as Tibia sprang onto Leo's desk, her four charcoal-gray paws daintily avoiding the pile of typed certificates, Leo eyed a manila envelope pinned beneath her chipped teacup and saucer. It had been on her desk that morning when she'd arrived at the morgue, though it had not been there when she'd left the previous evening. At first, she'd wondered if Mr. Sampson, the night attendant, had left it for her. However, upon opening the envelope, the sight of a ten-pound note inside had cured her of that idea. That, and the folded piece of paper accompanying it.

Once unfolded, the scrawled words had seemed to spool from the page and wind around Leo like a rope plagued by burrs.

A token of my gratitude. You'll make a fine spy, Detective Spencer.
Must be in the blood.

It hadn't been signed. Nevertheless, she knew who had left it for her.

"It's nearly six o'clock." Connor swept into the office, pulling Leo's attention from the envelope.

The protective canvas coat and tall, rubber boots that he'd worn during the autopsies of three corpses that day had been replaced with a suit of herringbone wool in a shade of chocolate brown.

Leo straightened her back as he tugged at the lapel of his coat. "That is a new suit," she observed. Or at least, she'd never seen him wearing it before.

"Is it too stuffy?" He looked down at himself. "I fear I resemble my father."

"Not at all." She stood and pulled the last certificate from the platen. "Then again, as I haven't met your father, you very well might resemble him."

He arched his brow, as though not appreciating her remark. But Leo only grinned.

"Are you wearing that suit for any particular reason?" she asked.

"I have dinner plans," he answered with a gratified quirk of his mouth. "With Miss Brooks."

Their interest in one another had been evident when they'd met after the tumult at Gleason's Department Store, and although Dita commented while visiting a recuperating Leo at Duke Street that she found his occupation distasteful, there had still been a glimmer of interest in her eyes. Leo hadn't seen that side of her friend for quite some time and was glad to see it again.

"Dita adores dancing," she told Connor as he removed his fob and checked the time. "In case you were looking for something to do after dinner."

Instant alarm rounded his eyes. "I'm not sure she would enjoy dancing with me. I'm embarrassingly clumsy on the dance floor."

"That shouldn't be a problem," Leo replied. "Dita also loves to laugh."

She stifled a smile as he shook his head good-naturedly and tugged on the brim of his bowler. "Then I shall strive to make the lady laugh. I've locked the front door. You'll be fine finishing up for the evening?"

Leo assured him she would be, and he hurried off with a spring in his step.

There wasn't much else to see to before putting out the lamps. Leo pocketed the envelope from Mr. Bloom, curious if it had been delivered while Mr. Sampson was on duty, between the hours of ten o'clock and four in the morning. How else would his man have been able to gain access to her desk? Unless Mr. Bloom's men were trained in lock picking, which was entirely possible. They were criminals, after all.

As she fed Tibia, refreshed the cat's water bowl, and

laid out clean newspaper in her litter box, Leo mulled over the last line in his brief message. *Must be in the blood.* Had he been referencing her *family*?

Eddie Bloom had been the one to warn her against digging into her father's activities, specifically what had led to him being murdered. While Leo knew it was the Carter family who ran the East Rips that had given the order to kill her family, she hadn't been able to tell Mr. Bloom how she knew that information—as it would have given away Jasper's own involvement. But he'd clearly known more about the night of the Spencer family murders than he'd divulged.

Jasper only knew that Leonard Spencer had betrayed the East Rips, not in what manner. Had her father been involved in some sort of *spying*?

Leo was inside the supply closet, checking that the shelves were fully stocked for the next day's examinations when the scuff of feet behind her had her wheeling around, a firestorm licking her back and neck.

Jasper, his Thames-green eyes sparking with mischief, stepped into the closet. His lips formed a coy smirk. "How many times have I advised you to lock that back door?"

Leo's heart buoyed at the sight of him even as it raced. The dizzying effect wasn't altogether unpleasant.

"Numerous times, if I recall," she replied, relieved that it wasn't another intruder. "I may even take your advice one day."

"I won't get my hopes up."

After several heartbeats spent grinning at one another, Leo held out her hand. Jasper tossed his hat onto a shelf, slid his fingers into her palm, and tugged her to him.

For the last few weeks, Leo had grown increasingly

bold in her private thoughts of Jasper, especially at night when she lay abed, waiting for sleep to claim her. Remembering the electric rush through her body as his mouth explored hers in a kiss, or the prickling of heat wherever his hands touched next, had been both pleasurable *and* frustrating. The things Leo saw might be seared into her brain, but feelings were disappointingly elusive.

She'd forgotten the exact scent of his cologne—pine forest and sandalwood—until she was standing against him now, inhaling it deeply. The memory of the smooth bussing of his lips against hers, and the coarse, if thrilling, graze of his stubbled chin had elapsed until now, when he kissed her again.

As Jasper's palms pressed possessively over the hips of her cotton skirt, Leo gave in to the warm, honeyed delight of his affection. And to her own longing for him. He'd missed her just as keenly as she'd missed him. The soft groan from the base of his throat when she pulled her mouth from his gave her confidence in that.

"There are dead bodies to think of," she whispered.

"They do not care if I kiss you."

"It might be considered disrespectful."

Jasper chuffed a short laugh, then rested his forehead against hers a moment before stepping back. His hands, however, kept her waist firmly within their grasp.

"I'm happy you're finally home," she said.

"As am I." His palms glided lower, along her hips again. They paused as they came upon the outline of the envelope in her pocket. There was nothing inherently dodgy about storing something in her skirt pocket, but Leo's knee-jerk reaction—to shift away, out of his hold—stirred his suspicion.

He peered at her. "What is wrong?"

"Nothing," she said as she slipped past him and out of the closet. But while she could lie convincingly to others, she had never been able to with Jasper. The note from Eddie Bloom had worked its way under her skin, and it showed.

Before Jasper had returned to Liverpool, Leo had come clean about Eddie Bloom's interest in the Lydia Hailson case. Unsurprisingly, he had been furious and worried. He did not like or trust Mr. Bloom, and while Leo didn't trust him either, she did not believe the man was an outright danger to her.

"What is in your pocket?" Jasper asked in the notably deep, serious tone he reserved for suspects as he followed her from the closet. Leo supposed she shouldn't have been surprised at how observant he was; he hadn't been made a detective inspector for nothing.

Not wanting to keep anything from him—even things that might upset him—she sighed and reached into her pocket.

"This was on my desk this morning," she explained, extending it to him.

His jaw clenched in preparation of bad news, then opened the envelope and withdrew the ten-pound note. A dark blond brow shot up. Then, when he extracted the message within and read it, he let out a long exhale.

"Bloom."

"Yes," she replied.

Jasper returned the money to the envelope but took a second look at the message. He was reading that last line, no doubt.

"What do you think it means?" she asked. "About it being in my blood?"

He folded the paper along the crease and stuffed it alongside the money. "It's probably just Bloom playing games."

"Do you think my father might have been acting as a spy of some kind?" she pressed on. "He betrayed your family—"

"The Carters are *not* my family." The sharp words flayed, and Leo lifted her chin, startled. Jasper swore underneath his breath and tempered himself visibly. "Forgive me, Leo." He held out the envelope, and she took it.

"You're right, they aren't," she said. "The Inspector was your family. As is Mrs. Zhao. I know that. My point is that if my father betrayed the Carters, maybe it was because he was spying on them."

Jasper hesitated, then turned to retrieve his bowler hat from the shelf in the closet. He appeared conflicted when he came out again, and it took him another moment to speak.

"I understand that you want to know why your family was killed. But Leo, as much as I distrust Eddie Bloom, he was right to tell you to stop asking questions. I don't know why he'd bait you with this," he said, gesturing toward her pocket, where she'd put the envelope again. "I can only think it's for his own benefit."

She blinked back a sudden pricking of tears. For years, Leo had struggled with not knowing why she'd survived the night of the murders. Why the shadowy figure in the attic had saved her. Now that she had an answer for that long-held question, her mind had turned to a new quandary. If her father was the reason her family had been brutally murdered, *why*? What had he done to deserve such punishment?

As much as she yearned for the truth, however, she valued Jasper's safety more. So far, his cousin, Andrew, was the only one in the Carter family who knew who he truly was. Poking around for answers about her father would draw the attention of other Carter family members. If they looked too closely at her, they would see Jasper, too. She couldn't risk it.

Andrew Carter's attention was enough of a risk to manage as it was. Now that Jasper was back in London for good, Leo wondered how long it would be before Andrew approached him. Then again, she knew it was useless to worry about something before it even happened.

"You're right, I'm sure," she said with a nod. "I'm half-inclined to send back his ten pounds."

"I wouldn't go that far. You earned that fee." Jasper tensed his brow and frowned. "I was wrong when I suggested you couldn't solve a murder inquiry on your own. Even though it was dangerous, and I will always object to anything that puts you in danger, you did well, Leo."

She hadn't expected such praise, and it flustered her for a moment. "That means a great deal to me, Jasper." She smiled, slightly abashed. "Though, I admit, working alone was not as satisfying as the times we've worked together."

He had confessed something similar to her at St. Thomas's. It had been lovely to hear, even if his sentiment would not change the rules set out by the London Metropolitan Police against lady investigators. Before

Jasper could remind her of that, she turned her attention to putting out the gasoliers in the postmortem room.

"Now that you're back, we can move forward with leasing the murder house," Leo said as she turned for the office, with Jasper in her wake.

They hadn't had a chance to discuss what to do with the house on Craven Hill before he'd left for Liverpool, but they had touched on the subject in correspondence while he was there. As two murders had been committed at the house, it seemed an apt name for the place. Though it was a fine home in a superb neighborhood, neither of them wished to ever set foot inside it again.

At first, Leo had puzzled over why Francine Stroud would bequeath it to them. But when Jasper explained what Mrs. Zhao had confessed—that Francine had been helping the Inspector pay the property taxes on the Charles Street home so that he could keep it, and that theirs had been a romantic relationship, hidden from what would have been judgmental eyes of the world—Leo thought perhaps her reason had been slightly more pragmatic.

"I wrote to Stockton," Jasper said, referring to his solicitor. "He agrees the yearly lease for a Craven Hill address will provide a nice income for us both."

Leo had thought of that too, and how the money could be put toward the care her Aunt Flora would soon require. Mrs. Zhao and Claude were doing what they could for her at the house, but over the last several weeks she had become more detached, and her bodily functions were also becoming more irregular and a chore for them to see to.

"I'd been considering selling 23 Charles Street," Jasper said. "But now, I'm not sure I have to."

Leo, too, had worried that he might need to sell the Inspector's home, and the idea had filled her with sorrow. Perhaps Francine had seen the gift of the Craven Hill house as a way for her generosity toward the Inspector to keep going, in perpetuity.

"Selling it might still be for the best," Jasper continued as she reached for her coat and hat on the stand. Leo lowered her arm and stared at him, dismayed. "It is far too large for one man and his housekeeper. It would be wiser to find a smaller home in a more reasonable neighborhood," he explained.

"But…it is your home, Jasper." Her chest grew heavy with regret. "It was the Inspector's home. He loved it."

She knew it wasn't the structure, however, that he'd loved. It was the memories the house held of his wife and children. Perhaps he'd clung to it because he could not let go of *them*. For a man as proud and independent as Gregory Reid, accepting Francine Stroud's financial help must have been humbling. But his desire to remain in the home that he'd shared for nearly a decade with his beloved wife, where his young children might have grown into adults, had been strong enough to endure whatever shame or embarrassment he might have felt.

As though Jasper saw all these thoughts swirling in her watery eyes, he stepped forward and reached for her cheek. His tender touch threatened to spill the gathering tears.

"Memories are not stored within the walls of a house, Leo. We take them with us, wherever we go." He sighed.

"And truthfully, I'm thinking more about what is ahead than what lies behind us."

At his slow, sly grin, excitement simmered to life, pushing out the grief she'd been feeling over what might come of 23 Charles Street. Jasper wanted a future with her, and there was nothing to lament on that topic.

His hand lowered to rest gently against her bandaged throat, his palm warming her through the linen.

"The last time we spoke about…the future," Leo began, thinking of the evening in her front sitting room, when Jasper had confessed to having spoken to Claude about courting her.

"We didn't speak," he interjected. "We argued."

"I don't want to argue again."

"I don't either."

"And I don't want to join a detective agency like Dita has," Leo continued. "I shouldn't have said that I did. I was only being contrary."

He raised a brow as if to say, *Were you now?*

"But I want to work, Jasper. At the morgue, or taking on another private inquiry, if I'm asked. I understand that if you and I are to be together, change will be inevitable, for both of us," she said. "But I won't become someone I'm not…someone I haven't ever been…just to please your superiors at the Yard."

Jasper's thumb coasted over her linen-wrapped neck where Connor had, only yesterday, removed the few sutures from her healing wound. The spot was sore still, and there would be a scar. But Jasper's touch seemed to soothe the pain, and she had a few scars already anyhow. What was one more?

Jasper nodded, and at his next words, her whole body

went numb with radiant wonder. "I cannot ask you to be someone you are not. I didn't fall in love with whoever that might be." He angled his head, and vulnerability flickered in his eyes. "I fell in love with *you*, Leonora."

Once, when she'd been younger, Leo and her uncle had been caught just steps away from their home in a sudden downpour. As they shrieked and laughed on their race to the front door, a bolt of lightning struck the pavement nearby. So close, in fact, that a current of electricity reverberated through their limbs, up their spines, and even into their teeth. She and Claude had stared at each other in shock for several seconds before realizing they were not injured. And then, as euphoria at their good luck gripped them, they could not stop grinning.

A similar hot shiver of electricity fired through her now at Jasper's confession of love. As he held her in a searching stare, awaiting her response, euphoria claimed control, and all Leo wanted was to kiss the lips that had just formed those words.

She lifted onto the tips of her toes and did just that. Her mouth was still against his when she whispered, "I love you."

The words felt entirely at home between them, and as she had after that close encounter with lightning, Leo knew how fortunate she was. Jasper pulled back, just enough to look into her eyes.

"Does this mean you are giving me permission to court you?"

Leo smoothed his collar, slightly embarrassed by her inability to stop smiling. "I already thought you were," she said, then shrugged lightly. "But for officiality's sake, my answer is *yes*."

He pressed his mouth to hers again, hard and fast, his lips turned up in a smile. "Good," he said, then took her coat from the stand and held it up for her. "As my first act of official courtship, I'd like to take you to dinner."

Leo was not so caught up in the moment that she forgot what she was wearing. She peered down at her dark, utilitarian, cotton gown, lacking a single ruffle or feminine frill, as she slipped her arms into the sleeves of her coat.

"I'm hardly suitable for dinner out."

Jasper next presented her with her hat. "You look perfect."

She knew she did not, but on second thought, she decided it didn't matter. "Very well, I'm sure a chophouse won't turn me away."

"Or..." He opened the back door for her. "We could go to Charles Street and see what Mrs. Zhao has made."

Her cooking was better than anything a chophouse might serve. "That sounds lovely." Leo put out the gas lamps and joined Jasper in the doorway.

"Perhaps afterward, you'll join me in the study for a drink. There is plenty of cherry cordial," he reminded her.

She peered sideways at him, affecting a look of shock. "The study? Alone?"

"We could invite Mrs. Zhao," he said, closing the door behind them. "But she might object to my kissing you."

"Then she is not invited," Leo replied.

Jasper's bark of laughter echoed down the dirt lane behind the morgue. The rare sound was a gift, one she would wrap up and keep safe forever.

Thank you for reading Tears for the Forsaken, book 5 in the Spencer & Reid Mysteries.
Please leave a rating and review on amazon to help other readers discover the series.

Keep up with me and the Spencer & Reid Mysteries by joining my newsletter.

You can pre-order Leo and Jasper's next book, hazard of the pursuit, coming April 2026.

Also by Cara Devlin

The Spencer & Reid Mysteries

SHADOW AT THE MORGUE

METHOD OF REVENGE

COURIER OF DEATH

CLOAKED IN DECEPTION

TEARS FOR THE FORSAKEN

HAZARD OF THE PURSUIT

The Bow Street Duchess Mysteries

MURDER AT THE SEVEN DIALS

DEATH AT FOURNIER DOWNS

SILENCE OF DECEIT

PENANCE FOR THE DEAD

FATAL BY DESIGN

NATURE OF THE CRIME

TAKEN TO THE GRAVE

THE LADY'S LAST MISTAKE (A Bow Street Duchess Romance)

The Sage Canyon Series

A HEART WORTH HEALING

A CURE IN THE WILD

A LAND OF FIERCE MERCY

THE DARING TIMES OF FERN ADAIR

A Romantic Historical Fiction Novel

THE TROUBLE WE KEEP

A Second Chance Western Romance

About the Author

Cara is the author of the bestselling Bow Street Duchess Mystery series. She loves to write romantic historical fiction and mystery, especially when the romance is a slow burn and the mystery is multi-layered and twisty. She lives in rural New England with her husband and their three daughters. Cara is currently at work on the rest of the Spencer & Reid Mysteries.

Printed in Dunstable, United Kingdom

79248123R00170